CATCH YOUR DEATH

Also by Lissa Marie Redmond

Cold Case Investigations

A COLD DAY IN HELL *
THE MURDER BOOK *
A MEANS TO AN END *
A FULL COLD MOON *
THE PARTING GLASS *

Novels

THE SECRETS THEY LEFT BEHIND

** available from Severn House*

CATCH YOUR DEATH

Lissa Marie Redmond

SEVERN
HOUSE

First world edition published in Great Britain and the USA in 2022
by Severn House, an imprint of Canongate Books Ltd,
14 High Street, Edinburgh EH1 1TE.

Trade paperback edition first published in Great Britain and the USA in 2022
by Severn House, an imprint of Canongate Books Ltd.

severnhouse.com

British Library Cataloguing-in-Publication Data
A CIP catalogue record for this title is available from the British Library.

ISBN-13: 978-0-7278-9132-7 (cased)
ISBN-13: 978-1-4483-0755-5 (trade paper)
ISBN-13: 978-1-4483-0754-8 (e-book)

All Severn House titles are printed on acid-free paper.

Typeset by Palimpsest Book Production Ltd.,
Falkirk, Stirlingshire, Scotland.
Printed and bound in Great Britain by
TJ Books, Padstow, Cornwall.

For Missy

Seventeen Years Ago

'Shane,' said the salt-and-pepper-haired homicide detective, leaning in across the rickety old table to crowd the teenager, 'if you know anything about Jessica Toakase's murder, now is the time to tell me.'

Eighteen-year-old Shane Reese rammed the heel of his hand into his red-rimmed left eye, as if he could grind away the situation he was in. He'd been in the interrogation room for an hour, still in his pajama pants, answering the same questions over and over again. The older detective would ask questions, while the younger one with the huge bushy mustache sat at a computer and typed what was being said.

Shane had been in his bed when his mom came into his room at eight fifteen, saying that police were at the house. Maybe if his dad had been home and not at the fire station he wouldn't be here now. All he wanted to do was get out of police headquarters, away from these detectives, and find his friends. Were they talking to the police as well? For all he knew, they were already in the other rooms he'd passed as the detectives led him through the Homicide office.

He'd seen a lot of closed doors.

Shane swallowed hard before he answered. There was a lump in his throat that wouldn't go away. 'I don't know anything else,' he insisted. 'How many times do I have to say it?'

The older detective lit a cigarette, even though there was a no smoking sign directly above his head. Other than that sign, the walls were bare, painted industrial gray. A window across from him was cracked half-open to a view of a red brick wall.

They'd sat him down at a long scratched-up table with metal legs and a plastic top made to look like wood. The only other furniture in the room were three chairs: the one he was occupying, the one the detective was perched on, acting as if he was ready to pounce, and the one the mustached detective sat on in front of the computer monitor and keyboard on the other end of the table. Mounted up in the corner of the ceiling, a video camera pointed right at him. He'd passed a handwritten notice taped to the wall on his way into the room stating that any and all conversations may be recorded.

The wall behind the detective was a big mirror. Shane assumed another detective was watching him through it. Every time he glanced at it, he had to look away quickly. He wasn't handcuffed, but between his image in the glass and the camera he felt trapped.

Salt-and-Pepper exhaled a cloud of smoke that seemed to hang in the air in the closed room. Shane stifled a cough. The detective offered the pack to Shane, who shook his head. Ashing the cigarette in an empty Pepsi can on the desk, he told the teen in his gravelly voice, 'This is some serious shit, kid. Maybe the most serious shit you're ever gonna have to deal with. Jessica was murdered. And then dumped in the river like garbage. In my twenty-three years on the job this is one of the worst scenes I've ever had to work.' He slapped a hand to his chest. 'Because I have a sixteen-year-old daughter. And to see that little girl, just graduated from high school with her whole life ahead of her snuffed out, well, that makes this personal for me. And if you have to tell me about yesterday a hundred times, then you're gonna tell it a hundred times. So spare me your righteous indignation and tell me *again*, when was the last time you saw Jessica Toakase?'

On the desk, next to the Pepsi can, Shane could see a manila folder marked 'Crime Scene Photos'. A picture stuck out from the corner. Shane could just make out a foot lying on what looked like a blue plastic tarp on the ground. The skin was white and mottled with splotches. Bile rose up in his throat. The detective noticed Shane looking at the photo and quickly stuffed it back inside, out of sight. A shudder ran through Shane as he tried not to throw up, making him crumple forward a little in his hard plastic and metal chair. 'I last saw her at around six thirty at Memorial Park. I had a baseball game earlier at the diamonds there and I was hanging around, waiting for my girlfriend's shift to end. They worked the concession stand together.'

'But you never saw Jessica after you left with your girlfriend last night, correct?'

Shane kept his eyes down. 'We didn't leave together. I walked her to her car, held the door open for her, then kissed her on the cheek and watched her pull out of the parking lot. Then I hopped in my car and went home.'

The detective's crisp white shirt was unbuttoned at the neck. Thick gray hair curled up from the opening, almost to his Adam's apple. Shane watched it bob up and down as he spoke, feeling like every time he looked the detective in the eye, the man was dissecting him. 'I'll repeat the question. Did you see Jessica after she stormed off by herself at six thirty last night?'

All the air seemed to disappear from Shane's lungs. 'No.'

'Because you got in a heated argument with her, right?'

'It wasn't like that. She was my friend,' Shane insisted, raising his voice a little. 'I didn't kill Jessica.'

The detective exhaled another cloud of gray smoke. 'So where were you exactly when Jessica Toakase disappeared?'

Outside the window that faced the brick wall a small green leaf flitted by.

The younger detective with the big mustache made a notation on the statement form that Shane Reese looked away and hesitated before he answered.

ONE

Now

There was an old saying in the Cold Case Homicide office: never be the person to answer the phone first thing on a Monday morning.

Buffalo Police Detective Lauren Riley had forgotten what day it was when she snatched up the receiver on her desk. She and her partner, Shane Reese, had come in for overtime the day before and it had thrown off her internal calendar. When the caller started talking without even saying hello, she knew she should have let it go to voicemail.

'My ex-old lady set up a guy for a mob hit. It happened in 1988 or 89, I think.' The voice on the phone sounded agitated and put out, as if Lauren had called him about an offer for an extended warranty for his vehicle, rather than him calling the Cold Case office to give them information on a homicide. 'They found him duct taped to a tree behind Baro's Pawn Shop off Military Road in Riverside.'

'I know the case,' Lauren replied, pen hovering over the yellow legal pad on the desk in front of her. 'Julian Fatta.' She bit back the urge to correct the man on calling someone his 'old lady.' It had always been one of those phrases that pissed her off. And while this man sounded much older than her forty-one years, she doubted he ever called his significant others anything else. The restraint in her tone of voice made her partner look up from the iPad he was working on across from her.

Reese cocked an eyebrow at her as the caller went on. 'Do you know she got fifty thousand dollars to keep him at his shop after closing time until one of the Magory brothers showed up? She was there when Salvatore Magory beat him to death, then took him out back behind the shop and taped him to a tree with his hands over his head. That was a warning to anyone else who might want to skim a little off the top of their money-laundering scheme.'

The Magory family had been high up in the Buffalo mob food chain from the Fifties all the way to the late Nineties. Then the patriarch, Paul, decided he wanted to go legit and move to Florida. He'd realized that their rackets had been declining for years and they could make good money from their legitimate businesses without the risk of going to jail or getting wacked. There was an entire file cabinet dedicated to mob-related cold cases in the office.

'Can you elaborate on who *she* is?' Lauren was familiar with the file. She was familiar with almost all of the mob-related cases. None had been cleared with an arrest since she'd been in the Cold Case Unit, even though every single case she had looked at had a suspect named. She tapped the end of the pen against her lips. Knowing who did it and proving it were two very different things.

'Shirley Gizzo.' The older man made a HRUMPH noise on the other end of the line. 'That bitch went out for a steak dinner afterward. She was together with Julian for five years and didn't bat a false eyelash while he was getting beaten to death in the backroom of the pawn shop. She's a real piece of work.'

The niece of a made man, Shirley Gizzo was an infamous mob hanger-on. Lauren refused to use the word 'moll' to describe her. She believed that glamorized what Shirley really was, an opportunistic gold digger who seemed to always be in the background of the mob cases that came in during the Eighties. Her name had popped up in a couple of the files. Lauren was actually a little surprised to hear that Shirley Gizzo was still alive. Even with her tenuous connection to the mob through family, her lifestyle choices hadn't been conducive to longevity. *But*, Lauren thought, *a woman like Shirley is a survivor. Fatta got whacked and she moved on to the next guy who could give her status. It was Shirley's MO.*

'Can I get your name, sir?' Lauren asked, her icy blue eyes traveling to Reese's face. He was pitched forward, hanging on her every word.

'I'm the asshole who paid for her boob job. I just gave

you what you need to know. Now go do your job.' The caller hung up.

Reese leaned back in his creaky chair and put his feet up on the desk. The Cold Case Unit was an office within an office, a room along the long hallway that made up the homicide squad, with each crew having their own separate space. Their crew was made up of Reese and Riley, Major and Avilla. However, Reggie Major was using up his vacation time in anticipation of retiring in a month, and Hector Avilla had come in early to chase down a lead in an old liquor store robbery gone bad, leaving Reese and Riley in charge of returning all the phone messages that had come in over the weekend. Lauren had returned exactly one before being interrupted by the disgruntled caller. It was 8:11 in the morning.

'Who's slipping us tips on the Julian Fatta case?'

'He wouldn't leave his name.' She scribbled her notes as fast as she could before she forgot anything. 'He said Salvatore Magory beat Fatta to death.'

'I think I got the gist from your end of the conversation,' Reese said. Old-fashioned landlines made it harder to hear both sides of a conversation than cell phones. It seemed every time Lauren stood in a checkout line at a store, the person behind her had to have an in-depth conversation with their best friend on a ridiculous number of personal tragedies. And always, both sides of the conversation rang out loud and clear.

'That's been the word on the street since it happened.' The skepticism in Reese's voice was evident. 'Even the paper at the time named him as a suspect.' Lauren knew he didn't put much faith in mob tips. Not one had panned out since he'd been up in Cold Case. He was convinced the callers were mostly armchair detectives regurgitating what they read in online forums. Lauren had to remind him from time to time that if you shake every single tree, eventually a coconut is going to fall out.

'They didn't say Shirley Gizzo was an eyewitness though.'

Reese let out a low whistle and dropped his feet back on the floor. 'No, they did not. She was at the bar in the Cranston case when Pauly Gates was gunned down outside and was the alibi for Jimmy the Pig in the Barberi homicide. If memory serves, Shirley wasn't even mentioned in that file.' When Reese had first come up to Cold Case, their captain at the time had made him go through all the mob-related files and make copies for the feds who were trying to put together a RICO case against a couple of key players. The case fell apart, but not before Reese had become intimately familiar with every mob hit in the past fifty years.

He got up and crossed the room to a huge olive-green cabinet. Twisting the handle, he threw the doors open, revealing box after box labeled in green writing, Reese's own personal filing system designed to denote organized crime cases. 'Fatta, Fatta, Fatta,' he mumbled, his finger dragging down from one box to the next. Lauren knew they had exactly fifteen unsolved mob cases going back to 1975. The older ones were archived.

'Here it is.' Reese turned back, waving a thick manila file at her. It wasn't the original. Reese had all the originals stored away in the file room under lock and key and video surveillance. It was one of the copies he'd made for the RICO case. He took it over to the mess table and started to pull pieces of paper out, one by one, arranging them in separate piles, all the while muttering under his breath.

Lauren watched him work furiously for a moment, then walked over. Reese was a ball of nervous energy when nothing was going on; throw a hot lead at him and he exploded into action.

'Here's the medical examiner's report,' he said, angling it up in the left-hand corner. 'Statement, statement, evidence report, neighborhood canvas, statement.' He quickly and methodically sorted every piece of paperwork, talking his way through the process.

The mess table was simply a plastic and metal folding table, the kind used for basement church party planners to set crockpots on or to display your treasures in your driveway during a garage sale. Some long-retired detective had brought it in before Lauren had transferred to Cold Case and Reese had made sure it survived the move from the old headquarters building. Hector and Reggie didn't use it as much as Reese and Riley, but every cop had their own way of doing things.

Reese examined a statement, let it drop back on its pile, then picked up another report. 'Nothing,' he said, putting that one down and grabbing another. 'No mention of the infamous Shirley Gizzo anywhere.'

'Fatta was married. It is possible she was having an affair with him at the time.' Lauren had a passing knowledge of most of the mob cases, but she'd actually read the Fatta file a couple of years back at Reese's urging. Reese had resubmitted all the evidence for further DNA testing and had gotten some interesting results. After months of combing over the original file, the new evidence and reinterviewing witnesses, nothing had panned out. When the higher-ups in the Bureau decided against trying to put together a RICO case, they handed all of their findings back to Reese, and he found that he didn't have enough evidence to make an arrest in any of the individual cases either. The mob knew how to cover their tracks. The Fatta case got added to the file cabinet, where it sat getting colder by the year.

'Shirley Gizzo wasn't opposed to dating married men,' Reese replied. 'And she wasn't opposed to doing favors for them either. She could have been dating one of the Magory brothers at the time as well. Either way, it's not out of the realm of possibility she was involved somehow.'

'The big question is, will she talk to us?' Lauren asked, absently running her fingers through her short, choppy hair. 'How loyal is she after all these years?'

'Loyal enough to still be alive.' He dropped the crime scene photos on his desk. 'Still, we should take a shot at talking to her.'

Lauren took a sip of cold black coffee from her hot pink mug that said, 'Greetings from Fabulous Las Vegas'. She'd have Reese stop for a refill at Tim Horton's on the way. 'Let's go then. No time like the present.'

Walking back over to his desk, he straightened a picture of his almost five-month-old son and snatched up his keys. 'You always said all it takes to break a cold case is one thing. Let's see if this is that one thing.'

TWO

Shirley Gizzo had an address in Kenmore, New York, just north of the city line. 'One square mile of heaven,' its residents liked to joke. Lauren drove the unmarked car up Delaware Avenue, out of the city, while Reese rode shotgun.

'It looks like she lives in that big brick apartment building across from Teagan's Dry Cleaning,' Reese said, staring at Google Maps on his phone.

'That's a nice building,' Lauren commented as they passed strip after strip of stores and businesses.

'Nice enough,' he said, putting his phone back into his jacket. 'But it's November. And freaking cold out. Most of her contemporaries are living or snowbirding in Florida. Something's keeping her here.'

'She doesn't have any kids,' Lauren said, stopping at a red light. 'Maybe she's short of cash. Maybe a guy.'

'Maybe both. Up there, on the left.' Reese pointed to a huge stately brick apartment building that took up the entire corner. Lauren spied a man pulling out of a parking spot half a block down. It wouldn't be a long walk, but the wind had kicked up and she'd left her hat at home. The first flakes of winter hadn't landed yet, but you could feel them coming. The sky was a steel, overcast gray and the wind was whipping in from over the lake, ripping down the streets and through the trees, carrying dead leaves and the occasional white plastic bag along with it.

Lauren was glad Reese bit his tongue while she parallel parked. He knew it was distracting to mock her while she performed that maneuver. He'd wait until after they left to critique her on it. She also knew he didn't want her to punch him in the shoulder. It was one of the last uninjured parts of his anatomy.

Pulling the collar up on her jacket to shield her ears as much as possible, she put the car in park and exited the unmarked vehicle. When she'd started the job almost twenty years ago, she could jump fences in snowdrifted backyards without a hat and just her thin leather gloves. No thermal gear, just the heavy black boots provided by the city. Now that she was over forty, she found herself in a state of perpetual cold, even in the summer. Her best friend, Dayla, assured her that would all come to an end once the hot flashes started. She didn't know if she should look forward to that or dread it.

'Says on the printout she lives in Apartment Twelve,' Reese said, leaning forward into the wind, holding onto his Buffalo Police ball cap with his left hand so it didn't fly off his head.

Lauren had been to these apartments a couple of times before, when she was in the Sex Offense squad. She'd had a victim on the third floor and had been to her apartment to talk to her a couple of times. She remembered it as clean and comfortable, but not particularly homey. It was the type of apartment you rented in-between life events: saving to buy your first house, waiting for your divorce to finalize, your first apartment after college with friends. The apartments on the first floor had their entrances on the outside of the building. Lauren and Reese crossed from the public sidewalk to the walkway that encircled the perimeter, checking the numbers on the doors as they walked around the square of the building.

Number 12 ended up on the backside, facing the tenant parking lot. They bladed themselves on either side of the painted green door and Reese knocked three times with the butt of his hand-held radio.

Immediately they were assaulted with the barking of what sounded like a very small dog with a big sense of self. The noise covered over any sound of footsteps approaching the door, so when it cracked open just wide enough for the occupant to peek out, Lauren took a step back. The door closed again, the dog stopped barking and then came the unmistakable sound of a chain lock being slid open.

Shirley Gizzo stood in her doorway holding a cigarette in her right hand and a growling Chihuahua in the crook of her left arm. She blew a cloud of smoke at their faces. 'Can I help you, detectives?' she asked in a raspy voice that betrayed her age more than her Botoxed forehead did.

She was in her seventies, the kind of woman Lauren's dad would have called 'well put together', with perfectly done white-blond hair, thick makeup that showed off every crow's foot around her eyes, and long red manicured nails. Spray-tanned to a brownish orange complexion, Shirley Gizzo was wearing more gold jewelry with her red tracksuit at eleven in the morning on a Monday than Lauren owned.

'Shirley Gizzo?' Reese stepped front and center. He usually did better with women like Shirley so they'd agreed in the car that he should take the lead. Shirley's appraising glance slowly ran Reese up and down but her slight frown signaled that his usual charm wasn't going to be enough.

'What can I help you with?' She didn't confirm or deny who she was. Lauren thought, *This woman doesn't just know her way around the block, she's got a map of it tattooed on the back of her hand.*

'We're detectives with the Buffalo Police Department,' Reese forged ahead. 'Can we come in and speak with you?'

She flicked the ash of her cigarette toward them and her little brown dog let out a menacing snarl. 'No.'

There was no follow-up, no excuse or explanation.

'Aren't you even curious about why we're here?' Lauren asked.

She shrugged her shoulders and took a long drag off of her smoke. 'Not particularly.'

'It's about an old homicide, ma'am,' Reese said. 'Julian Fatta.'

'It's got nothing to do with me. And I've got an appointment to get my eyebrows waxed at noon, so I've got to go.' She started to close the door, then paused, looking at Lauren. 'I should give you my waxer's number. She could get you in right away as an emergency case.'

Lauren willed her hand to stay by her side instead of flying up to touch her unruly brows. 'Come on, Shirley. Don't you want to get ahead of this thing?' she asked.

'A little piece of advice to you, dear,' her smoker's voice rasped, 'besides go to a salon and get yourself a makeover as soon as humanly possible. The things you're asking about? They're ancient history. Do you remember back when they found King Tut's tomb? The head archaeologist was told it was cursed, but he opened it anyway. Within weeks he was dead. Sometimes when you meddle with things, they come back and meddle with you. Is it worth dredging up the past if all it does is stir up more trouble?'

'Is that a threat?' Reese asked, stepping slightly in front of Lauren. 'Or is someone threatening you?'

'Neither.' She flicked the butt out onto the sidewalk, where the ember still glowed a cherry red until Reese stepped on it. 'Just a friendly observation from someone who's seen a thing or two. Bad shit happens when you don't let things go. You can't change the past. Sometimes it's better to just move on.'

'We can't just move on,' Lauren said. 'It's our job to find out the truth.'

'Well, that's a good way to catch your death, honey,' Shirley said. 'Go find someone else to harass.'

With that, she shut the door in their faces.

THREE

'I have been sweating for Amichi's calamari for months now,' Reese said, flipping the menu over in his hand. 'I'm glad we had to come out this way. It was worth it just for the food.'

Lauren could feel herself frown as her eyes jumped from the grouper to the eggplant parm. 'Good food aside, Shirley Gizzo could be holding the key to solving this case and it pisses me off. She's not cooperating and we can't make her.' She took a sip of water and immediately regretted it. She'd forgotten to tell the waitress no ice. A cough rose up from her lungs, threatening to spray Reese. Cold drinks often triggered her coughing fits; she didn't know why and was too chicken to ask her doctor. The city's physician had only cleared her to return to work three weeks ago, and just barely. She suspected Howard Whitney, a person involved in the last private investigation she'd handled with Reese, was to thank for that.

They'd recovered a stolen painting for him and his ex-wife. The two were still battling out the ownership in court, but he'd told her that he'd get her reinstated. She'd replied with a 'no thank you', but here she was. Lauren knew her lungs weren't any better. Getting stabbed two years ago and having one lung collapse should have been a career-ender. Owing that terrible man a favor kept her awake at night. Choking down the cough, she tried to push those thoughts to the back of her mind. She'd just have to take it one day at a time and hope that eventually she'd heal.

The pretty young waitress, whose nametag read Julia, tried to walk by their table with her arms full of plates. Reese shot out a hand to stop her. Even though that move was an absolute no-no, up there with snapping your fingers at a bartender, she smiled down at him. 'Can I help you?'

'Could you throw an order of calamari in for us? Make that two heaping orders, on one giant plate, please.'

She blew a strand of dark hair that had come loose from her ponytail out of her eye. 'Just let me serve this table and I'll get that right in for you. Anything else?'

He looked over at Lauren, who shook her head. 'Nope. That's it. Thank you.'

'My pleasure,' she replied, and went to the next table to hand out their lunches.

Now that ordering was out of the way, Reese got back down to business. 'Don't take it personally,' he said, dipping his piece of warm bread in the little dish of olive oil in front of him and ripping a chunk off with his teeth. 'Shirley Gizzo's been playing this game since before either of us were even born.'

Lauren had encountered women like Shirley Gizzo before. They would have to find something to use as leverage against her or she'd never talk. The problem was discovering the one thing she cared enough about to risk her life by going against a made man. While the mob in Buffalo had diminished its presence, there was no doubt they still had a foothold in the city.

'Shane? Shane Reese?' a deep baritone voice called from behind Lauren. They looked up simultaneously at the man who'd approached their table. Reese squinted for half a second then bounced from his seat to embrace the handsome dreadlocked man.

'Chris Sloane! I can't believe it! I almost didn't recognize you with all that hair.' Reese clapped him on the back. 'I thought you were somewhere out west, brother.'

Chris gave a deep laugh as they broke apart. He had on a crisp green shirt, buttoned to the neck, and khaki cargo pants tucked into fashionable black boots. 'I was, but now I'm home.'

'I dig the new look,' Reese told him.

Chris ran a hand over his knotty locks. 'These are my pride and joy. Most of the guys our age are going bald so I'm not cutting these beauties for anything.'

Reese grinned and lifted up his baseball hat, showing off his scarred, shaved head. 'I resemble that remark.'

Chris winced. 'Yeah. Sorry about that. I saw on the news about you getting shot. I hope you're all right now.'

Reese pulled out one of the empty chairs. 'Have a seat. And I don't know if I'm all right, but I'm definitely OK. It would take more than a bullet to shatter this thick skull of mine.'

'I hear that,' Sloane laughed, sitting down. He turned to Lauren, who was seated next to him, and extended his hand. 'Shane has no manners. I'm Christopher Sloane, but you can call me Chris.'

Lauren shook his hand. It was strong and warm. 'Lauren Riley. I'm Reese's partner on the police department.'

Chris was the type of person who made you feel special the moment you met him. Lauren was reminded of a television interview she'd watched once where a casting director was talking about some people having that 'it' factor – a presence no one could quite define that drew people immediately to them. Whatever it was, Chris definitely had that factor. 'I've known Shane since high school. I'm glad he's partnered up with someone who can rein him in.'

Reese had been in the process of taking a sip of water when Chris spoke, causing him to snort and shoot liquid out of his nose. He grabbed his napkin and mopped his face while correcting his friend. 'Other way around, brother. Other way around.'

Lauren couldn't help but be amused watching the two of them play off each other. 'So you and Reese went to high school together?' she prompted, wanting more details about the early life of her partner.

Chris nodded. 'Down at Public School 91, also known as the Patrick J. Stanton Academy, in the Old First Ward. It's closed now. I took a drive by where it had been two days ago. Developers are gobbling up the Old First Ward.' He paused, as if reflecting on that fact, then went on, 'Shane and I were part of a pilot curriculum. Some of the parents thought there was a brain drain, with all of the smart kids going to City Honors, so they grabbed a bunch of us and put us in a Gifted and Talented program.'

Reese elaborated. 'It was loosely based on some European model, where the same kids are in all the same classes together all four years of high school. We were the only class to actually graduate from the program. Two years after we left the funding ran out.' He raised his shoulders in a slight shrug. 'Then a year after that the school closed altogether.'

'The program really didn't make much sense,' Chris said. 'We were in a regular school, going to class alongside regular students. We participated in school sports and clubs and activities with the other kids. All it meant was that the eight of us spent six hours a day staring at each other in class.'

'And competing against each other,' Reese added.

'That too.' Chris reached across the table and clapped Reese on the shoulder. 'This guy. I thought this guy would be playing Division 1 Baseball somewhere. I was shocked when I heard he enlisted in the army.'

'I was done with school,' Reese said. 'College ain't for everybody. If anything, that program proved higher education wasn't for me. I nearly lost my mind having to look at your ugly mug every single day.'

'You're gonna give me a complex,' Chris said, trying to cover his face with a napkin. 'It's a good thing my wife Veronica fell in love with my personality.' Lauren knew he was being self-deprecating. He was an extremely attractive man, with smooth dark skin and wide, expressive brown eyes sporting lashes so long they nearly grazed the top of his eyebrows. She could picture the younger versions of him and Reese and knew that neither of them was an ugly duckling.

Reese ripped the napkin from his hand and Chris took a playful swipe at him across the table.

'But seriously,' Chris said. 'I'm opening a luxury spa in Inverness, in Cattaraugus County. I've invited our whole group to join me as my special guests the Friday after Thanksgiving. Running into you was serendipity, brother. I need you to come to my new place.'

'Last time I saw you, you were home from working at some high-end hotel in Colorado. Now you're opening one of your own?'

Chris's smile turned down in the corners slightly. 'I had a rough patch financially for a while. I almost lost everything. Then I found the right investor.' Now he seemed to puff with pride as he went on, 'It's going to be the most exclusive spa and boutique hotel outside of New York City. Let me stuff you with food and drink. We're still in the process of hiring staff, but I have my chef. We're just trying to nail down the menu and I need guinea pigs. Our whole class is coming.'

Reese raised an eyebrow. 'The whole group? You managed to track down everyone?'

'There's only seven coming so far, including me.' He started ticking off on his fingers. 'I know Tonya is still in Toronto, so she won't be there. But Erica will be in town with Raphael, so will Amanda and her husband, Owen. Tyler is coming up from Cleveland. Seth will be there. You were the only one I hadn't heard back from. I must have sent you six emails.'

'You probably sent them to my old address. If it was the one I gave you last time I saw you, I haven't used that in over ten years.'

'I was on the verge of emailing you at the police department. Wasn't sure how you'd feel about that.'

'Let's just say I'm glad it worked out this way,' Reese said. Departmental emails could be read by the brass at any time. Reese and Riley tried never to use them for personal correspondence. A couple of cops had been embarrassed into retirement by misusing work email addresses. 'What made you think to do this?'

'My mentor out in Colorado used to tell me that if he wanted someone to tell him his hotel was wonderful, he'd call his mother. I've been hosting mini events: a bridal party, a family get-together, and a small corporate retreat, trying to work the kinks out since September. I'm nowhere near ready to open to the public; sometime after Easter, in the spring, I'd guess. But for the prices I expect to charge, everything has to be perfect. What better way than to ask people with no skin in the game for their honest opinion?'

'I can't ask you to pay for everything,' Reese said. 'That doesn't feel right.'

Chris shook his head so hard his dreads swung a little. 'It's a business write-off. Listen, bring your partner here, too.' He turned to Lauren. 'You wouldn't mind spending the weekend at my resort in a luxury room, eating gourmet food with good company, all for the price of an honest critique, would you?'

Lauren was flustered for a split second. Was he being serious, or merely polite? 'I wouldn't want to intrude on you and your classmates—' she began.

'Nonsense,' Chris waved his hand as if to brush the ridiculousness of Lauren not coming out of the air. 'I think you'd fit right in. We were a bunch of oddballs, our little class.'

'Gifted and talented, my ass,' Reese agreed. 'It was more like competitive and over-aggressive.'

'Hence my invitation. It's been seventeen years since we were all together. Who needs a relaxing weekend together more than our little class? Although the spa section won't actually be open yet. My wife is the spa manager and hasn't hired all the staff yet. She's pretty picky. Almost every other amenity will be available though.' He was talking to both of them but looking right at Lauren. 'Say you'll come.'

Before Lauren could answer, Julia set the plate of calamari down in front of her. Reese reached over with his fork and immediately stabbed a ring and popped it in his mouth.

'Still a charming bastard,' Chris said as Reese chewed with his mouth open.

'Being a cold case detective is a hard job,' he protested, and shoveled another piece into his mouth. 'You have to eat when you can.'

'Speaking of that . . .' Chris's voice took on a somber tone. 'Do you think you'll ever solve Jessica's case?'

Reese paused for a long moment before answering. 'The original detectives put a lot of work into it. I had all the evidence retested two years ago.' He shook his head. 'I got nothing usable. She was in the water for about twelve hours, long enough to wash away DNA evidence. And the murder weapon had been submerged too.'

Lauren realized they were talking about one of their classmates.

Chris took a moment himself to digest what Reese had just told him before asking, 'She was stabbed, right?'

Lauren vaguely remembered looking at the file they were talking about when she first got up to Cold Case. Jessica Toakase was found caught on tree roots in the Buffalo River. She hadn't come home from her summer job at a local park. No witnesses, no DNA, no strong suspects. It had gone back to the file cabinet in favor of cases with more solvability factors. Lauren's mother had once asked how many cold cases could the city of Buffalo actually have? Lauren had patiently explained that if, on average, they had forty homicides a year and they solved thirty of them, that left ten unsolved cases. In ten years, that meant they had a hundred cold cases. From now until 1970, that meant well over five hundred. It was a sad, sobering statistic. The fact that cases had to be prioritized meant that some victims continually went to the back of the queue as new homicides were added to the list every year. It wasn't fair and it wasn't justice, it was lack of personnel and resources, which Lauren was constantly fighting for.

If Reese's name had been in Jessica's file, she didn't recall it. She'd looked at it years ago, before Reese had come to the Cold Case squad. He would have been a young patrolman she'd never met. There would've been no reason to remember his name, especially since she hadn't spent much time with that particular case. And no family members had ever called asking for an update. With no similar crimes in the area and no leads, there was nothing to do but file the case away and hope for a phone call with some information like what had just happened in the Fatta case.

'Yeah,' Reese replied, his mouth turning down into a grim frown. 'She was stabbed.'

Lauren knew he was understating it. She was stabbed multiple times.

'I still can't believe it, even after all these years. That was so messed up.' Chris ran his hand over his long dreadlocks again, smoothing them back off his forehead. 'I hope you get a break in that someday.'

'I'm working on it, brother.' Reese stood and extended his hand. 'It was great to see you.'

Christopher grasped his outstretched hand and pulled him into a man-hug, clapping him on the back. He reached into the back pocket of his cargo pants and handed Reese a business card. 'You'll come to my place, right? It'll be the class reunion we never had. Everyone else has already said yes.'

'I think I can manage to squeeze it in.' Reese's face broke into a wide smile now, showing off his perfect, straight white teeth. He opened the faux leather folio he'd set against his chair leg and fished out his own business card. 'That's my cell number there.'

'Good.' Chris tucked it away and turned to Lauren. 'And you, too. The spa section won't be open, but the rooms themselves are amazing and the views are breathtaking. Our guests also have privileges at the Mount Blanc ski slopes in Ellicottville. Just what you'll need to wind down after all that cooking on Thanksgiving.'

'I'm not cooking this year.' She glanced over at Reese. 'He is.'

Chris's dark eyes twinkled. He didn't ask why Reese was cooking Thanksgiving dinner for her. 'Then you'll really need a mini-vacation.'

'If you're sure you have room for me.'

He gave her a wink. 'I'll make room. Just make certain this one shows up.' He jerked a thumb in Reese's direction as he began to back away from their table.

'I'm coming, I'm coming!' Reese laughed, sitting back down.

'I'll text you the details!' With that, Christopher Sloane exited the side door and was gone.

As soon as Sloane left, the mood at the table swiftly changed. Reese wouldn't meet her eyes because he knew what would come next. He threw four twenty-dollar bills down and got up without a word. Lauren motioned to Julia that their money was on the table, then scurried after Reese. Her legs were longer than his, but she still had to hustle to catch up with him in the parking lot.

They were quiet the entire way to their car. Reese remained silent as Lauren put it into reverse and backed out of the parking spot. Usually he began to spout nonsense to fill uncomfortable silences between them; it was one of his nervous ticks. When no words were said as she drove down Delaware Avenue back into downtown, she began, 'Reese—'

He cut her off mid-sentence. 'Don't lecture me on this, Riley. What was I supposed to say? Was I supposed to stick my hand out on my first day in Cold Case and announce, "I'm Shane Reese and I was questioned in an old homicide. Now that I'm here in the squad I'm going to pick up that file and start looking into it on the side." What would you have said about that?'

She clenched and unclenched the wheel. She was gripping it so tight her fingers were going numb. 'That you shouldn't have touched it. You should have asked me to do it.'

'I was never arrested, never charged with anything. I obviously have no police record or the department never would have hired me. I was just a witness and not even an eyewitness at that.'

'Did you ever talk to Reggie about it?' Reggie Major was the most senior detective in the Homicide squad; surely he would have remembered Reese.

'No. He was on a different crew at the time and didn't work on the case. And there was no Cold Case squad back then. By the time I got to Homicide, all the original detectives were retired.' He ran a hand over his scarred head, like he did when he was agitated. 'I'd appreciate it if you didn't tell him, or anyone else in the office, that I was once questioned in a homicide.'

'A homicide you decided to work on in secret.'

'A homicide that needs to be solved.'

'You know it's a conflict of interest.'

'You scolding me on conflicts of interest is hilarious,' he scoffed, looking out the car window. 'Every case you get involved with is a conflict of interest.'

Lauren tried to tamp down her anger. If he was never eliminated, his involvement could contaminate the entire case if they ever did come up with a suspect. She knew he knew better, but she also knew what it was like to be consumed by an unsolved homicide. Every detective had those particular files that stuck with them, that they worked on from home and lay awake in bed going over all the details every night. She'd been there. More than once. And nothing anyone had said to her stopped her from following those cases to their conclusions, for better or worse. She softened the tone of her voice. 'Where's the file now?'

Reese let out a long breath. 'The original is in the big cabinet. I made a copy and put it in the file room.'

Just like the mob cases, she thought. Turning the wheel, she eased around the traffic circle in front of police headquarters. 'Would you mind if I took a look at it again?'

He was still staring out the window. 'I can put it on your desk when we get upstairs.'

'OK.'

'It should probably go without saying, but I didn't kill her.' There was a hint of anger in his voice. 'Jessica was my friend.'

'I believe you.' Because if she'd read the file all those years ago and Reese had been a serious suspect, she would have remembered his name. It seemed, from what she could remember, that a couple of the other kids Jessica had graduated with were more likely persons of interest. But even that supposition was thin. In truth, no one had ever been considered a prime target of the investigation. The case had stalled within weeks and then gone completely cold.

But that didn't change the fact that he'd kept his involvement in the case a secret from her.

FOUR

Reese put two cardboard boxes containing the files on the chair next to her desk as soon as they got back to the office, then announced, 'I'm going to the gym.' Grabbing his army green duffel bag up off the floor next to the door, he left without another word.

She'd seen the boxes a thousand times. There were twenty boxes and files stuffed in the black metal cabinet against the far wall, all cases that were on hold for one reason or another. Not cold enough to go back into storage, but not hot enough to be considered active. Add those to the cases they had out and were working on at any given time and it was easy to lose track of them, especially when the family wasn't working with the detectives and calling for updates.

Lauren's curiosity was piqued as she lifted the lid of the first box and looked down at the files within. She remembered when the murder happened. Her own daughters had both been little at the time, so it had hit home for her. Whenever and wherever a young girl or boy is brutally murdered, the community is wrapped in a collective fear, at least until some other newsworthy event happens and knocks it out of the headlines. It had dominated the news for a week or so and then got lost in the never-ending cycle of twenty-four-hour coverage.

Lauren pulled out a slim folder she knew from experience would only contain interdepartmental reports and opened it. The original incident report was the first page. It listed the victim as Jessica Toakase, white female, seventeen years of age, one month shy of her eighteenth birthday. It gave an address of 2109 Sidway Street, down in the Old First Ward where the park was located. There was a note along with the names of next of kin: victim had been in foster care. Lauren flipped a couple of pages in and found a P-73 detailing the death notification, in which the detective recorded that Jessica had been with the family for less than four months and was planning to leave them for good once she went off to college at SUNY Potsdam. Her parents had moved to New York State from Arkansas when she was thirteen. Both were heroin addicts who'd heard New York had the best welfare system. According to the foster parents, they both overdosed within a year. Jessica was bounced between group homes as the State tried to locate family members, finally being placed with a local family she stayed with for three years. They moved to North Carolina the spring of her senior year without her.

Her new foster parents had given statements the day after her body was found, July 3rd. Lauren scanned those carefully. The foster mom had phoned the police at ten o'clock, July 2nd, to report Jessica missing. The foster father was a nurse who worked the overnight shift at a local hospital. He was already at work when his wife called. Each of their whereabouts were established all the way back to noon that day. They both took polygraphs within two days of Jessica's body being discovered and were ruled out. Her foster mom described her as a sweet girl who kept to herself. She went to school, work, came home and went right to her room and worked on her secondhand computer a lot.

The foster mom and dad, who had three small children of their own, couldn't contribute much as to whether Jessica had a boyfriend or who her friends were. All they could definitively say was that she was very sweet, smart, loved computers, and caused them no trouble at all.

There were notes from her case worker, but it was pretty much the same: she was a good kid who'd been born into a shitty life with shitty parents and appeared to look at college as her only way out. Good kids didn't generate much paperwork in the foster care system. Lauren thought of her own two daughters, both away at college, and what would have happened to them if something had happened to her. Their dad had never been a part of their lives and died when they were both very young. Technically they were adults now, but moms can never bear the thought of their kids having to go through life without them, or worse yet, all alone.

It was heartbreaking to Lauren that Jessica had no one to fight for justice for her back then. But then she saw the newer files, printed in the latest format the department had adopted about four years ago, and she realized how much work Reese really had done on the case behind her back. There were updated DNA reports, printouts of every call to the park for a month prior and after the homicide, and he'd pulled the records of every sex offender who lived in a five-mile radius.

Outside their Cold Case office door Lauren could hear snippets of conversation, the rumble of their ancient copy machine, and the sounds of footsteps walking up and down the long corridor that was the backbone of the Homicide unit. Every office off the main spine had its own little drama going on, every homicide crew was working on their own three-act tragedy. A door slammed somewhere at the far end. It should have felt like any other day in the unit. *What else is going on that I have no idea about?* she wondered. *If my own partner can keep such a big secret from me, how good a detective can I really be?*

Lauren sighed into the empty space of her office. Not empty because it wasn't filled from floor to ceiling with the detritus of decades of police work, but because without Reese's big personality flooding it, it was just another room in headquarters. She opened the envelope of crime scene photos, hoping that working on the case would take her mind off the way she and Reese had left things.

The first ones she pulled out were pictures of the Underwater Recovery unit removing the body from the river. One of the divers had taken hold of Jessica under her armpits, her white arms drooping, and was lifting her to another officer standing on the shore. He was reaching out to take her. Long brown hair hung in knotted strands from her head, dripping wet. Her face was turned away from the camera. Slender, pale legs dangled from black shorts. She was barefoot, the water having carried away whatever shoes she'd been wearing. Lauren studied the photo for a moment longer, then placed it face down on the desk.

The next photo was of Jessica's prone body laid out on a blue plastic tarp, her brown hair tangled and knotted around her shoulders. A thin brown branch was twisted in her hair near her right ear. In the missing persons report her foster parents had filed the night before, it said she wore glasses. They were gone. Several dark stains dotted the front of her pink work shirt. *Stab wounds*, Lauren thought, turning the picture over and looking at the next one, a close-up of her hand. Deep, ragged gashes crisscrossed her palms. *Defense wounds*, Lauren noted. *She fought hard for her life*.

She turned the photo face down on top of the last one and realized there was another, smaller envelope inside the first. Written in the police photographer's familiar scrawl across the front was: *Here ya go, Reese. Let me know if you need anything else*. Inside was a cropped photo, a close-up of Jessica's face, pale but beautiful, even in death. Her eyes were closed, her mouth slightly open. He must have needed a picture of her face to show to potential witnesses. She flipped the photo over. Across the white paper backing were multiple black and brown smudges, like the picture had been handled a lot.

Of all the people who came into Jessica's life, Lauren thought sadly, *Reese is the only person who ever cared enough to keep looking for her killer*. She returned the photo to its envelope and started to dig into the homicide file.

FIVE

Seventeen years ago, the Homicide office had not yet started videotaping interviews and interrogations. The Buffalo Police Department was always fifteen years behind on the latest technology. Rumor had it that a camera had been installed in the interview room for two years before it was actually hooked up. They'd even had a sign on the wall cautioning that everyone was subject to video monitoring, but the city hadn't wanted to pay the technicians to wire the system. If Jessica's murder had happened twenty-four months later, there'd be a box of VHS tapes or shiny CDs with the files. Yet because of red tape and bureaucracy, interviews at that time were memorialized only by type-written statements produced by the investigating detectives.

It pissed Lauren off that all that potential evidence was lost because some penny-pinching accountant in city hall wouldn't approve a work order.

Lauren shuffled through the box until she found a paper file marked STATEMENTS. While she marveled at the bare-bones simplicity of the statement form they used to use, she also cringed at its antiquated format and horrible grammar. Any English teacher would develop a migraine just reading the opening pedigree information. Finally updated about ten years ago, the same form had probably been in use since the 1960s. An old-fashioned Polaroid picture was stapled to the upper right-hand corner of each first page. That was a habit the interviewers only lost when all suspect and witness interviews had to be recorded on video. It had been the only way to know for certain who the person you were talking to really was. As hard as it was to believe today, a lot of people didn't have or didn't want to have proper identification on them. The Homicide squad still had three dusty square cameras fully loaded with film in one of the storage closets. *You never knew when something like that might come in handy*, Lauren thought as she jotted the names of everyone who had given a statement on July 3rd, the day Jessica's body was found, on the yellow legal pad at her elbow: Shane Reese, Christopher Sloane, Erica Taviani, Raphael Diaz, Seth Creehan, Amanda Sabria and Tyler Owstrowski. She then added someone named John Branson, who was interviewed on July 5th.

She also made note of the detectives assigned to Jessica's case: Ralph Masterson, Henry Wiley, Kenneth LaBlanc and Tobias Lake. It was quite the cast of characters. Lauren had known all of them before they'd retired, having worked as a detective in the Sex Offense squad on the same floor in the old police headquarters building. She'd watched them do interviews and interrogations as a young detective, trying to learn. Every one of them was retired by the time she transferred to Homicide. And that was long before Reese got there.

Each one of the detectives had had his own unique style of questioning. Ralph was thorough and methodical. Lauren had witnessed Henry Wiley use his tough old father persona while he chain-smoked Marlboro lights. LaBlanc was kind and understanding. Tobias 'Toby the Stache' Lake, the youngest of the crew, was famous for two things: getting confessions and his massive walrus-like mustache. As soon as he got his twenty years in he retired to become a bartender at a biker joint in Sturgis, South Dakota.

She flipped back to Reese's statement and looked at his picture. He was sitting in one of the hard-backed chairs in the main interview room, a white Buffalo Bisons baseball hat on his head. He looked impossibly young in a plain T-shirt and grey pajama pants. His eyes were wide and blank, like the detectives had roused him from a sound sleep and he wasn't fully awake yet. The time on the statement said his interview had begun at 8:52 a.m. And although she hadn't seen it happen very often over the years they'd worked together, she could tell he was afraid. As much as she wanted to dive into it, she decided she'd read his statement last. She didn't want what she knew about Reese now to color her view of his words then. It was better that she read everyone else's first and get the big picture, than read his and want to believe everything he said was true. She needed to be impartial and unbiased. At least as much as she could be.

She slipped his statement back into the folder. They were in no particular order, having been rifled through over the years. The next one in the stack was Christopher Sloane's. Contrasted against Reese's half-asleep-and-scared pose, Chris looked awake and alert. Lauren noted that he'd been interviewed at 1:11 p.m. He hadn't been pulled right from his bed like Reese had been. He had a mint green T-shirt on and the long, baggy jean shorts that were all the rage that summer. Instead of the well-kept dreadlocks, his hair was cut short with a neat part shaved into one side. She flipped to the actual statement page. The form was yellowing with age and had a coffee stain in the upper corner. Ralph Masterson had interviewed him and typed the notes. Sometimes one detective did both, sometimes one asked the questions and another detective silently transcribed. Either way, they were taught to type everything the interviewee said verbatim, sometimes stopping them after a sentence to get everything in exactly as they said it. It was tedious, but necessary.

CITY OF BUFFALO – POLICE DEPARTMENT – HOMICIDE SQUAD

STATE OF NEW YORK	**DATE: 7/3**
COUNTY OF ERIE	**TIME COMMENCED: 1:11 p.m.**
CITY OF BUFFALO	**Incident # 03-976421** **File # 03-058**

I, **Christopher Antwan Sloane,** residing at 5940 South Park Avenue, Buffalo NY 14204, telephone 716-278-0566 being duly sworn deposes and makes the following statement while at the Buffalo Police Department Homicide Office. The questions are asked and typed by Detective Ralph Masterson.

RM (Ralph Masterson): Can you read and write, and how far have you gone in school?
CS (Christopher Sloane): Yes, I can read and write. I went to 12th grade. I start college in the fall.
RM: The Buffalo Police Department is investigating an incident that occurred on July 2nd. Can you answer my questions about this incident?
CS: Yes.
RM: Can you tell me what you did yesterday, July 2nd?
CS: I was working at Memorial Park in the Ward on the groundskeeping crew. I got there at noon and left when my shift ended at six thirty.
RM: Did you drive there or get a ride?
CS: I drove my mom's Dodge. What is this about? Is my dad still out there?
RM: He's still out in the main office. Did you see Jessica Toakase yesterday?
CS: Her and Amanda Sabria work at the concession stand together.
RM: How do you know she was working?
CS: Shane Reese had a baseball game yesterday afternoon with his summer league. He goes out with Amanda. He stopped by the groundskeeper building and told us

he was going to hang around and wait for her to get off work at six thirty. He said her and Jessica were both working. So later when we were making our rounds on the golf cart we drove by them.

RM: Who was working the grounds crew with you?

CS: It was me, Seth Creehan and Tyler Owstrowski. We all got hired together through the Mayor's summer youth program, same as Jessica and Amanda.

RM: Just the three of you on grounds for the whole park all day?

CS: From noon until six thirty. It's not that busy on weekdays but there were a couple of baseball games scheduled and the fans are total slobs. They leave garbage everywhere. Hey, am I here because of what Tyler did?

RM: What did Tyler do?

This writer notes the subject hesitates before answering.

CS: He said he saw Jessica and Amanda walking to the concession stand on his way into work and started messing with them. He grabbed Jessica around the waist and she yelled at him.

RM: Tyler Owstrowski grabbed Jessica Toakase yesterday?

CS: Yeah and he was really nervous about it. He said he was only fooling around, but he was afraid she'd make a complaint. He said she should be grateful any dude was paying attention to her at all. I told him he had to cut that shit out, oh sorry, stuff out or he'd get fired or worse. He could lose his football scholarship.

RM: Is that what he told you?

CS: Yeah and I guess he was right, if she called the police. That's why I'm here, isn't it? She made a complaint.

RM: Is Jessica the type to make a complaint?

CS: I don't think so, but I don't know. We're not tight like that. We don't hang out. There's nothing interesting about her. She's like a blank piece of paper, really into computers. Kinda nerdy. Tyler has a football scholarship,

Division 2, but still. He was really scared she'd tell her boss. And since I'm here, I guess she did.

RM: You never spoke to her about it though.

CS: The concession stand is over by the main entrance to the park, don't ask me why. You'd think it'd be right by the baseball diamonds. The groundskeeping building is all the way over on the other side, so I only saw her from a distance. Me and Seth waved at them, they waved back. Am I done? Can I go now?

RM: Jessica Toakase was found dead this morning.

This interviewer notes subject did hesitate for several seconds before responding.

CS: Damn. Jessica's dead? That's messed up. What happened to her?

RM: I thought maybe you could help us piece that together. What time did Tyler tell you that incident between them occurred?

Interviewer notes that subject shrugged his shoulders.

RM: That's not an answer.

CS: I don't know. When he first came in around noon.

RM: Did he ever leave your presence the rest of the day?

CS: No. The three of us rode around on the golf cart between games. We use the bathroom in the groundskeeper building because the port-a-potties are nasty. So, no. He was with me and Seth until we punched out at six thirty. After that, I don't know where he went. I went home. You can ask my mom and dad. I was home by eight o'clock.

RM: Did Tyler say where he was going after work?

CS: No and neither did Seth. Can I go now? I really want to see my dad.

RM: You got off at six thirty but didn't get home until eight o'clock. Where were you during that time?

CS: I stopped at the store on South Park Avenue, got some pop and chips. Drove by my friend Marcus's house, but his car wasn't there so I went home. It's not like I have a curfew or anything.

RM: Did anyone see you at the store that can back up your story?

CS: It's not a story. I was there.

RM: Can anyone corroborate you were at the store from seven until eight last night?

CS: That's not what I said. I was only in the store for a few minutes. Marcus lives over off of Jefferson Avenue. I came right home after I didn't see his car.

RM: So Marcus can't back you up either.

CS: I don't think I want to talk to you anymore.

RM: Don't you want to help me find out what happened to Jessica?

CS: How can I help you? You're the cop. I told you everything I know. I want to go now. Please.

RM: Is there anything else you can tell me about Jessica that I haven't already asked?

CS: No. Can I leave now?

RM: You're free to go. Here's my card. Please call me if you remember anything.

Subject does take interviewer's card.

Interviewer ends questioning.

***** Statement ended 1:57 p.m. *****

I understand that any false statements made herein are punishable as a class A misdemeanor, pursuant to section 210.45 of the New York State Penal Law, of the State of New York. Subscribed and verified under penalty of perjury.

Signed: Christopher Sloane

Sworn and Subscribed before Me

Ralph Masterson
Commissioner of Deeds in and for
The City of Buffalo, New York,
County of Erie

Lauren knew that everyone processed death differently, but still she was surprised at the seemingly casual way Chris was described as taking the news about Jessica. She didn't expect him to break down in sobs, but for Ralph to jot down the shrugging of the shoulders, that meant he also noticed a note of detachment. Chris might not have hung around with Jessica, but she was someone he'd seen every day for four years of high school. It seemed a stark contrast to the warm, open man she'd met at Amichi's. The one who'd asked Reese about the progress of Jessica's case. She understood his frustration at the end. Ralph's questions might have seemed like accusations to a kid sitting in the Homicide office's interview room. Hell, they'd seem like accusations to her if the roles were reversed.

The real point of interest though was Chris's statement about Tyler Owstrowski. Losing your summer job at the local park was one thing, losing a football scholarship equaled motive. Lauren fished out his statement. He was also interviewed on July 3rd by Ralph, but in the morning, at 10:58, before Chris had given his statement. The detectives must have sent a car crew out to grab him right away, given that either Amanda or Reese, who'd been interviewed first, would have told them about Tyler grabbing Jessica.

Tyler's Polaroid showed a beefy-looking teenager wearing a football jersey and athletic shorts. His brown hair was buzzed close to his head, making his forehead look huge. It was hard to tell from his expression what he was feeling. His mouth was set in a tight line. His eyebrows were knitted together. It could be fear, concern or anger. Maybe a mix of all three. She neatly folded the Polaroid over the back of the statement and started going through the pedigree information at the top.

CITY OF BUFFALO – POLICE DEPARTMENT – HOMICIDE SQUAD

STATE OF NEW YORK	**DATE: 7/3**
COUNTY OF ERIE	**TIME COMMENCED: 10:58 a.m.**
CITY OF BUFFALO	**Incident # 03-976421** **File # 03-058**

I, **Tyler Owstrowski,** residing at 2077 Kentucky Street, Buffalo NY 14202, telephone 716-349-4345 being duly sworn deposes and makes the following statement while at the Buffalo Police Department Homicide Office. The questions are asked by Detective Ralph Masterson and typed by Detective Henry Wiley.

RM (Ralph Masterson): Can you read and write, and how far have you gone in school?
TO (Tyler Owstrowski): Yes, I can read and write. I graduated from 12th grade.
RM: The Buffalo Police Department is investigating an incident involving Jessica Toakase that occurred on July 2nd. Can you answer some questions about this incident?
TO: I guess.
RM: It's a yes or no question.
TO: Then yes.
RM: Tell me about your day yesterday.
TO: My whole day? Like getting up and brushing my teeth and stuff?
RM: Let's skip to the park. Do you work at Memorial Park?
TO: Yes. I'm on groundskeeping.
RM: Did you work yesterday?
TO: Yes, from noon to six thirty. I worked the six to noon last summer and it killed me to get up that early.
RM: Did you happen to see Jessica Toakase at the park yesterday.

This writer notes subject does hesitate before answering.

TO: Yes.
RM: Tell me about that.
TO: Uhhhh, I saw her when I was walking in the park entrance. Her and Amanda Sabria were getting out of Amanda's car. I went over to them and said hello. Then I went to the groundskeeping building.
RM: Did anything else happen?
TO: Uhhhh, I worked, we cleaned up the diamonds after the games, Raphael came by. Shane Reese stopped over after his game.
RM: Did anything happen when you saw Jessica?

TO: Uhhh

RM: Uhhh is not an answer.

TO: I mean, I said hi to them and I put my arm around her and she went nuts. I was only joking around.

RM: Where did you touch her?

TO: I didn't touch her anywhere! I put my arm around her waist, that's not touching her.

RM: Did you say anything when you put your arm around her waist?

TO: I was kidding! I was just being stupid. What is she saying?

RM: What time did you work until yesterday?

TO: Six thirty. Ask Seth Creehan or Chris Sloane. They were with me all day.

RM: Did you see Jessica again after you put your arm around her waist?

TO: Just from the golf cart. I was like, a mile away from her. What did she say I did?

RM: How about after you got done with work? What did you do?

TO: I walked to my car. I park it on Ohio Street because a lot of the cars in the lot have been getting broken into, even in broad daylight. It's a rusted-out Chevy, but they'll smash the windows just to get the change in your console.

RM: So Chris Sloane wouldn't have seen you get into your car?

TO: No. Why? What is Jessica saying I did? Because I didn't see her again yesterday.

RM: Where did you go after you left the park?

TO: I went to my house.

RM: Were your parents home when you got there?

TO: No, my grandpa is in Mercy Hospital. He fell and broke his hip and wrist and he's in really bad shape. They've been there all week. Visiting hours end at nine but the nurses let them stay until nine thirty, so they got home close to ten.

RM: So no one can vouch for your whereabouts between 6:30 and 9:45?

The door to the Cold Case office swung open. Reese came in, threw his duffel bag in the corner and flopped down at his desk. 'I can't work out. I tried. I can't concentrate.'

Lauren slipped Tyler's statement back into the folder. She was troubled by how Tyler tried to minimize his interaction with Jessica. 'I know this is upsetting to you. I can see how hard you worked on this file.'

'I spent every school day from ninth grade to my senior year with her. The little group of us? We were more than classmates.' Reese leaned his head forward and rested it in his hands. 'I still can't believe someone killed Jessica. And that no one's been caught yet. Or that I can't even develop a good suspect.'

'Maybe you couldn't develop a good suspect because you're too close to the case.' That old, tired trope from every cop movie and TV show snapped into Lauren's mind. The ornery captain screaming at the troubled detective in front of his desk, 'You're too close to this one! You're off the case!' and the vengeful cop angrily slamming down his gun and badge while secretly vowing to pursue justice on his own. Reese didn't look vengeful, he looked distraught.

He nodded into his hands. 'I know you're right. Barring a wandering psycho killer, all the suspects are my friends. I don't want to believe one of them could have done this, but I pulled every registered sex offender within miles, checked similar crimes from ten years previous to ten years after, had all the physical evidence retested, rechased every lead, and I got nothing.'

'You didn't reinterview any of your friends,' Lauren pointed out.

'How could I? That would have been crossing an even bigger line. I thought if I could come up with something, anything, I'd turn the file over to you and let you run with it. I know now that was stupid of me.'

She tried to sound comforting without being condescending. 'You did the wrong thing, but from what I see I don't think you corrupted the case.'

'My alibi is that I walked Amanda to her car and we said goodbye. Not very solid.'

'She corroborates it, right?'

Reese nodded. 'I waited for Amanda to get off work. I walked her to her car, which was parked near mine and we both went home. It's in both of our statements. Our parents confirm we were each home by eight o'clock.'

Lauren gathered up the folders she'd been looking over and put them back in the box. 'I'm going to have Marilyn scan this whole file into the system for me. Put it in the Cloud so I can download it.'

'I made individual files on all my classmates. I tried to keep tabs on where they've been and what they've been doing. I haven't updated them in over a year. I put the case away for a while, tried to get it out of my head.'

'We have been very busy.'

He rubbed the scars on his scalp with his left hand, fingers lingering on the angry-looking raised red lines. 'That we have,' he agreed.

Standing up, Lauren slipped her hands into the box handles. 'I'll get this taken care of right now. You relax. You're not alone in this anymore.' She hitched the box up a little and headed for the door.

Just as she was balancing the box on her hip and trying to turn the door handle, she heard Reese call out to her. 'Hey, Riley?'

She turned her head to look at him. 'Yeah?'

His warm green eyes met her icy blue ones. 'Thank you.'

SIX

Lauren didn't need the original files to go over to the spot where Jessica's body had been pulled from the Buffalo River. When she'd dropped the boxes off on Marilyn's desk, the report technician had looked up from the payroll she was typing into her computer. 'What fresh hell is this?' she'd asked.

'I need all of this scanned into the computer and saved in the Cloud so I can access it.'

Marilyn stood up from her chair and looked over the contents. 'Well, princess, I have two files ahead of yours.' She motioned to the newer-looking boxes sitting on the floor behind her desk. 'I'll try to have them done by Thanksgiving. I'm a one-person show here.'

'You are wonderful and I owe you lunch.'

She sighed, sinking back down into her seat. 'I know I'm wonderful. And I'd like to go to that new place on Pearl Street tomorrow.'

Lauren snapped her fingers with a smile. 'You got it! Oh, and Marilyn . . .'

'Hmmm?' she murmured, typing in some more numbers.

'You're going to see a familiar name in those files. I'd appreciate it if you kept that to yourself.'

Marilyn looked up at Lauren over the rim of her red glasses. 'I keep a lot of secrets, my dear. I'm a vault of dark knowledge. I'm surprised someone doesn't have a hit out on me.'

Lauren laughed out loud at their report technician. 'You've always been a little dangerous.'

'Girlfriend . . .' she said, and turned back to her screen. 'You don't even know.'

With that taken care of Lauren went back to her office where she and Reese pretended it was just another shift. Sometimes silence worked better for them instead of barbs and jabs. When they had finished up for the day, Reese told her he wanted to take a ride to McCarthy's Brew Pub to check on his fantasy football pool stats. Lauren guessed that was as good an excuse as any to have a beer or three, especially after everything that had come out that day. She knew he wanted to go somewhere anonymous to try to forget for a couple hours. Lauren waited until after he left the office, made her way to her personal car down in the lot, and then drove over to his old neighborhood to try and remember.

Lauren slowly drove past the site of Public School 91. The main building was now an empty lot used for parking for the new microbrewery. The football field behind the school had been transformed into a beer garden. Most of where Memorial Park had been now consisted of high-priced condos that rose up along the river front. It was on the Riverwalk in front of the newest addition that Lauren found herself staring down the rocky bank.

Using the crime scene photos she'd studied at the office as reference, she knew from the skeletal remains of an ancient warehouse the city refused to tear down across the river that this was the right spot, despite the huge bar/restaurant complex that had been built beside it, separated by only a parking lot. The developers had left the old tree, with its twisted, gnarled roots reaching for the rushing water that marked where the fire department's dive team had laid out Jessica's body. The Michigan Street lift bridge was visible downriver, just before a brand-new waterfront wedding venue and another set of condos.

A heaviness seized her chest. Revisiting the scene was an essential part of any cold case, but with it came the realization that even though Jessica's case had remained cold, the rest of the world had continued on without missing a beat. The young couple strolling past her on the footpath with their Goldendoodle barely glanced at her, absorbed in their own world, one where Jessica Toakase had never existed. That was the burden cold case detectives carried: it was their job to remember the dead, to look for forgotten people and things. Sometimes, like today, it weighed more heavily on Lauren. Another bloom of darkness took hold in her heart, along with all the others that had accumulated there over the years – a bouquet of black roses with names that whispered to her in her sleep. Jessica had only been a couple of years younger than her own two daughters were now. It was hard not to feel an acute ache of loss for her in this spot. Reese must have felt that ache for seventeen years.

She looked behind her through the break between buildings. The new pool and clubhouse for the condominiums stood where the baseball diamonds used to be. This was where Reese had grown up, where he'd gripped his first bat and developed his love for the game. She knew that where she was standing had been a network of walking paths carved out between scrubby trees and high bushes between the park and water. She wondered if the new residents of Queen's River Towers knew that a young girl's broken body had been recovered here.

She wondered how many times Reese had come and stood where she was standing now. She wondered how many times he'd almost told her about Jessica, but didn't.

Lauren had snapped pictures of the autopsy report into her phone before she'd turned the boxes of files over to Marilyn. A cold wind blew her hair around her face. Wishing she'd worn a jacket with a hood, she thumbed through her photos, stopping and pinching the screen to zoom in on the faded ink of the report.

She reminded herself what the autopsy terms meant. *Postmortem meant the injury occurred after death. Perimortem meant at or near the time of death. I shouldn't be mixing those terms up*, she thought, *I should be a walking glossary of death terminology. Maybe, after seeing too many dead bodies, you start to block things out. Maybe you don't have a choice, if you want to stay sane.*

She focused on the pages on her cell phone.

Perimortem blunt force trauma to the head. The crude drawing of a prone figure showed a line from the back of her head marking the injury. Other arrows pointed out post and peri stab wounds to the upper back and chest, defense wounds to both hands, and notes scribbled along the margin declared the wounds consistent with a blitz-style attack. Lauren swiped over to the typewritten portion of the report. Jessica's toxicology had come back clean, no drugs had been found in her system. The cause of death was listed as stabbing, the manner of death: homicide. Her killer had hit her in the head to incapacitate her and then furiously stabbed her with a metal stake even after she was dead. The weapon, a wicked-looking green metal stake about three feet long used around the park to anchor newly planted trees, had been recovered thirty yards upstream on the riverbank, caught between some rocks, all DNA washed away by the rushing waters. The autopsy report had concluded it was also the instrument used to cause the wounds to her scalp.

Lauren lowered her phone. A red leaf sailed by her head, followed by a yellow one, the old tree next to her shedding its foliage like a wet dog shaking off the rain. She sank down on one knee and looked down the path. She pictured the trajectory of the crime: the killer yanking the stake out of the ground as they stalked after Jessica, the ambush by the big boulders where they hit her in the head, the stabbing and then the dumping of Jessica's body. In her mind's eye Lauren saw the killer drop the stake into the rocks next to them and push Jessica's lifeless body into the water. She got caught by the current and dragged down the river, tangling up in tree roots – the roots of the tree Lauren was standing next to now. Lauren pictured the water flooding over Jessica, taking her shoes, her glasses, her blood.

Lauren closed her eyes and inhaled deeply. The smell of Cheerios from the nearby General Mills plant filled her nose. She imagined the sun, still high enough on a summer July evening to see everything and everyone clearly. Jessica had seen her attacker. Seen and knew and struggled against him or her. The Old First Ward hadn't yet started its renaissance when the crime occurred. Memorial Park wasn't a destination like Buffalo's famed Delaware Park designed by Frederick Law Olmsted. It had been a shabby neighborhood hangout, barely maintained by the city until they finally sold it off altogether. Only the local residents frequented the park – the children playing baseball there during the day and the teenagers drinking and necking in the shadows together at night. A stranger hanging around in the bushes while it was still light would have stuck out like a sore thumb. Lauren opened her eyes.

Everything she knew about homicide, how it was committed and by who, told her this was no random attack. She felt the weight of the darkness in her chest. She let out the breath she hadn't realized she'd been holding and turned into the wind to walk back to her car. No, Jessica had known her attacker.

Which meant so did Reese.

SEVEN

Thanksgiving dinner was blessedly stress-free for Lauren since Reese had volunteered to do all the cooking this year. It was just her, her daughters and him. Her parents had gone to her sister Jill's house out west, Dayla was hosting dinner for her kids and grandkids a few doors down, and Reese had negotiated having his son the night before. Lauren suspected he'd offered to do all the cooking to take his mind off the fact that the baby wouldn't be with him.

The product of a very brief relationship, five-month-old Gabriel was the love of Reese's life. What had started out as amicable between him and Gabe's mother, Charlotte, in the glow of a new baby coming, had dissolved over the last few months into a tense give-and-take. Lauren knew it was headed to Family Court soon for custody and visitation, even though Reese had wanted to avoid that at all costs. He gave Charlotte more than the court would have awarded for child support, hoping that would delay the inevitable. He picked up Gabe whenever she asked, taking vacation days if necessary.

Lauren had warned him before he walked into the delivery room that he was about to lose his heart forever and, sure enough, he had. Watching Reese parent his baby boy brought her back to the days when her own girls were tiny and helpless and depending on her for everything. Now they were both grown, sitting across from her at the dining room table, talking about college, exams and spring break plans between shoveling bites of turkey into their mouths. Watching Lindsey's head tilt toward Erin's, Lauren still marveled at how it was possible that she had given birth to such beauty. She recognized the same look in Reese's eyes as he held Gabe – that feeling of love mixed with awe that constantly threatens to overwhelm you.

Now Reese sat at the head of the table, one hand on his

fork, the other on his West Highland Terrier's head. Reese had become even more attached to his dog, Watson, since Gabe's birth. Lauren suspected he'd become Gabe's stand-in during the long absences.

'How is it?' Reese asked, surveying his handiwork in front of them.

'The food is excellent,' Lauren replied. 'You should have been a fireman.'

'Where do you think I learned to do all this?' He spread his arms wide over the table of food. Reese's father had been a captain in the Buffalo Fire Department and had done most of the cooking in his house.

'I love the stuffing,' Erin told him, scooping more onto her plate. 'I can't wait for Gabe to be able to be with us on the holidays.'

'You and me both, kid,' he replied, and began to pile food onto the decorative plate adorned with turkeys that Lauren had found at HomeGoods. Five years ago she wouldn't have even thought about buying holiday dishware, complete with matching gravy boat, but the events of the last few years had reminded her that life was fragile and time flew by. She'd never get back all the holidays she'd had to work as a single mom. Seeing Reese struggle to spend even a little time with his son made her resolve to make every get together with her daughters more special. The last three days with them had been fantastic. It was strange and wonderful to hear them talk now. They'd become adults, but she hoped they still needed her in some way, if only for advice on what *not* to do. She could give plenty of that.

'What time are you heading to that spa place tomorrow?' Lindsey asked.

'We're thinking around noon. It's about an hour and a half drive.'

'Are you going to go skiing? It's supposed to snow tomorrow night. Some of my friends are renting a condo in Ellicottville to go snowboarding.' Erin had been an avid snowboarder in high school but had had a really bad fall. Lauren tried to encourage her to try it again, but even though she hadn't been seriously hurt, she'd been seriously scared and still wasn't ready to brave the slopes. 'They're super excited. It's not the same when the snow machines make it.'

'Chris says he has a deal with one of the resorts in Ellicottville if anyone wants to go skiing on Saturday,' Reese said. 'I'd like to go, but I'll wait and see what the group wants to do.'

'I'd like to go to the lodge at least,' Lauren said. She took a sip of her wine and immediately started coughing and couldn't stop. Lindsey liked her white zinfandel ice cold and had put the bottle on the back steps to chill.

Erin pounded on her back. 'Mom? Are you OK?'

Tears welled up in Lauren's eyes. She managed to smile as she finally caught her breath. 'It went down the wrong pipe,' she said, dabbing her mouth with her napkin. 'Sorry about that.'

'Don't be sorry,' Reese said, looking at her hard but keeping his voice light. He knew her lungs were still damaged from getting stabbed. He also knew she never should have been cleared to come back to work three weeks ago. Lauren smoothed her napkin over her lap and hoped Reese would let it drop. Her daughters had no idea about the state of her physical health, and she intended to keep it that way.

'It's too bad the spa section isn't open yet,' Lindsey said, adding some butter to her mashed potatoes. 'You both could use a nice massage. Maybe some aquatic therapy.'

'The indoor/outdoor pool won't be ready until at least next fall, so the entire wing to the spa section is closed off. I'm actually kind of bummed about that,' Reese said.

'I was looking at the website online after Mom told me you were going up there. It looks amazing. The fireplace in the third-floor atrium is like something out of a movie,' Erin said.

'The whole place is like something out of a movie,' Lindsey amended. 'It's like someone plunked a luxury resort from the Swiss Alps in the middle of the Southern Tier.'

Reese raised his wine glass, took a drink and smiled at the girls. 'Looks like my friend did.'

'Are you excited about seeing your old classmates again?' Erin asked, reaching for the wine bottle in the center of the table. Lauren's hand shot out, grabbing it first. She poured herself another glass and set the bottle next to her plate. She knew Erin probably drank at college, but that didn't mean she got to drink at home. Erin gave her a goofy I-had-to-try smile and Lauren smiled back.

Reese ran a hand over his head, rubbing his scars, that gesture Lauren knew so well. 'Yes and no. I've been on the phone texting and talking to Chris all week. It's been great catching up with him. Seth and I weren't that close, he was really into computers and I was a jock. Tyler was obnoxious. I learned to ignore half the crap that came out of his mouth a long time ago. Erica is just Erica.' He glanced over at Lauren. 'You'll see what I mean as soon as you meet her. And Amanda, well, that might be awkward.'

'Was she your high school sweetheart?' Lindsey teased, elbow on the table, resting her chin in the heel of her hand.

'She was, but it was kid stuff, you know? Chris says her husband worships the ground she walks on.' A slight smile turned up the sides of his mouth. 'I hope that's true. She deserves it.'

'You haven't seen her since you left for the army, right?' Lauren asked.

'Since before that. Since . . .' His voice trailed off, then he caught himself. 'We broke up before that. I enlisted in the army the September after I graduated. I started dating the girl I almost married right after.'

'You almost got married?' Lindsey asked, with a look of extreme interest. 'Why did I not know this?'

'Because it was most certainly a rebound relationship,' Reese told her, and flicked some mashed potatoes at her, hitting her squarely in the forehead. 'And it's none of your business.'

Lindsey laughed while trying to get the potatoes out of her hair with her napkin, wisely letting the subject drop. Lauren was glad her daughter could tell by the tone of his voice that he didn't want to discuss it. After reading some of Jessica's case file, she had a few questions about his relationship with Amanda as well. In fact, she had questions for every single one of his classmates that were going to be at the spa that weekend. She'd been troubled by the case since she picked it up. Something about the statements she'd read so far just didn't sit right with her.

Thankfully, Marilyn had finished scanning most of the file into the Cloud for Lauren just the day before. Now she could review the paperwork on her iPad or even her phone, in case she was with Reese and didn't want him to see what she was doing. As close as she was with him, there were things his friends had told the police about Jessica's case that needed to be rechecked. She'd agreed to come for a relaxing weekend, but as she got deeper into the homicide file, in her mind it morphed into a fact-finding mission.

What had Shirley Gizzo said? Lauren asked herself. *When you meddle with things, they sometimes come back and meddle with you? Or was that only true if you had something to hide?*

EIGHT

That night, after she'd said goodnight to her daughters and Reese, she lay on her bed and opened up Jessica's homicide file on her iPad. She was exhausted in a good way, from running around with her girls, shopping and eating. It was the kind of family time she craved now that both of her daughters were away at school, and she savored every second of it.

She stayed up past her bedtime listening to them talk about sororities and professors and mid-terms, just inhaling their very presence in the house. She'd managed when Lindsey went off because she still had Erin at home to mother for another year. After Erin went to Duke, Lauren was left alone in her big house with no one to take care of, no one to run to soccer practice or the movies. She only realized now what a dark place she had been in, how her empty nest had contributed to her getting mixed up in the David Spencer case. She'd spent so many years as a single mother that suddenly finding herself alone was unbearable at first. It took her a long time to get to a good place again, only to get stabbed in her office and have Reese and Watson move in. Very few people on the job understood their relationship. They assumed Reese and Riley were lovers who just denied it, even though they lived together. Lauren had never really cared what gossiping cops had to say about her. Their living arrangement worked for them. He had his first-floor bedroom and bath with his own entrance, and she had the entire second floor when her daughters weren't home. Gabe's crib was in Reese's room for now, but the little guy had his own bedroom upstairs waiting for him, decorated in green dinosaurs. Watson, of course, had the run of the house. They weren't a traditional family by any means, but so far, they'd been happy.

Until Jessica's case came up. Since that revelation there'd been a distance between them that she hadn't felt since he'd threatened to end their partnership over her joining the David Spencer serial killer task force. He'd felt she was putting herself in danger and leaving him out of the loop. And he'd been right. It had almost gotten them both killed. Maybe if she could make some headway on Jessica's murder, identify some piece of evidence that singled out a suspect, he could stop feeling like she were looking at him as though he was a perpetrator.

Now as she lay under her covers with her iPad propped on her chest and her daughters and Reese all safely ensconced in their own beds, she scrolled through Jessica's file. She'd already read Chris's statement, taken the afternoon her body was found. She saw that Seth Creehan's statement was also taken that morning, after Reese and Amanda Sabria's. The order of the statements made sense to her – Amanda first because she was Jessica's best friend and co-worker. Reese right after her, because he was Amanda's boyfriend. The foster parents would have steered the police right to them, especially since they'd stated they hadn't learned much about Jessica's social life in the short time she'd lived with them. Logically, the three boys who worked in the groundskeeper section would be next, followed by Erica and Raphael. The detectives had also located an independent witness who was brought in last. One person's statement always led to someone else being questioned, if you did it right.

Using the touch-screen, she pulled up Seth Creehan's statement. In his Polaroid he was sitting ramrod straight, staring right into the camera. A skinny kid with thick, coke-bottle glasses that magnified his eyes, he looked like a terrified baby owl. His mouth was shaped in a little 'o', as if the picture had been snapped just as he was about to say something.

Lauren ran her eyes over his information. Seth had lived in a house in the Ward that was no longer standing. She knew this because she recognized the address as one that now belonged to a popular bar where she'd gone to at least two police retirement parties. Things had changed a lot in the last seventeen years in Buffalo's Old First Ward. People sipped IPAs on outdoor patios in the shadow of abandoned grain elevators where they now held poetry slams. She wondered if Seth came home and drove around the area, taking in the new condos and kayak launches on the river and wondering what the hell happened to his working-class neighborhood.

Seth's interview was taken by Kenneth LaBlanc, an old-timer who seemed more suited to being a librarian than a homicide detective. Lauren had only worked with him for a short time before he retired. A wearer of thick glasses and out-of-date suits, Ken was mercilessly teased by the other detectives for having a slight stutter. 'L-L-LaBlanc!' She'd hear them mimic him when she first became a detective, before she was brave enough to open her mouth and tell them to shut the hell up, like she'd do now. She was ashamed she'd been such a coward. As she read over the statement in her head, she could hear poor Ken getting caught on the *s*'s, trying so hard to push the words out. He was a genuinely kind man, the guy the other detectives had interview females and children, while they opted for the hard-core felons who knew the system inside and out. She wondered if that was why he was the one who took the statement, so as not to give poor Seth a heart attack.

CITY OF BUFFALO – POLICE DEPARTMENT – HOMICIDE SQUAD

STATE OF NEW YORK	**DATE: 7/3**
COUNTY OF ERIE	**TIME COMMENCED: 11:45 a.m.**
CITY OF BUFFALO	**Incident # 03-976421**
	File # 03-058

I, **Seth Creehan,** residing at 4671 O'Connell Street, Buffalo NY 14204, telephone 716-318-6759 being duly sworn deposes and makes the following statement while at the Buffalo Police Department Homicide Office. The questions are asked and typed by Detective Kenneth LaBlanc.

KL (Kenneth LaBlanc): Can you read and write, and how far have you gone in school?

SC (Seth Creehan): I just graduated in June from PS 91. I can read and write.

KL: The Buffalo Police Department is investigating an incident that occurred on July 2nd. Do you consent to answer my questions about this incident?

SC: Yes.

KL: Seth, the Buffalo Police Department is investigating an incident involving Jessica Toakase. Is there anything you can tell us about that?

SC: No. I didn't even know she was missing until the cop told me on the way here.

KL: So you have no idea what happened to Jessica Toakase?

SC: No. My mom woke me up and said the cops were at our house and we had to come with you. I don't know what's going on. I saw Jessica yesterday. When did she go missing?

KL: She was last seen in Memorial Park.

SC: That's crazy. Did she run away? She was a foster kid you know.

KL: How well did you know Jessica Toakase?

SC: We went to School 91 together. We were both in a special gifted and talented program and we both worked at Memorial Park in the Ward.

KL: Did you see her last night?

SC: No, I only saw her during the day. When I came home from work, I played *Call of Duty* all night. I just got it and I was up until four in the morning playing it. It's a sweet game.

KL: But you did see her yesterday?

SC: Yeah, like I said, during the day, for like, a second when we drove by the concession stand.

KL: You didn't stop and talk to her?

SC: I wasn't driving the golf cart. Chris Sloane was. Me, him and Tyler Owstrowski work groundskeeping and we have to clean the baseball diamonds after every game. We waved to her and Amanda Sabria as we went by.

KL: Was Tyler Owstrowski with you when you saw Jessica and Amanda?

SC: Yeah, but he was hiding in the rear seat.

KL: Hiding?

SC: Well, not hiding. He just ducked down when we went past them. Something happened with him and Jessica, and Tyler didn't want her to see him.

KL: What happened?

SC: Nothing really. Tyler said he was joking around with her and she took it the wrong way. He was afraid she was going to get him fired.

KL: Did he tell you what he did?

SC: He said he saw her and Amanda walking into the park on their way to work and hugged her and she freaked out.

KL: Do you believe him that he only hugged her?

SC: I kinda do because Tyler is all talk, you know? He's always bragging about girls, but I don't think he does most of the stuff he says he does.

KL: You don't think it's serious to touch girls without their permission?

SC: I do think it's serious. I just don't think he meant it like that.

KL: Then why would he be afraid he'd get fired?

SC: I think he was just trying to make it look like a big deal. Like he's some kind of stud. I think he was more scared of Raphael finding out.

KL: Who's Raphael?

SC: Raphael Diaz. Now he's the real deal. All the girls love him. He went to school with us too, but he wasn't in our program. His girlfriend, Erica Taviani, was though. Him and Jessica were hooking up behind her back.

KL: Is that a rumor you heard?

SC: No, that's the truth. Raphael told me himself. Me and him live on the same street and sometimes he stops by and he tells me things.

KL: He told you he was cheating on his girlfriend with Jessica?

SC: Yeah. He told me a couple of weeks ago. He'd never tell Tyler or Chris because they're friends with Erica, but she doesn't bother with me much, so I guess he trusted me to keep it a secret. He's been with Erica for, like, years.

KL: Did you see Raphael Diaz yesterday?

SC: Yeah, Erica came by the groundskeeping building around 3 o'clock to ask some questions about an article she's working on, then Raph came around later. He told me he was meeting up with Jessica after she got off work last night. Hey, you should talk to Raphael. He probably knows where she is.

KL: What time did he tell you that?

SC: I think it was around five thirty. Do you think something happened to Jessica, because from the questions you're asking, it sounds like you think something really bad happened to her.

KL: Something bad did happen to Jessica and I'm trying to figure it out. Did you see Tyler leave the park after you were done with your shift?

SC: You don't think Tyler would hurt Jessica, do you? Because he wouldn't. He's all talk, like I said. He wouldn't hurt anybody.

KL: Did you see Tyler leave the park?

SC: No, because it was my turn to stay and clean up. Tyler and Chris left right at six thirty. I didn't get finished until about quarter to seven.

KL: How did you get home?

SC: I walked.

KL: Did you see Raphael when you were walking home?

SC: No, but he was supposed to meet Jessica on the big

rocks by the river when she got done with work. That's in the opposite direction.

KL: Did Erica Taviani know Raphael was cheating on her with Jessica?

SC: No. No way. She'd have gone ballistic.

KL: When you saw Erica earlier in the afternoon, did she seem mad or upset?

SC: No. Erica was kind of bitchy, same as always.

KL: Was it unusual for her to be in the park?

SC: In the summer, even when we're not working, the park is our hangout. All of us are always hanging out by the playground. Me, Chris and Tyler have worked there since we were sixteen. That's three summers now. Raphael worked one summer and hated it, so he quit. Amanda and Jessica worked last summer and this summer. Erica is doing an internship for some online blog and she babysits her brothers a lot, so she just comes and finds us.

KL: Did you notice anyone suspicious in the park yesterday?

SC: Nope. It was just like every other day this summer. Same people, same mess to clean up.

KL: Do you consider Tyler and Raphael your friends?

SC: Yes.

KL: Even though you're not exactly the kind of kid they'd hang out with?

SC: I used to get mocked out a lot, before I got in the gifted program, and Tyler still mocks me out, but he sticks up for me too. It's like he can punk me, but no one else is allowed to, you know? And Raphael was one of the most popular guys in our high school. He's lived down the street from me my whole life and until I started the program with Erica, he totally ignored me. Now he's my friend. Shane Reese calls me on the weekends to hang out. Chris Sloane, too. He never spoke a word to me until we were in that program together and we'd gone to school together since kindergarten.

KL: You say it like you're proud.

SC: If it wasn't for that program, I'd have never gone to one high school party. Raphael Diaz would never have spoken to me. Shane Reese wouldn't have known I existed. Guys on the football team with Tyler would have kept sticking my head in the locker room toilet. So yeah, for a guy like me, having them for friends is great.

KL: Would you lie for Tyler or Chris or Raphael or Shane?

This writer notes that subject did hesitate before answering.

SC: What happened to Jessica?

KL: Just answer the question.

SC: I wouldn't lie for them but I wouldn't get them in trouble either.

KL: This is a very serious matter, son. Maybe the most serious matter you'll ever deal with in your life. If you know something, now is the time to tell it.

This writer notes subject stares out the window for almost a full minute.

SC: I don't know anything.

The rest of the statement was just Ken asking the same questions in different ways. Lauren could picture nerdy Seth Creehan, seeming to realize halfway through his statement that he was saying too much, trying to backtrack on Tyler and Raphael. His status depended on the friends he'd made in the program, and from the way he was responding, those friendships were tenuous at best.

Seth's statement seemed to inadvertently point to both Tyler and Raphael as suspects. He also brought up that Erica Taviani was volatile when it came to her relationship with Raphael.

Lauren looked at the time on her iPad. It was after one in the morning. She wished she'd gotten the file from Marilyn sooner. She intended on staying up and reading all the statements. Otherwise, she'd feel like she was heading to Sloane's Spa and Retreat without finishing her homework.

She dutifully read through every single page, forcing herself to finish. Closing the file, Lauren put her iPad on her nightstand. She checked her cell phone for any missed calls, then turned out the light. Jessica Toakase deserved better than the hand she was dealt. Hopefully Lauren could make some headway on the case this weekend. One thing she'd learned from all the time she'd worked in the Cold Case squad was that the name of the killer was almost always already in the file. Maybe the detectives at the time weren't asking the right questions. She needed to meet these people in real life and figure out what the right questions might be.

NINE

'Inverness, New York is an unincorporated town south and west of the village of Ellicottville, known for its ski resorts,' Reese read from a Wikipedia page on his phone.

'That's great,' Lauren replied as she stared at the twisting road ahead of her. 'Does it say how to find it?'

'Chris says if we've hit Salamanca, we've gone too far and missed the turn-off,' he told her, now staring at Google Maps on his screen.

'Is it even on there?' Lauren asked as a semi-truck passed her on the two-lane road, causing her to involuntarily hug the right side of the lane.

'Not the private road to the spa. Not yet. He said we'll see a sign for Rock City State Forest with a bullet hole in the "O" of Rock. The turn-off's a quarter mile past that.'

'A bullet hole. Charming.'

'Hey! Chris said he's trying to get it replaced. The State says it's the town's sign, the town says it's the State's. Inverness doesn't even have a volunteer fire department or a post office, let alone a highway department.'

'You'll have to excuse me if I'm a little leery of that. You do remember what happened a few months back when we got caught in a half-finished hotel.'

'That was an abandoned resort on the coast of Ireland,' Reese pointed out.

'We almost got shot.'

'But we didn't. And now we're here at a luxury boutique hotel for a weekend of relaxation. Chris says that we won't even notice the unfinished spa because that area is closed off to guests now.'

'I swear if you say "Chris said" one more time this week, I'm going to turn this car right around and go home,' Lauren complained good-naturedly, then mimicked Reese, '"Chris says the optimum temperature in the hotel is seventy-three degrees exactly. Chris says satin pillowcases should always be an option at check-in. Chris says soft lighting sets the mood."'

'I haven't talked to the guy in years. I'm sorry if I'm a little excited we rekindled our friendship after all this time. You spend hours FaceTiming Marie and I don't say a thing.' Marie was Lauren's high school friend she'd found on Facebook after she'd gotten stabbed and her daughters had made her join social media so they could keep tabs on her. She and Marie had a standing date every other Wednesday night where they drank wine and talked about their kids, pets and whatever TV shows they were binge-watching. She looked forward to their twice-a-month meetings and felt a little pang of disappointment every time they had to sign off.

'I'm sorry. I was just teasing. Of course, it's great that you two seem to have picked up where you left off.'

'I have to have someone to brag about Gabe to besides you,' he said. Bragging about his adorable baby son was now his favorite pastime.

'You have a ton of friends. I have two, besides you and my daughters,' she pointed out.

'I think that's the sign there, coming up.' Reese aimed his phone at a spot down the road. 'Look for Hidden Loch Way on my side.'

The Southern Tier of Western New York is ski country. There are no mountains in that area, but the hills are substantial enough to support a thriving ski industry, especially in the town of Ellicottville. The rolling, forested peaks stretch down into Pennsylvania and dominate the landscape. The words *winter wonderland* would always pop into Lauren's head when she'd pile Erin and three of her friends and all their gear into the Ford Explorer she had at the time. She'd drive the fifty minutes to the slopes in Ellicottville on a Friday night and sip hot chocolate in the lodge while the girls snowboarded. They usually didn't get the best snow until after Christmas, so a random snowy day at the end of November or in December was always welcome. The flakes right now were fat and falling steadily. Reese planned to rent a pair of skis the next morning at the Mount Blanc resort and hit the slopes with Chris and some of the others. She pictured herself waiting in the lodge watching Reese instead of Erin and thought it was funny how time had a way of turning things back around into a circle.

'There it is,' Reese said.

Right before a break in the trees was an ornate blue and gold sign announcing the SLOANE SPA AND RETREAT. Lauren took a right onto a newly paved road, marveling at how beautiful the trees on either side of her looked dusted with snow. 'We're a little early,' she said, glancing at the time in the right-hand corner of the screen in her dashboard that showed them turning off the main road onto nothing. Navigation systems were great, but this was a private road, which was probably an unpaved driveway until the spa was built. Lauren remembered Reese telling her that Chris had bought two hundred acres of land that bordered the state forest from an older man who had a small hunting cabin on the side of the hill. That cabin had been demolished and the spa was built in its place. *Another 'Chris says'*, she thought with a smile. *I hope Chris says we're going to have a fantastic time this weekend.*

After a half mile the trees thinned out to expose an enormous chalet-style building that sat halfway up a large hill. 'I thought you said there were only seven rooms in this place,' Lauren said as they approached.

'Six guest rooms and one massive bridal suite that covers most of the third level.' Reese pointed to the top floor. 'See those floor-to-ceiling windows? I bet that's it.'

'I don't know how he expects to turn a profit with seven rooms.' Lauren followed the curve in the driveway and drove right up to the giant glass front doors under a covered car port.

'By charging obscenely high prices,' he replied, unbuckling his seat belt. 'And catering to the ultra-rich.'

'Why would the ultra-rich want to come to some obscure spot in Western New York when they can go to Vail or Aspen or the Swiss Alps?' Lauren put the car in park and turned it off. She pulled on her fur-lined black leather gloves and then her bright orange knit hat that Lindsey hated. Lindsey had seen the hat on the hallway table when she came home for Thanksgiving, snatched it up, and informed her mother she was going to burn it for her own good. Lauren had replied that it was a perfect fall color, thank you very much. Lindsey had tossed it back, telling her, 'Only if you want to look like a traffic cone.'

Reese didn't seem to mind Lauren's lack of fashion sense. He went on with his explanation without giving the hat a second glance. 'Because his silent investor has a lot of friends who demand discretion, luxury, and most importantly, privacy. There are no paparazzi in Cattaraugus County.' He popped the back hatch and pulled out their suitcases.

'Lauren! Shane!' Chris came out of the double doors, clapping his hands together. 'I'm so glad you made it. Ward, my manager, will take your bags up to your rooms. Lauren, if you give me your keys, I'll park your car in the guest lot.' His eyes roamed around the front of his hotel. 'When we're up and running, I'll have a valet for all this, but for now, it's on me.'

'Where do we check in?' Lauren asked.

'You're already checked in.' Chris held out his hand to Lauren, who dropped her car keys into his palm.

Another man suddenly appeared next to Chris. He wore black pants, a black vest over a white shirt, with a satiny dark green tie. A Sloane Spa and Retreat name tag pinned over his heart read: WARD – Manager. 'Welcome,' the middle-aged man said in a pleasant, formal voice. 'I'm Ward and I'll be taking care of you this weekend.' He managed to grab the handles of both the rolling suitcases. 'If you'll follow me, please.'

As soon as Ward stood in front of the doors the motion sensors kicked in, opening them. He rolled the cases inside with Reese and Lauren at his heels, not even pausing in the small entryway, instead triggering another set of double doors, taking them right into the lobby.

If understated opulence was what Chris was going for, he'd achieved it magnificently. Lauren had never been to a high-end resort and spa, not even when she'd been married to Mark, who surely could have afforded it. They'd done amusement parks, bed and breakfasts and all-inclusive resorts in Jamaica because she had two young girls that would have found all this luxury frightfully boring.

A huge chandelier made of horns – moose? Elk? Lauren didn't know and could only hope they were faux – hung in the center of the lobby ceiling, which was a gorgeous combination of exposed beams and knotty pine. Straight ahead was the front desk, and to the immediate left of it was a staircase that twisted upwards. To the right was a stone fireplace with a long leather couch in front of it, flanked on either side by matching wing chairs. The color palette was a soothing combination of browns, creamy tans and soft greens. Ward wheeled the suitcases behind the front desk with him, set them aside, and began to type away at his computer.

'Ms Riley, you'll be in room 202.' He handed a plastic key card across the desk to her. 'Mr Reese, you'll be in room 204, right next door.'

'Hey, Shane!' A woman's voice carried through the lobby. Reese and Lauren turned to see a lovely strawberry blond coming down the stairs towards them.

Reese's face lit up at the sight of her and Lauren knew this must be his high school sweetheart, Amanda. They met each other halfway across the lobby and hugged.

'Look at you!' Reese exclaimed, holding her out at arm's length. 'You look exactly the same.'

'Well, not exactly the same. Three kids definitely changed the landscape.' She waved a hand down the length of her body. The simple sheath dress's shade of pink matched the flush of her cheeks perfectly. 'But I've never felt better.'

'You look great,' he affirmed with his thousand-watt smile.

'And you,' she said, reaching out and giving the brim of his cap a playful tug, 'still wearing the baseball hats, I see.'

He laughed. 'You know me. This is one from my vast collection.'

'We all thought you were headed to the major leagues,' she teased. 'Then you joined the army.'

'I did play some baseball in college when I got out of the service,' he told her. 'Unfortunately, I wasn't nearly as good as I thought I was.'

She put a hand to her chest in mock surprise. 'Shane Reese being humble? I never thought I'd live to see this day.'

'Maybe sweet Amanda Sabria throwing shots at me has shaken my confidence.'

'It's Amanda Carter now.' She jokingly made a menacing voice. 'And I've changed *a lot* since you last saw me.'

He popped his Buffalo Bisons cap off, revealing the scars that crisscrossed his head. 'A few things have changed on me, too.'

'Oh, Shane.' Her pretty mouth turned down into a frown and her demeanor became serious. 'I live in Tampa now, but my mom sent me links to the articles about you getting shot. I'm so sorry.'

'Don't be. I'm still here, right?'

She nodded a head full of tumbling curls. 'Right. That's all that matters.'

'Now I'm really glad I said yes to coming this weekend.' His voice was warm and full of nostalgia. Lauren could see and hear how much Amanda must have meant to him back in the day.

A beautiful blush spread across Amanda's cheekbones. Obviously, she could hear it too. 'I was shocked to get that email out of the blue from Chris inviting us. It took calling in some favors, but I managed to get a babysitter on short notice for my kids.'

'Hey! I've got some good news to report. I'm the proud papa of a brand-new baby boy named Gabriel,' Reese said. 'Gabe just turned five months old. I'll bore you with lots of pictures later.'

'Wow!' The girlish thrill had crept back into her voice. 'I can't wait to see them. Believe me, I'm prepared to bore you with some of my own. Is this your lovely wife?' She turned toward Lauren with an outstretched hand. 'I'm Amanda Carter.'

'Lauren Riley.' She shook Amanda's soft, warm hand. 'It's nice to meet you.' She waggled a finger between her and Reese. 'And we're not a couple. We're partners on the police force. But thanks for introducing yourself. If we'd waited for Reese to do it, we'd still be strangers on Monday.'

Amanda laughed out loud, a genuine belly laugh that made her bend at the waist. 'Oh, Shane! Some things *don't* change!'

'Hey!' he protested. 'Don't you two go ganging up on me.'

Chris suddenly appeared behind the front desk. *Must have another entrance from the parking lot out back*, Lauren thought, as he came around to their threesome and held out her car keys to her. 'If you need anything from your vehicle, just go out the front doors, follow the sidewalk around the main building to the guest lot.' Lauren noticed snowflakes melting along the length of his dreadlocks, which he had neatly tied back with a tan leather string.

He clapped his hands together. 'It's supposed to snow tonight and tomorrow. If you want to sled or ski and didn't bring your equipment, we do have some on hand for guests. It's a little limited right now so we made an agreement with a ski lodge in Ellicottville, and you can rent whatever else you need there and charge it to the Sloane tomorrow.'

'Sounds great,' Reese told him and slapped him on the back again. 'And should I refer to this place as The Sloane? It makes it sound so very upscale and exclusive.'

'Call it whatever you want. I aim to please,' Chris said. The pride in his new venture was written all over his face. *As well it should be*, Lauren thought. *This place is amazing.*

'Thank you.' She pocketed the keys and turned toward Reese, who was still gabbing with Amanda. 'I'm heading up to my room. I'll see you at dinner time.'

'Don't forget cocktail hour starts at five in the lounge right through there,' Chris said, pointing to an archway to the left of the check-in desk. 'The elevator is behind you. Ward will be right up with your bags.'

TEN

Lauren left Reese talking to his old friend in the lobby. Out of the corner of her eye she spied another man coming down the stairs wearing khaki pants and a navy-blue golf shirt. He had the look of a Ken doll, with perfect light brown hair swept over his forehead. Hopping in the elevator, she hit the button for the second floor and looked at herself in the mirrors that surrounded her on three sides. Lauren rarely compared herself to other women, but Amanda naturally had a shade of strawberry blond hair that most women paid top dollar to achieve, with soft curves and huge blue eyes that radiated kindness and warmth. Lauren was tall and skinny with black-rimmed glasses and short, choppy brown hair that looked like it could have been combed with a fork. Gone were her days of being a blond head turner, but she didn't miss it. The last few years had aged her and for that, she was grateful. It was better than the alternative.

The elevator doors chimed open. She stepped into an expansive hallway with three doors on each side. At the very end of the corridor was a rough-hewn wood table with a display of fall flowers mixed with pinecones and red and yellow fall leaves, framed by a picture window that overlooked the small valley.

Her room was the first one off the elevator to the immediate left. Waving the key card in front of the lock, it clicked open.

As impressed as she had been with the lobby area, her eyes widened at the sight of the room. It was more of a studio apartment, a really expensive studio apartment, with an open-floor plan, minus a kitchen. She admired the front sitting area, dominated by a floor-to-ceiling gas fireplace. Sliding glass doors led out to a balcony. A beautiful dark wood desk with a heavy-looking matching chair took up one corner. You could relax on the couch in front of the fire or work at the desk and still see the expansive view of the valley and trees. To her left a huge king-sized bed was made up in tasteful shades of green bedding. The door to the bathroom was open, revealing a soaking tub, separate shower stall and double vanity. Everything was new, everything was immaculate, everything was exquisite. Now it made sense to her why there were only six rooms and a bridal suite.

A knock on her door interrupted her wonder at the room. Ward stood outside with her bag. When she went to dig out some money from her pocket, he waved her off with practiced politeness. 'We're not allowed to accept tips, ma'am. Your satisfaction is all the tip I require.'

'Thank you,' she replied. 'You can put that right here.'

He gave a nod, set the suitcase just inside her door and left.

Alone with her suitcase and thoughts, Lauren sprawled on the bed. Sank into it was more like it. The fluffy comforter and pillows seemed to want to swallow her whole.

Amanda, Amanda, Amanda, she thought. She'd already read the statement Amanda had given to the original detectives, but she wanted to refresh her memory. She and Jessica had been cheerleaders together, although Amanda had been captain. She claimed Jessica was her best friend.

Lauren pulled her phone out of her pocket and opened the file. She never ceased to be amazed at technology. Thanks to the Cloud, that huge cache of paperwork was completely accessible on her phone. She could flip through the pages, look at the crime scene photos and peruse the scanned autopsy information, all from her mobile device. She pulled up the folder labeled STATEMENTS and opened it.

Amanda's statement was the first one the detectives had taken the morning they'd found Jessica's body, which made sense. Jessica's foster parents told the police when they reported her missing that she'd been working with Amanda at the concession stand that day. They had called Amanda's house looking for her, but Amanda had said she had no idea where Jessica could be.

Amanda had also been Jessica's best friend, making her privy to all the secrets teenage girls loved to hoard like gold.

The homicide detectives must have had patrol pick her up as soon as the body was discovered. Ken LaBlanc had started questioning her at 8:40 a.m. He'd stapled Amanda's Polaroid to the top right corner. She looked scared and lost, mascara tracks lining both sides of her round cheeks. Her curly hair was pulled back in a ponytail, one errant strand hanging over her left shoulder. Amanda Sabria had her arms crossed tightly in front of her, as if to keep the person taking her picture as far away from her as possible.

The statement itself was set up just like Chris Sloane's and Tyler Owstrowski's, in the standard question-and-answer format. Lauren pulled up the report on her phone screen.

CITY OF BUFFALO – POLICE DEPARTMENT – HOMICIDE SQUAD

STATE OF NEW YORK	**DATE: 7/3**
COUNTY OF ERIE	**TIME COMMENCED: 8:40 a.m.**
CITY OF BUFFALO	**Incident # 03-976421** **File # 03-058**

I, **Amanda Ann Sabria,** residing at 1298 Katherine Street, Buffalo NY 14202, telephone 716-427-1984 being duly sworn deposes and makes the following statement while at the Buffalo Police Department Homicide Office. The questions are asked by Detective Kenneth LaBlanc. Also present and typing the questions and answers is Detective Ralph Masterson.

KB (Kenneth LaBlanc): Can you read and write, and how far have you gone in school?

AS (Amanda Sabria): I graduated high school and I can read and write.

KL: The Buffalo Police Department is investigating an incident that occurred concerning Jessica Toakase on July 2nd. Can you answer my questions regarding this incident?

AS: Yes.

KL: Do you know why you're here today, Amanda?

AS: They said something happened to Jessica. My mom

got a phone call from her foster mom last night looking for her. She put me on, but I didn't know where she was. What happened to her?

This writer notes subject is crying.

KL: Did you see Jessica Toakase last night?

AS: We worked together at the concession stand in Memorial Park.

KL: Down in the Old First Ward?

AS: Yes.

KL: What time did you start work?

AS: I picked Jessica up just before noon. We worked until six thirty.

KL: You drove her to work? Were you supposed to take her home?

AS: No. She said she had a ride home.

KL: Did she say with who?

AS: No. But I thought maybe with Raphael.

KL: Who is Raphael?

AS: Raphael Diaz. He went to high school with us. He stopped by our stand yesterday and they talked for a while.

KL: Was it unusual for her not to come home with you?

AS: The last couple of weeks she hadn't been coming home with me. And Raph kept coming to see her at work. We got into an argument about it because he's Erica Taviani's boyfriend. She went to school with us too. Erica was in our program, but Raph wasn't.

KL: So you had an argument because she might have been sneaking around with your friend's boyfriend?

This writer notes the subject breaks down into sobs.

AS: I don't know. We fought about that. Then later my boyfriend, Shane, came by and she accused us of spending too much time together. She said I was blowing her off for him all the time. He told her to butt out and get a life. She was already upset because Tyler Owstrowski grabbed her on the way into work.

KL: Tyler Owstrowski grabbed her? Grabbed her how?

AS: He works in groundskeeping. We were walking to the concession stand yesterday and he came up and grabbed her around the waist and said something dirty in her ear. She pushed him away, but she was upset. And that made matters worse because she said I didn't care if she was happy or not, or if a guy like Tyler grabbed her, that I only cared about myself. Shane tried sticking up for me and it got really bad. I was so mad. I told her she was being stupid, that I did yell at Tyler, and I did care about her.

KL: How bad is really bad?

This writer notes that subject looks toward door and doesn't answer right away.

KL: Amanda, please explain to me what you mean by really bad.

AS: She threatened to tell my dad I'm going out with Shane.

KL: Your parents don't know you're dating him?

AS: My mom knows. She likes Shane a lot, but I don't live with my dad. He has a new family in Garden Valley. I hardly ever see him. He doesn't know about Shane.

KL: Is that why you keep looking at the door? Because your dad is out there with your mother?

AS: Please don't tell him. Please. He's awful enough to my mom as it is. If he found out she was letting me go out with Shane he'd make things worse for her.

KL: He doesn't want you to date yet?

This writer notes that subject shakes her head no.

KL: What then?

AS: Shane is biracial. His mom is black and his dad is white. My father is such a racist. I don't want to have anything to do with him anymore. I'm eighteen but my little sister is only twelve. He's always threatening to take my mom back to court and get custody of her, even though he really doesn't want either of us. If he knew I was dating Shane he'd lose his mind and take it out on my mom.

KL: Did Jessica know how your father felt about Shane when she threatened to tell him you were dating?

AS: Yes. I couldn't believe she said it. That's why Shane

got so mad. And then she just walked out of the stand and stormed off toward the river. I called after her but she didn't turn around. Shane stopped me, told me to just let her go. He couldn't believe she said that either.

KL: What happened next?

AS: Then Shane walked me to my car and we both left. Her foster mom called my house last night around eleven looking for her. I wanted to call Shane and tell him, but my mom said not to, that Jessica could get in trouble for running away because she was in foster care. And now I know something awful has happened to her because I'm in the Homicide office, right? What happened to Jessica?

This writer notes subject does break down into tears. This interviewer does get subject a glass of water, which she does drink, then continues the interview.

KL: Are you OK to continue?

AS: I know she's dead. I know it. And the last thing I said to her was that she was stupid.

Another unexpected knock on her door startled Lauren out of her concentration with Amanda's statement. 'Riley? You in there?'

Lauren threw her phone down on the bed and walked to the door. Sliding the security bar back, she opened it for Reese. 'What's up?'

He walked in without waiting to be asked. 'I think I just caused some tension between Amanda and her husband, Owen.'

'What? Why?'

She backed up and Reese made himself comfortable, flopping down on the couch in front of the fireplace. 'This place is insane. Chris spared no expense, that's for sure. Can you believe we're here?'

Lauren came around to the back of the couch. 'Focus, Reese. You just told me you thought you caused trouble between Amanda and Owen.'

He exhaled loudly. 'Amanda's husband came downstairs when we were talking and, man, he did not seem happy she was reminiscing with me.'

'I saw him as I was getting on the elevator. Do you think he's the jealous type?'

'I'm going to assume that's a yes.' Reese kicked off his boots and swung his legs on the couch. 'Amanda introduced us and his smile just kept getting wider and wider, like his face was going to split in two.'

'You were her high school sweetheart,' Lauren pointed out, leaning both hands on the back of the couch, looking down at her partner.

He cocked an eyebrow at Lauren. 'You married your high school sweetheart. Do you still have feelings for him?'

'He's dead, but the short answer would have been no, if he were still alive.'

'Exactly. There's a reason why people are your exes. I'll always have a fond place in my heart for Amanda and I'm sure she has one in hers for me, but that's it.'

Lauren couldn't argue with that logic. Her first husband had left her with a baby and one on the way. If she had ever seen him again after he took off they wouldn't have been hugging in a hotel lobby, that was for sure, but she was grateful for the two beautiful daughters she got out of their brief time together. 'You've never met him before, right?'

'No,' he said. 'I just think he's got a little of the green-eyed monster in him. And who can blame him when confronted by all of this?' He waved his arms down the length of himself.

'Out.' Lauren pointed to the door. 'I want to grab a power nap before the cocktail hour. You can go stand in front of the mirror in your own room until then.'

'You're brutal,' he replied, swinging his legs down and grabbing his boots. He didn't bother putting them back on, just marched toward the entrance in his stocking feet. 'Don't forget to put the security bar back in place.'

'There are eight guests in this hotel, plus Chris.' She held the door open for him.

'Still,' his voice became serious. 'Put the bar on the door.'

And then he was gone. Puzzled at that reaction, Lauren let the lock click back into place and pulled the metal bar over the knob sticking out from the door frame. Even if someone had a key card, the door would only open a crack. It was the hotel's stronger version of a chain lock.

A disturbing idea began to form in Lauren's head as she lay back down on the bed. It was a nagging hunch that maybe Reese was suspicious of one of his classmates in particular, but sleep overcame her, even as she was reaching for her phone, still open to Jessica Toakase's homicide file.

ELEVEN

Lauren had fallen into one of those short, deep, dreamless sleeps that leave you disoriented when you wake up. For a full five seconds she had no idea where she was. Finally, her eyes focused on her suitcase, still standing sentinel by the door, and she remembered.

Never one to pass up a golden opportunity, Lauren realized she still had an hour and a half until she had to be downstairs, so she drew a hot bubble bath in the oversized tub.

While she was waiting for the tub to fill, she grabbed her phone off the nightstand and then picked up a brochure that was sitting next to it. The picture on the front showed the Sloane Spa and Retreat surrounded by fall foliage that crept up the hills behind the building in stunning reds, oranges and yellows. There were the compulsory photos of the lobby and bar, the guest rooms and even the spa area that was closed to them. What she hadn't seen yet was the view from the third-floor atrium. A picture showed round tables in front of another stone fireplace. Floor-to-ceiling windows covered the entire west-facing wall, surely to capture spectacular sunsets over the hills. The brochure also stated the grand bridal suite was located on the third floor, complete with a hot tub that overlooked the east side of the landscape. That was where Chris was staying.

Sunrises and sunsets, Lauren contemplated, *Chris has thought of everything.* The back of the brochure declared the indoor/outdoor pool would be ready by the fall of next year and included an artist's rendering of what that would look like. *It appears I won't be able to afford to stay here then*, she mused, tossing it on the vanity next to her toiletries.

She put her phone down on the edge of the tub. Testing the water with her hand, she judged it was just hot enough. She wriggled out of her clothes and let them fall on the bathroom floor in a heap.

Slipping into the water, Lauren wished the spa music that had been playing in the elevator, acoustic guitar against the backdrop of falling rain, was on. Smooshing down some bubbles, she picked up her phone and opened Jessica's file to the statement section. There was one oddball among Jessica's old classmates' statements that she wanted to review again, a man named John Branson.

Branson's statement was odd because Ken LaBlanc and Tobias Lake had taken it two days after her body had been found and it listed his age as eighty-two years old. Lauren thumbed back to the Polaroid that had been stapled to the corner of the original. The man had longish, combed-over white hair and a scraggly gray beard. His heavy-lidded eyes looked small and tired but determined. Both of his hands were crossed over the top of a cane in front of him. Staring directly into the camera, he looked like a tired man who had something to say. She scanned the pedigree information, noting that Mr Branson lived only two streets away from the park.

Lauren reread the interview.

CITY OF BUFFALO – POLICE DEPARTMENT – HOMICIDE SQUAD

STATE OF NEW YORK	**DATE: 7/5**
COUNTY OF ERIE	**TIME COMMENCED: 2:05 p.m.**
CITY OF BUFFALO	**Incident # 03-976421** **File # 03-058**

I, John Eugene Branson, residing at 1002 South Street, Buffalo NY 14202, telephone number 716-336-1174 being duly sworn deposes and makes the following statement while at the Buffalo Police Department Homicide Office. The questions are asked by Detective Kenneth LaBlanc. Also present and typing the questions and answers is Detective Tobias Lake.

KL (Kenneth LaBlanc): Can you read and write, and how far have you gone in school?

JB (John Branson): I went until the 8th grade but I can read and write pretty good if I have my glasses on.

KL: Mr Branson, the Buffalo Police Department is investigating the homicide of Jessica Toakase on July 2nd. What can you tell me about this incident?

JB: I called you folks when I saw that little girl's picture on the television last night. I seen that girl the night she died. I seen her in the park.

KL: Tell me what you saw.

JB: I was walking my dog down by the Buffalo River. I walk Hans every night. He's a German Shepherd. He's getting up there now, but he still likes to get out and sniff the rocks and trees down by the water in the park. I usually take him right after supper, but my son called and we talked for a while. It's so rare I get a call from him, usually he's asking for money. This time he just wanted to see what I was up to. I was on the line with him until almost seven o'clock. Poor old Hans was begging to get let out by the time we hung up. Whining and scratching by the back door. He's a good boy though, keeps me company, so I grabbed his leash and he pulled me all the way to the park. That's where I saw her.

KL: Who did you see?

JB: The girl from the television news they found in the river. She stormed down the footpath right past me. She was moving fast too, bumped my shoulder a little and didn't say sorry or excuse me or nothing. It was right at the fork by the NO DUMPING sign. Me and Hans cut down the side path there. I figured whoever she was mad at was coming next, so we'd better get out of the way. About ten feet along Hans stopped to piss on his favorite bush and I heard a man's voice call out, 'Jessica!'

KL: Are you sure it was a man's voice?

JB: Not an old man's voice like mine, or even a lived-in voice like yours. It was a young man's voice. Strong and high, not too deep.

KL: Did you see the person who was calling to her?

JB: Can't say that I did. He must have been moving pretty fast too because by the time I looked up, both of them were gone. Farther up the path, I reckon, into the wooded spot by the big rocks. It's all overgrown there. The Parks Department should really clear that area out.

KL: Would you recognize that voice if you heard it again?

JB: I'd like to lie and tell you I would. I'm not sure. At my age, you learn not to make promises you can't keep.

KL: You seem to have a pretty good memory.

JB: That's a laugh. The only reason I knew that was the same girl was because she had on a Parks Department shirt, like all the workers wear, and the name, Jessica. Jessica was my wife's name. I remember thinking it was a sign that my son had called and I heard my bride's name on the same night. I thought maybe it was my time to get called to be with her again. A young man calling for a young Jessica.

KL: You're sure you heard the name Jessica?

JB: I'd bet my life on that. I can't tell you how many times my Jessica had stormed away from me when I did something foolish and I had to go chasing after her, calling for her to stop.

KL: You didn't see anyone else on the path?

JB: No. I saw a couple of kids when I first walked into the park, looked like they were heading for the bleachers. That's where they go to drink beer and leave their bottles all over. But that's in the opposite direction of the walking paths I was heading to. Except for the girl and whoever was calling after her, me and Hans were the only ones out there.

This writer notes that subject does start to wipe his eyes and stops to collect himself for a moment.

KL: Do you want a tissue, Mr Branson?

JB: No, thank you. Pure evil, what happened. She had a whole life ahead of her. I want you to catch whoever did this to that young girl. Catch him and throw him in jail forever and maybe then some.

KL: That's what I'm trying to do, sir.

JB: Try harder.

KL: Is there anything I should know about this incident that I didn't ask you?

JB: No. That's all there is. The park gets pretty desolate once the baseball games are over. The city barely gives it enough money to keep it open. If they did, them paths would have been cleared and that little girl would be alive now.

KL: Do you swear you have told me the truth today?

JB: I wish it wasn't so, but yes. I told the truth today.

******Statement ended 2:59 p.m.******

I understand that any false statements made herein are punishable as a class A misdemeanor, pursuant to section 210.45 of the New York State Penal Law, of the State of New York. Subscribed and verified under penalty of perjury.

Signed: John Branson
Witnesses: Tobias Lake

Sworn and Subscribed before Me

Kenneth LaBlanc
Commissioner of Deeds in and for
The City of Buffalo, New York,
County of Erie

There was a Post-It-Note Marilyn had scanned in after the last page of the statement. It was in Reese's handwriting. Lauren felt a lump rise in her throat. Reese had tried to track the witness down, but he'd passed away five years after Jessica's murder. There was no date on when he'd tried to find him, but the fact of the matter was if Branson was alive now, he'd be ninety-nine years old. Even though he probably wouldn't have added anything new to the case, Reese had still tried to track him down. His commitment to finding Jessica's killer made Lauren even more determined to follow through.

She realized she had stayed in the tub reading until she was pruney. She put her phone on the edge of the tub then got out, careful not to knock it into the draining water, and toweled off. She immediately began to stress about how to dress. The place screamed formal wear and expensive casual at the same time, probably by design. After a good ten minutes of staring at the clothes in her suitcase she finally chose a pair of cream-colored corduroy pants and a camel-hued turtleneck sweater. Lauren had never been one to care much about fashion, she was very much a jeans and T-shirt type of person on her days off, so packing for this weekend had been a little stressful. With a closet full of fifteen black suits that all looked exactly the same and an array of multicolored button-up blouses to wear underneath the suit coats, she was pretty much set when she got up to go to work every morning.

She felt a little better when she opened the door to Reese's knock and he was standing there in khaki pants and a dark blue collared shirt he'd managed to tuck in all the way around. He'd replaced his baseball cap with one of the tweed Irish hats he'd gotten in May when they'd gone to Ireland on a case together. He was still self-conscious about the scars that crisscrossed his head. Finding new ways to hide them was something he took seriously.

'Ready, Ice Queen?' he asked, cocking his arm out to escort her.

'Ready,' she replied, letting the door shut and lock behind her with an electronic click. He'd been calling her Ice Queen since they met, current weather conditions notwithstanding. Ice Queen, Big Bird and Slim were just a few of his pet names for her. She balanced it out by calling him Slob, Mouth-Breather and Heartbreaker. Heaven forbid they should show actual affection for each other unless absolutely necessary. It would have thrown off the delicate balance of their relationship.

They took the stairs instead of the elevator, twisting down the flight, Lauren trailing her fingers along the smooth wooden railing. The landing into the lobby fanned out, taking up the entire corner to the left of the check-in desk. The grand fireplace was roaring, casting the room in a cozy yellow glow. Outside the double glass doors was nothing but white.

'We're getting more snow than they predicted,' Lauren said as they crossed the lobby. A wicked howl followed up her statement.

'A lot more,' Reese agreed, eyeing up the fast-moving snow. 'And wind.'

They were the last to show up at the bar, where Chris was serving his guests. 'Don't you have an employee for that?' Reese called.

'I've interviewed about twenty bartenders,' he explained as Reese and Lauren approached, pouring a pink drink from a metal cocktail shaker into a martini glass in front of Amanda. 'My wife says I'm too picky, but I say I'd rather do it myself and do it right than hire someone who doesn't know a Manhattan from a Cosmopolitan.'

A chorus of hellos came up from the seated guests. Reese walked over and embraced one after the other, while Lauren hung back.

'There are books for that,' a man pointed out to Chris, tipping back his glass, his beer belly touching the bar. His square jaw gave his face a blocky look. He was bald, but still had two patches of brown hair over each ear that he wasn't giving up for anything. Lauren could picture him sporting an elaborate comb-over in later years. He was definitely the type of guy who was trying to hold onto his youth, yet too lazy to take care of himself at the same time.

Chris shook his head. 'Not on my watch.'

Reese slapped the balding man on the back and said to Lauren, 'This is Tyler Owstrowski, star linebacker for the Screaming Eagles.'

'I'm Lauren Riley,' she said, holding out her hand. 'Nice to meet you.'

'Tyler,' he replied, eyes traveling the length of her. His hand was clammy and gripped hers a tad too long before letting go. 'You're the one who works with Shane at the police department.'

'I do,' she replied, and resisted the urge to wipe her hand on her pants.

'I've never met a female cold case detective before,' a beautiful, dark-haired woman called to Lauren, leaning back in her chair to get a better look at her. She had a jaw that could cut glass and high, angular cheekbones to match. The words *fierce* and *striking* immediately popped into Lauren's mind. The woman gestured to the handsome Latino man next to her. 'I'm Erica Diaz and this is my husband, Raphael.'

'Nice to meet you both,' Lauren said. 'And I've never met a real podcaster before.' She'd been approached many times via phone or Internet for interviews but had always declined. Lauren had no interest in bringing any more media attention to herself.

'I'd love to get you on my broadcast sometime,' Erica continued. 'It'd be great to pick your brain on some things.'

Before Lauren could answer, Reese had moved down to greet another man. He was on the short side, and slightly built, with neatly combed brown hair and silver wire-rim glasses. 'And this is Seth Creehan,' Reese told her. 'Our computer genius, all the way from Silicon Valley.'

He raised a rocks glass in Lauren's direction. 'Cheers.'

She smiled back. 'Cheers.'

Reese had a hand on both of his shoulders, giving them a friendly shake. 'I used to try to cheat off this guy all the time. He always covered his papers.'

'You should have paid more attention in school,' Seth countered with a grin.

'Would I be as rich as you are now?' Reese teased.

He shrugged and shook his head. 'Probably not.'

'You were a huge nerd!' Tyler playfully taunted. Seth balled up a cocktail napkin and threw it at him. 'All you ever did was play computer games.'

'Well, now I'm a huge, rich nerd,' he countered, holding up his drink in a cheers gesture to him. 'Those games paid off.'

'Come sit here,' Amanda called to Lauren, and tapped the empty stool next to her.

Her husband sat on Amanda's other side, still in his golf shirt, sipping beer from a glass. He too raised his drink to her in greeting. 'Owen Carter. It's a pleasure to meet you.'

'Likewise,' she responded, detecting a slight southern drawl in his speech.

Lauren slid into the swivel chair. Reese plopped down next to her, Seth on the other side of him. She took a second to have a look around. The bar area was bigger than Lauren had expected and the dining room that spread out behind her was large enough to sit at least fifty people. Thinking back to the brochure in her room, it made sense since the hotel was advertising itself as a wedding venue, also available for baby showers and bachelorette getaways. There were enough hotels and inns thirty minutes away in Ellicottville to handle overflow guests once all the rooms were rented.

Round tables that sat four each in leather-backed chairs dotted the room. In the far-left corner, a single long table sat at an angle to the fireplace. It was already made up with nine place settings for their dinner, white napkins fanning out from long-stemmed water glasses at each setting. Lauren found herself imagining a wedding party seated there, the firelight reflecting off their glasses as they raised them to the bride and groom in a toast. Yes, this place was all Chris claimed it was and then some.

'What can I get for you?' Chris's smooth voice interrupted Lauren's daydream.

'Do you have any Jameson on hand?' she asked. 'I'd love a Jameson and ginger ale.'

'My lady,' he replied, running his hand over the gleaming wood bar, 'whether I have one guest or a hundred, I will always have a completely stocked bar.' He turned to the shelves behind him, pulled a bottle off and held it up.

'Can I have that neat, actually? With *no* ice?' Lauren asked.

'You can have it any way you'd like. I aim to please,' he responded, and started mixing her drink.

'I'll take another muddled Old Fashioned when you're done with that,' Erica called to him, pushing her empty rocks glass forward on the bar next to an oversized book.

'Is that our yearbook?' Amanda asked her.

'Oh,' Erica laughed, picking it up. 'It is. I thought it might be fun to look through it together.' She held it out across her husband, who leaned back so Amanda could grab it.

'I'm so stupid I didn't think to bring mine,' Amanda said, opening it up on the bar. Her husband bent in to get a better look. 'To tell you the truth, I don't even remember where they are. We've moved so many times in the last ten years, they could be anywhere in my wreck of a house.'

Erica got up and stood behind Amanda so they could look through it together. Lauren was surprised at how small Erica was, barely five feet tall if she had to guess, with black hair cut short to frame her face. 'There's you,' Erica pointed. 'Captain of the cheerleaders.'

'I thought I was so fat back then,' Amanda said, staring at the photo. 'I struggled so much with my weight all through high school. It wasn't until after I had my first child that I finally looked in the mirror and liked what I saw.'

Her husband leaned over and kissed her cheek. 'You're perfect just the way you are,' he said.

'I'll never be a size eight.' She slung an arm around her husband's shoulder. 'But I've got three amazing kids and I'm finally happy in my own skin.'

'That's a great life view. I wish more women felt that empowered,' Erica told her. 'And for the record, I always thought you looked healthy.'

'That's the goal I've set for myself. Healthy.' She smiled. 'Mind and body.'

Lauren felt herself stiffen a little. She'd always been naturally thin, it ran in her family, but after she'd gotten stabbed, thin had turned to gaunt. She'd managed to put a couple of pounds on, mostly because living with Reese meant he had to have a constant stream of food, but she still had a sickly look to her. Compared to Amanda, who radiated self-acceptance and the tiny but fierce Erica, who exuded confidence, Lauren imagined she looked like a wreck.

Tyler, Seth and Reese all crowded around Amanda, gazing down at the book, while Chris bent over the bar, palms down on the polished wood to catch a glimpse, the whiskey sour sitting on a beverage napkin.

'Hey,' Chris said, squinting to get a better look. 'This is our junior yearbook.'

'I thought it was more interesting than our senior one,' Erica said, stepping back so that the others could see. 'The candid shots of us are much better.'

'I hate how we had our own little section in our senior yearbook,' Reese said. 'Like we were space aliens and not really a part of the graduating class.' The book was open to a group shot of them standing on some risers on a stage, boys in back, girls up front. Underneath the picture their names were listed. Lauren assumed the pretty dark-skinned girl between Amanda and Erica was Tonya, the Jamaican immigrant whose family eventually settled in Canada.

The opposite page was full of candid shots of the group: Amanda in her cheerleader outfit putting up a crepe paper streamer in a hallway; Reese in his baseball uniform standing with Seth by a drinking fountain; Chris, Seth and Tonya bent over a model of a molecule; Jessica smiling over her shoulder as she sat in front of a computer monitor.

'They did keep you brains separate from the rest of us,' Raphael agreed. 'If they hadn't let you participate in the extracurricular activities, I wouldn't have even known you guys went to our school.'

'Looking back, I don't think it fostered learning the way they said it would. By the time we graduated I was done with school,' Reese said.

'I'm of the opposite opinion,' Seth countered. 'I feel like the program allowed me to explore my interests more. I never would have been able to build such an impressive portfolio for my computer science major if I hadn't had the freedom the program gave us.'

'I agree,' Erica said. 'My interest in journalism went from a hobby to a career path there.'

Tyler walked away from the group fawning over the yearbook and sat back down with his drink. 'I have mixed feelings about it. I got stuck with all you losers for four long years.'

A chorus of boos were hurled at Tyler, but he just smirked and kept sipping his drink. His eyes wandered over to Lauren, sitting two seats away from him. 'So what's your deal?' he asked. 'I heard you live with Shane but you two aren't a couple.'

Blunt and to the point, Lauren thought before she answered. Now everyone was looking at her. 'Reese moved into my house when I got seriously injured a while back, then he got injured.' *Because of me*, she wanted to add, but bit back the words. 'It just worked out that I have a big house and we make good roommates.'

'Not everyone has to be romantically involved,' Amanda told Tyler. 'It *is* possible for men and women to coexist without sex.'

'Whatever you say, Mama Bear,' he countered, not looking at her, just smirking into his beer glass.

Reese and Riley had only ever confessed to feeling more for each other once, standing on the edge of the sea in Ireland, a month before his son was born. The impossibility of their getting together had struck Lauren like a hammer at the time. It wasn't enough to want something, not if it meant you could lose everything. They'd both come to the conclusion that what they already had was what they needed. If they tried to take things to the next level, everything could fall apart. Reese needed to concentrate on the baby and Lauren needed to help him. That was the priority, she'd told herself. Lauren knew from experience that having a child meant every other thing in your life came second, or third, or fourth. Little Gabe had come and taken up every inch of Reese's heart, just like Lauren knew he would. She was just happy to be along for the ride now that her daughters were grown and off to college. Gabe filled the void in their relationship. When Reese got flustered because Gabe was being fussy, he'd hand him over to Lauren then hover over her shoulder as she rocked and cooed to him. When she handed him back, asleep and content, the look of love and gratitude on Reese's face made her heart swell. That was enough for her. It had to be.

Chris clapped his hands together, getting the attention of the group. 'I'd like to officially welcome everyone to the Sloane Spa and Retreat.'

That was met with a smattering of applause before he went on. 'If everyone will find their place card at the dinner table, my wonderful head chef, Diane Brady, has prepared a marvelous feast for us this evening.'

'Can Ward take a group photo of us before we sit down?' Amanda asked, holding up her phone.

'That's a fantastic idea,' Erica said, putting the yearbook on the bar and picking up her cell. 'I want one too.'

Ward came around the bar and collected the phones of everyone who wanted a picture. The group pulled together, arms draped across shoulders, smiles wide. Lauren could feel Reese's hand hugging her arm, his side pressed up against hers, and her heartbeat quickened for just an instant. One after the other Ward picked a phone from the small pile he'd made on one of the round tables and repeated, 'Say cheese!'

'Couldn't we have just taken one and sent it to each other?' Tyler grumbled after the fourth picture.

'Shut your pie hole,' Chris told him through his toothy smile. 'We're all done now.'

Yearbook abandoned on the bar, the group picked up their drinks, grabbed their phones and made their way to the long table, set up with beautiful linens in shades of autumn brown and decorated with an elaborate three-candle centerpiece. Fabric leaves in reds, yellows and oranges were scattered across the table. Reese picked one up and twirled it between his fingers as he sat down. 'I know you did not pick out these decorations,' he shot at Chris, letting the leaf fall onto the tablecloth.

'I must admit I have a designer who dictates the seasonal décor.' Chris slid into his seat at the head of the table. The place cards had the rest of them sitting boy, girl, boy, girl, which was fine with Lauren. Chris had her sitting between Reese and Tyler, and directly across from Owen, who was between Amanda and Erica, with Raphael on the end seat. Ward came by, blew out the candles and deftly removed the centerpiece so their views of each other weren't obstructed.

'It's beautiful.' Amanda plucked the napkin out of her water glass and smoothed it over her lap. 'You and your wife must be so happy.'

'It's our dream come true,' Chris said. 'And I'm happy to share it with all of you this weekend. I just wish Veronica wasn't still in Colorado. She's not moving here permanently until after the new year.'

Ward assisted Mrs Brady with the meal, balancing a huge round tray for her so she could pass out the first course, a creamy potato and leek bisque. The conversation died off as the guests dipped into the rich soup. Lauren noticed Tyler had the habit of slurping every other mouthful. It was hard to believe he'd found three women to marry him. Sitting so close their elbows occasionally bumped, Lauren could smell a mix of nasty cologne and cigarette smoke on him. She pictured him standing in the snow on his balcony, shivering and puffing away.

'That was delicious,' Raphael told Mrs Brady when she and Ward came around to clear their soup bowls.

Mrs Brady nodded, head down, smiling slightly. 'Thank you, sir.' *Raphael probably has that effect on most women*, Lauren thought. She'd read in his file that he was an actor in New York City. Despite his incredible looks – and he really did look like a movie star to Lauren with his jet-black hair and sultry dark eyes – he'd only appeared in a couple of guest episodes on some TV shows, done a bunch of commercials and a bit of modeling. In the last seventeen years he hadn't been able to break through, working full-time as a waiter in a swanky upscale West Side restaurant. Lauren wondered if his wife's success bothered him. She'd read that Erica's true crime podcast had over fifty thousand listeners. That kind of uneven terrain could strain a marriage.

Once the main course was served and another bottle of red wine was poured all around, the banter picked up. 'Lauren,' Erica said, leaning forward, elbow on the table, resting her chin in her hand, 'tell me about being a cold case homicide detective.'

Every other conversation around the table ceased and all eyes turned to Lauren.

'What are you curious about?' Reese jumped in, knowing how much Lauren hated to be the center of attention.

Erica waved him off. 'I don't want to hear it from you,' she said. 'I want a woman's perspective on detective work.'

Lauren set her steak knife next to her plate. She'd barely had three bites before Erica decided it was question time. 'It's not as glamorous as they make it seem on television or movies,' she replied. 'Especially in Cold Case. There's a lot of waiting for things: phone calls, DNA reports, witnesses to show up. It takes patience.'

'Until it doesn't,' Erica prompted, sitting straight up now. 'Until something breaks in a case, right?'

'Right,' Lauren agreed, feeling like she was being interrogated. 'Then everything is on fast-forward.'

'That's so fascinating,' Amanda said. 'I've only had contact with the police once in my life and it was terrifying.'

'That's because they woke up a bunch of seventeen- and eighteen-year-old kids, put us in a room and bombarded us with questions,' Tyler said.

'But suspects come in on their own, don't they?' Erica went on as if Amanda or Tyler hadn't spoken.

'All the time,' Lauren said, taking a sip of her drink.

'Why would they do that?' Erica pressed. 'Why would a guilty person voluntarily come to a police station and talk to the police without a lawyer?'

'To find out what we know,' Lauren said simply. 'They want to see what questions we're asking, find out if we're on to them. They want us to show our hand, let them see what kind of evidence we have. A lot of times they try to appear cooperative, maybe throw us a suggestion of a suspect other than themselves.'

'It does happen all the time,' Reese agreed with a mouth half full of steak. Nothing was coming between him and his dinner, not even police discussions.

'It's important work,' Seth said, wiping his mouth with his napkin. 'I give you and Shane a lot of credit. I couldn't do it.'

'I couldn't learn to code and produce computer games,' Reese countered, then turned to his partner. 'Did you know

Seth was the person who came up with the game *Random Mutual Destruction*?'

'I remember when that video game came out,' Lauren said, knowing full well from Reese's file what Seth Creehan had been up to. 'That was a long time ago. You couldn't have been out of college yet.'

'I wasn't. I finished the demo by the end of my freshman year and started shopping it around from my dorm. Luckily for me, a major software company picked it up. It sold like crazy and was named Game of the Year. With the money I made I founded BluHotPepper Games.'

'And the rest is history,' Chris said. History was the right word. Lauren remembered seeing an article in the file from the local newspaper about Seth Creehan after he won Game of the Year. There'd been a picture of a mousey-looking, thin young man with thick, black, coke-bottle glasses, not unlike the ones she wore now. He'd been standing in front of a row of computers, beaming with pride. Less than two years before, he'd been in the Homicide office, sitting on a hard plastic and metal chair, looking terrified as a detective snapped a Polaroid. Both looks were a far cry from the put-together, attractive man he had become. He'd gone from nerdy geek to intelligent chic.

'Seth is our self-made gazillionaire,' Tyler agreed. 'I shoulda went into tech instead of real estate.'

'I heard you were doing very well for yourself in real estate,' Seth said.

Tyler shrugged and ran a hand over his remaining hair above his right ear. 'I was, two ex-wives ago. They say third time's the charm, right? Well, wife number three took me to the cleaners. It's been five years since our divorce was finalized and I'm still paying out the nose.'

'I'm sorry to hear that,' Seth amended, sounding more like he was sorry he brought it up.

Tyler raised his glass of beer to his lips. 'It's cheaper to keep them.' He slugged back a huge gulp. 'Take my word for it.'

'I can't imagine why any woman would divorce you.' Erica's voice had a sharp edge to it.

'I think I like the idea of "until death do you part".' Tyler was looking at Raphael now, who was taking a sip of beer. 'It would have been easier.'

Raphael snorted and almost spit out his drink. Wiping his mouth with the back of his hand, he didn't notice the way Erica's eyes narrowed, but Lauren did.

'You've never been married, have you, Seth?' Amanda asked, trying to steer the conversation away from Tyler.

Seth shook his head. 'I lived with a woman for almost ten years. She was a professional model. She'd be gone for weeks at a time. I'd be gone for weeks at a time. It just didn't work out. Since we split, I've had a couple of short-term relationships. Nothing earth shattering. I'm still hopeful I'll find my soulmate.' He turned toward his classmate. 'You're very lucky, Amanda.'

Amanda practically glowed as she reached over and squeezed her husband's hand. 'Lucky and blessed.'

'I'm the lucky one,' Owen said. 'I saw her walking with her friends our sophomore year at the University of Tampa. I can't believe our paths didn't cross for an entire year. One of the guys I was with knew her and I made him introduce me to her.'

'But he didn't ask me out for almost two weeks!' she laughed.

'I was terrified. The last thing I wanted to do was scare her off.' He turned his adoring sky blue eyes to her beaming face. 'I knew she was the one.'

'When you meet the right person, you just know,' Chris agreed from his chair at the head of the table.

'And you'll do anything to keep them,' Erica added, reaching for her Old Fashioned.

TWELVE

'I still can't believe this is all yours,' Reese marveled, letting his eyes flow over the beautiful dark wood décor of the bar area. Ward had seated them in a semi-circle around the fireplace after dinner in rich brown leather chairs. They'd already been positioned for them when Mrs Brady began clearing their dessert plates. A bottle of high-end bourbon sat in the middle of the long oval table, with a cut crystal glass stationed in front of every chair.

'Mine and my wife's,' Chris amended as he unstopped the decanter. 'And a ridiculously bored billionaire investor who couldn't resist my charms.' Walking around the fireplace side of the table, he began to pour bourbon into the glasses.

'Has the investor been here and seen what you've done?' Lauren asked.

'He's more of a beach person,' Chris answered, and held the bottle out to Amanda.

'That's sad,' Amanda said, covering her glass with her hand. Her husband readily accepted the bourbon, watching Chris as he deftly poured the amber liquid into his glass.

'He has more money than he'll ever be able to spend. I'm sure that consoles him.' Chris moved on to Seth.

Erica held her glass out so Chris wouldn't have to bend over. 'I wish I were that sad.'

'You don't seem to be doing so badly,' Tyler told her. 'I read an article about your true crime podcast last month. It sounded like you were killing it. No pun intended.'

'Have you listened to the show?' Erica asked.

Tyler looked down into his drink. 'I never got around to actually *listening* to an episode.'

'What about the rest of you?' She turned and scanned the group. 'Have any of you ever listened to my show?'

'I'd heard about it too, but it always slipped my mind,' Seth said apologetically, trying to save the day 'It sounds like a very interesting concept though.'

At Reese, Chris and Amanda's guilty stares, she threw in, 'That's OK. My own husband hasn't even tuned in to one of my broadcasts.' Erica took a long sip of her drink. 'I've got enough listeners. And hopefully even more soon enough.'

'I told you, babe,' Raphael said, 'that's just not my thing.'

'That "thing" pays most of our bills,' she reminded him.

'True crime does pay,' Raphael admitted, taking a slug from his glass as Chris moved on with the bottle. 'Just not enough.'

'More than your acting jobs, I bet,' Tyler snorted.

'I was a guest star on an episode of *Law and Order* once,' he protested.

'Who hasn't been?' Tyler shot back. 'My mom has been a guest star on *Law and Order*.'

'Hey, Seth,' Raphael called. 'You know any rich Hollywood producers that want to make me a star?'

'Not offhand,' Seth remarked, then snapped his fingers and pointed at Raphael in a teasing way. 'Let my people check with their people and I'll get back to you.'

'You do that. I'm just waiting on my big break.'

Lauren caught the poisonous look Erica shot her husband as he gulped down the rest of his drink and forced a grin. She mashed her lips together and looked away. Being married to a struggling actor didn't seem to sit well with her.

Lauren wasn't the only one who'd picked up on the tension in the room. 'How about a toast?' Chris said, setting the bottle down in the middle of the table. He stood next to his seat at the end of the arc. 'To the success of the graduates of our little high school experiment. May we all continue to prosper.' He held his glass high and everyone raised theirs in turn.

'Hear, hear!' The call came up from the group and everyone drank to each other.

Lauren felt her muscles relax as she sank deeper into her chair, bathed in the glow of the firelight. The top-shelf bourbon sent a flush of warmth through her chest, rising up her neck to her face, taking the cold winter chill from her bones. She listened to the group as they reminisced about their glory days, adding nothing, content to be a fly on the wall.

Ward brought out a second bottle of bourbon, switching out the empty one on the table, then melted into the background again.

Lauren was on her second glass, sipping it slowly, meaning to enjoy every drop, when the conversation took a turn.

'I know it's the elephant in the room . . .' Amanda said, twisting a reddish-golden curl around her index finger. 'But I can't get what happened to Jessica out of my head. I think about her all the time. I can't be the only one.'

'I do too,' Reese admitted, more into his glass than to everyone in the room.

'Shane, have you looked into that case?' Owen asked. 'Is there a suspect or any leads?'

'It's not an elephant,' Erica said, draining the rest of her drink, then reaching over and pouring herself another. That sharpness had returned to her voice, only now it was a razor blade. 'It's a freaking Tyrannosaurus rex and it's coming straight for all of you now.'

'What?' Chris half laughed.

'What the hell is that supposed to mean?' Tyler demanded.

'It means,' Erica leaned forward so Tyler could see her face, 'that everyone in this room is about to be put on blast. I'm airing a two-hour special podcast this Wednesday night detailing her case, and all your dirty little secrets are about to come out.'

'Oh really?' Tyler challenged.

'Why did all of your wives divorce you, Tyler?' she asked him. 'Why don't you get to see your two kids?'

'That's none of your damn business,' he exploded, face turning a bright shade of crimson.

'Take it easy,' Seth said, trying to calm the situation down.

Her head whipped around. 'Seth, don't you dare pretend to play the innocent geek who grew up to be a benevolent soul. You don't get to be where you are today in the business world without being ruthless.'

'What the hell are you talking about?' Seth asked, his eyes wide behind his thin silver-rimmed glasses.

'I filed a Freedom of Information Act request over two years ago and got her homicide file. I've spent all my free time since then investigating the case and all of you.' Now she scanned the faces of the rest of her high school classmates with a crooked smile. 'And I pieced together what *really* happened that night.'

'Erica, I've been working Jessica's case since before I even got to the Cold Case squad. On my own time, going over every detail, every piece of evidence with cutting-edge technology and forensics.' Reese's voice raised an octave. 'So don't sit here and tell me you've solved it by doing a Google search.'

Erica's upper lip curled in a sneer. 'I wouldn't expect you to say anything else. The fact that you have access to all of that evidence raises the questions: what would you do to protect someone? What would you do to cover your own lies?'

Raphael reached over to his wife sitting next to him and tried to put his hand on her arm. 'Babe—'

She snatched her arm away, clutching the yearbook she had retrieved from the bar to her chest like a shield. 'Those questions are for you too, *Babe*. My loving husband. My so-called soulmate.'

'Erica,' Chris's voice was patient and calm, exactly the tone that would infuriate someone who'd been drinking for the last few hours. 'Why don't we put a pin in this conversation for now. Let's just enjoy the evening.'

'Really, Chris?' she challenged. 'Is that because your hands are squeaky clean? I read your police statement. I know how you felt about Jessica.'

'There's no call for any of this,' Reese told her. 'You need to stop.'

'"*I'm sorry she's dead and all but she wasn't really my friend*,"' Erica mimicked Chris's voice. '"*I never really bothered with her. She was like a blank piece of paper*."'

'That's enough.' Now Chris's voice was rising to match Reese's.

The smirk on Erica's face was absolutely wicked. She was enjoying this. 'That's all you had to say about her after she was just found murdered. That's pretty cold, considering that you asked her to our senior prom and she turned you down.'

'Where did you hear that?' Chris demanded.

'You didn't tell the cops that little story. I had to hear it from her best friend right here. Must have sucked to have to see her in the park every day, knowing she'd rather stay at home than go to a prom with you.'

'Stop it,' Amanda implored, tears welling in her eyes. 'I told you that in confidence.'

'You think I'd kill a girl over being turned down for the prom?' Chris spat out.

'People have been murdered for less,' she challenged. 'And

from the way you reacted to the news, you weren't particularly upset at her passing.'

'OK, Raphael,' Reese stood now, looking to Erica's husband. 'Maybe you should take your wife upstairs to sober up.'

'Coming to Amanda's rescue? I'm not surprised,' Erica said with a harsh laugh. Raphael was on his feet now, pulling on Erica's arm, trying to get her to stand. She rose, still clutching her yearbook. Then she twisted away from her husband and spat out, 'It was your girlfriend here who supposedly last saw Jessica alive, or so she says. The three of you argued that night. How heated did it get? Who's to say Shane really did leave the concession stand alone?'

'I'm to say,' Reese said hotly. 'I'm saying that's what happened.'

'We all know why you and Amanda didn't get your picture taken together at the senior prom. Amanda, your daddy would have lost his shit if he knew you were dating a person of color, wouldn't he? How far would both of you have gone to keep your relationship from him?'

'I thought we were friends,' Amanda sniffed.

'Enough of this bullshit,' Reese said, trying to cut her off.

His and Amanda's reactions only seemed to spur her on. She was actually smiling – a wicked, bitter grin that twisted her mouth, making every word sound like it was frozen in ice. 'Bullshit, huh? Maybe you and little Miss Susie Homemaker have some more explaining to do. You two did break up right after the murder. Which is weird, because you were so in love with each other. Maybe a secret got between you. A secret so bad, it drove you apart for good. Anything you'd like to confess to, Amanda?'

'That's it.' Owen jumped up on Erica's other side, getting into her face. His southern accent became more pronounced the closer his nose got to hers. 'I don't know who you think you are but leave my wife's name out of your filthy, lying mouth.'

Erica responded by dropping her yearbook to the floor and shoving Owen as hard as she could away from her. He stumbled back a few steps, then recovered enough to try to get at her. Amanda threw herself between the two, bracing her hands against her husband's chest. Erica snatched a glass off the table and whipped it at Owen's head, missing his face by only a fraction of an inch. It hit the wall and exploded in a shower of bourbon and glass. Before things could get any worse, Raphael scooped her up in a bear hug from behind, pinning her arms to her sides.

'I know the truth about all of you!' she heaved out between gritted teeth, trying to wrench herself from Raphael's arms. 'And it's coming out this week on the air!'

'Get that woman out of here before I wring her neck!' Owen yelled, still being restrained by Amanda.

With that, Raphael, apologizing profusely, carried her kicking and screaming from the room.

Everyone else was silent, staring after the couple. The ruckus continued until they heard the bong of the elevator doors closing. For several moments after, the only noise was the howl of the wind, the crackle of burning wood in the fireplace and Owen's breath coming in heaving pants.

'On that note,' Tyler said, pouring himself another drink from the carafe, 'I think Ward should bring us another bottle of bourbon.'

Seth reached over and picked the yearbook up off the ground where it had fallen, tucking it under his arm. Chris smoothed his shirt down, then briskly walked over and took it from him. 'Ward,' he called loudly, and his manager seemed to magically appear. 'Take this up to Erica and Raphael's room immediately.'

Ward nodded, accepted the book without a word and headed toward the lobby. Lauren surmised that Chris didn't want to give Erica any excuse to come back downstairs.

Amanda grabbed Owen's arm and pulled him down into his seat. She put her head close to his, her curls falling forward, and they began to talk quietly. Amanda put a hand on either side of Owen's face. Obviously wanting a moment of privacy to calm themselves, Lauren turned away. The last thing they needed was her gawking at them after the scene Erica had just made.

Chris walked over to the bar rail, popped it, grabbed a bottle off the shelf in front of the mirror and came back.

'What's that?' Seth asked.

'Who cares?' Chris said, mustering up his smile again. He began to pour amber liquid into the remaining guests' glasses. 'But you're welcome to help yourself from the bar.'

Tyler shook his head, bald pate gleaming in the firelight. 'I'm good,' he said, sipping his drink. 'Whiskey works for me.'

'Goodnight, everyone. We're going to head to our room.' Amanda spoke for her and her husband as they rose from their seats. Lauren watched her quickly wipe a tear from her cheek. 'Thank you for the wonderful dinner, Chris.'

'Amanda, Owen, I am so sorry—'

Owen cut him off, holding up a hand. 'Not your fault. We'll see everyone in the morning. Goodnight all.'

Amanda hooked her arm through her husband's and leaned into him as they walked together, practically holding each other up. It was a stark contrast to Erica and Raphael's undignified exit.

As they passed under the oversized clock above the door, Lauren noted it was only 10:30. It felt much, much later. Chris disappeared for a few seconds behind the bar and came out with a broom and dustpan. Bending down, he carefully began to sweep up the broken glass. A wet stain dripped down the mint green wallpaper. 'I'm surprised Mrs Brady didn't come out of her room and see what all the fuss was about,' he joked.

Reese and Seth started talking about good stock investments, politely ignoring their friend cleaning up their other friend's mess.

'Aren't the rooms practically soundproof for maximum relaxation?' Lauren quoted from the brochure.

'The guest rooms, yes. The staff quarters,' he pointed to a door behind the bar with the dustpan, 'which are just through the kitchen back there, not so much. They have to be able to hear what's going on to best serve our guests. They also have to know when to be discreet. Mrs Brady knows I'm out here with everyone so there's no need for her to intervene.'

Discreet seems to be the word of the weekend, Lauren thought, eyes still on the dark spot on the wall. Chris finished up and took the broken shards away. *Too bad everyone here demands it but doesn't practice it.*

Just so it didn't look like a mass exodus, Lauren finished her drink and waited another fifteen minutes before she decided to excuse herself to her room, leaving Chris, Seth and Reese drinking by the fireplace, with the newly returned Ward standing sentry near the door. Tired as she was, she was anxious now to reread Raphael and Erica's statements. The revelation that Chris had asked Jessica to the prom also warranted further examination of their relationship. Erica had implied Reese and Amanda were lying about something. She had the advantage over Lauren in that she knew all the players intimately. Erica's rage was rooted in something she'd found in those files she'd requested. Something Lauren had yet to connect to.

THIRTEEN

Even though Chris had bragged that the rooms were nearly soundproof, nearly is not totally, and Lauren could still hear the muffled argument coming from Erica and Raphael's room as she walked by. She waved her key card over the lock and slipped into her own room, eager to shut the noise out.

Sitting down at the fancy desk in the corner, she opened the files app on her phone and punched up Erica's statement. The interview was done by Henry Wiley, who she'd never worked with in Homicide, but she was familiar with some of his cases. He would have been the oldest of the detectives working the squad at the time. Erica's statement was typed by Ken LaBlanc. Her Polaroid showed tear-stained cheeks on a slight but intense-looking teenager with long black hair and huge dark eyes. She had on a hot pink T-shirt that practically glowed. Lauren imagined her grabbing the first thing off her bedroom floor when the police knocked. Lauren looked at the time of the statement. It read 1:03 p.m. It was now the afternoon and from the look on her face Erica had somehow gotten the news Jessica was dead before they sat her in the interview room.

CITY OF BUFFALO – POLICE DEPARTMENT – HOMICIDE SQUAD

STATE OF NEW YORK	**DATE: 7/3**
COUNTY OF ERIE	**TIME COMMENCED: 1:03 p.m.**
CITY OF BUFFALO	**Incident # 03-976421**
	File # 03-058

I, **Erica Maria Taviani,** residing at 6900 Miami Street, Buffalo NY 14204, telephone 716-361-8285 being duly sworn deposes and makes the following statement while at the Buffalo Police Department Homicide Office. The questions are asked by Detective Henry Wiley. Also present and transcribing is Detective Kenneth LaBlanc.

HW (Henry Wiley): Can you read and write, and how far have you gone in school?
ET (Erica Taviani): I can read and write and I start at Columbia in the fall for journalism.
HW: The Buffalo Police Department is investigating an incident that occurred on July 2nd. Can you answer my questions concerning this incident?
ET: I'll try. Yes.
HW: Erica, do you know why you're here today?
ET: Because someone killed Jessica.
HW: How do you know that?
ET: My mother's best friend is a cop. She called my mom this morning as soon as they found her. She said the police had been looking for her since last night.
HW: Were you in Memorial Park yesterday?
ET: I was. I'm writing an article on favoritism in getting summer youth jobs for my summer internship. I wanted to talk to my friends and other people who work in the park.

HW: What time did you get there?

ET: My parents let me take our minivan and I picked up my boyfriend at his house on O'Connell Street around three thirty. He lives right around the corner from the park, so he could have walked there.

HW: Who's your boyfriend?

ET: Raphael Diaz. We've been together since we were juniors. We were voted the prom king and queen this year.

HW: Did you see Jessica Toakase yesterday?

ET: Yes, I stopped by the concession stand where she works and saw her and Amanda Sabria.

HW: Was anyone else there?

ET: Just random customers.

HW: Was Raphael with you when you talked to Jessica?

ET: No.

HW: What was Raphael doing while you were talking to your friends?

ET: Hanging out with the guys at the groundskeeper building.

HW: Give me your exact timeline of yesterday at the park, if you can.

ET: I picked up Raphael from his house. We got to the park around three thirty. We walked around together for a while and then he wanted to go hang out with some of our other friends who work in the park, so I went to talk to Jessica and Amanda, then I interviewed some other park workers. We met back up around five thirty. I had to leave because I had to babysit my little brothers. My parents had a dinner to go to and needed the van. Raphael called me later and we talked on the phone until it was time for bed.

HW: What time did he call you?

ET: Around eight o'clock. You can check that though, right?

HW: Right. How old are your brothers?

ET: Eleven and thirteen. I don't really babysit them, I just have to keep them from beating each other up, mostly.

HW: How did Jessica seem when you stopped at her stand?

ET: Normal. Like she always was. Smiling, friendly. Just, normal.

HW: And you didn't notice anything unusual or any strange people hanging around?

ET: No, nothing like that. And I would, right? Because I'm a journalist and I'm supposed to pick up on details like that, right? So I guess I'm not a very good one.

HW: You weren't looking for anything like that. You might remember something later though, something that sticks out that didn't at the time. If you do, you call this office right away.

ET: OK.

HW: You said you drove to the park?

ET: Yes, in my parents' minivan.

HW: What time did you leave the park?

ET: Around six. I had to get back to babysit my brothers.

HW: Did you drive Raphael home when you left?

ET: No, he wanted to hang out with our friends some more after they got off work.

HW: So the last time you saw Raphael yesterday was around six last night?

ET: Yes.

HW: Who did he want to hang out with?

ET: Seth Creehan and Tyler Owstrowski and Chris Sloane.

HW: Not Jessica?

ET: No, he barely knows her. Only through me and we didn't hang out together that much. I liked her a lot but I hung around with Tonya Freeman in our gifted program, mostly. She's in Toronto with her family for the summer. I doubt I'll see her before I go off to school.

HW: Do you know of anyone who would want to hurt Jessica?

ET: Nobody. She was a really quiet person. She mostly did stuff with Amanda. Her and Amanda Sabria were best friends. Jessica didn't party or do drugs. I don't know why anyone would do this to her. I still can't believe it.

HW: Is there anything else you think I should know about yesterday, about Jessica?

ET: Just that she wouldn't hurt a fly. If someone attacked her, I doubt she'd fight back. She'd be too scared. She must have been so scared. So scared. Excuse me.

This writer notes subject did take tissue from box on desk and wipe her eyes and nose.

ET: I'm sorry. Excuse me. I just can't.

Lauren finished the rest of the statement, which was the detectives asking the same questions in different ways. It was obvious to Lauren that they were trying to nail down Raphael's whereabouts. Scrolling further into the file, she read a supplemental report the detectives filed a few days later, after they had gone to Erica's house and asked her brothers in their parents presence if Erica had left at any time that night. They both said no, that Erica made them go to bed at eleven o'clock and it was just another boring night with their crabby big sister, who spent most of the evening gabbing on the phone. Scrolling even further revealed Erica's phone records that did show a call from Raphael Diaz's phone to hers which started at 8:11 p.m. and lasted until 1:54 a.m.

It was clear that either Erica was unaware that Raphael was seeing Jessica on the side or she was good at lying about it. Lauren thought of Erica bragging about being the prom king and queen, because in an eighteen-year-old's mind that meant everyone in their world should view them as a solid couple. She valued her and Raphael's relationship above all other things in her life. Lauren remembered what it was like to be eighteen and in love. It could make you blind to a lot of transgressions. Lauren herself had married her high school sweetheart at eighteen, only to be abandoned with two babies by the time she was twenty. There was nothing anyone could have told her, not her friends, not her parents, that could have stopped her from being with him. And it was only after everything fell apart so quickly that Lauren saw her first husband for the person he really was.

She needed to read what Raphael had told the police. She pulled up his statement.

Raphael's statement was also taken by Henry Wiley later that afternoon, at 2:48 p.m. Raphael's Polaroid showed he was just as handsome a teenager as he was a grown man, with perfectly mussed black hair, big dark eyes and the lean, muscular build of a runner. He sat in the chair, looking right into the camera, eyes rimmed in red. He too looked scared, confused and upset in his Buffalo Bills T-shirt and knee-length denim shorts. He had one leg crossed over the other so that his white high-top sneaker showed.

CITY OF BUFFALO – POLICE DEPARTMENT – HOMICIDE SQUAD

STATE OF NEW YORK	**DATE: 7/3**
COUNTY OF ERIE	**TIME COMMENCED: 2:48 p.m.**
CITY OF BUFFALO	**Incident # 03-976421**
	File # 03-058

I, **Raphael Martinez Diaz,** residing at 3741 O'Connell Street, Buffalo NY 14202, telephone 716-375-9009 being duly sworn deposes and makes the following statement while at the Buffalo Police Department Homicide Office. The questions are asked by Detective Henry Wiley. Also present and typing the questions and answers is Detective Tobias Lake.

HW (Henry Wiley): Can you read and write, and how far have you gone in school?

RD (Raphael Diaz): I just graduated from PS 91. I can read and write.

HW: Raphael, do you know why you're here today?

RD: Because something happened to Jessica Toakase.

HW: Why would you say that?

RD: Because my girlfriend called me, my friend Tyler called me, my friend Shane called me. My phone has been blowing up since this morning.

HW: And what did they tell you?

RD: That Jessica got murdered last night and they had to come down here and give statements to the police.

HW: We had police come to your house this morning twice and you weren't there. Where were you?

RD: My mom and dad took me over to my uncle's when I told them what happened to Jessica. He's a clerk for Judge Weinstein. He told me to cooperate and tell the truth, so my parents brought me down here after they heard from the neighbors that the cops were at our house.

HW: Did you know Jessica Toakase?

RD: We graduated from the same high school together, only she was in a special gifted program and I was in with the regular kids. What happened to her? Do you know who did it? No one here will tell me what's going on.

HW: When was the last time you saw Jessica?

RD: Yesterday. I stopped by the concession stand in the park where she and Amanda Sabria work. I got a Coke and some chips.

HW: What time was that?

RD: Around five, I think. Maybe a little earlier.

HW: Who were you in the park with?

This writer notes that subject does hesitate before answering.

RD: I was with my girlfriend, Erica. She told me you talked to her this morning.

HW: Did Erica go to the concession stand with you?

RD: Not with me. We split up for a while. I wanted to see my boys down at the groundskeeper building and she wanted to interview people for a story she was working on.

HW: What was your relationship with Jessica Toakase?

RD: She was my friend.

HW: Raphael, we've talked to a lot of people today. People that know you and know Jessica. People that are friends with you and Jessica. I cannot stress enough how important it is for you to be one hundred percent honest with me. This isn't a game. And it's no time to lie, thinking we won't find out, so I'm going to ask you one more time: What was your relationship with Jessica Toakase?

This interviewer notes that subject does lean his head into his hand, shading his eyes. He does not answer for several seconds.

RD: I have a girlfriend, OK? I love Erica. But a couple of weeks ago me and Jessica started to hook up every once in a while. We'd meet up in the park or wherever. It was totally casual. No strings. She's leaving for college in a couple of weeks and me and Erica are going away to New York City. Erica is going to Columbia and I'm going to try to get an agent. I want to get into acting.

HW: Does Erica know about you and Jessica?

RD: No. No way. Erica would go nuts. She's really jealous, you know? She hates when she sees other girls look at me. That's one of the reasons I like Jessica. She's zero drama. Real chill. She just wants to hang out, no strings.

HW: What would Erica do if she found out you were having sex with Jessica?

RD: Hold up! We're not having sex. I mean, I'm willing and all, but Jessica isn't. Not yet. We only just started hanging out. She says she's not ready and that's cool. We do other stuff. I'd never, like, force myself on her.

HW: So you came to the park with your girlfriend to set up a rendezvous with Jessica?

RD: Don't say it like that. I didn't plan on us hooking up. She suggested it when I came to see her at the concession stand.

HW: What time did you meet her last night?

RD: That's the thing, I was supposed to meet her at seven by the rocks on the river. You know, the really big ones, like boulders, with all the spray paint on them? That's where she wanted to meet up. But she never showed. I waited for an hour and then I walked home.

HW: When you went to the rocks did you see anyone there? Anyone just hanging around or looking suspicious?
RD: No. The path along the river was deserted. It gets sketchy down there at night.
HW: Did you see anything out of the ordinary?
RD: Like what?
HW: Anything that could have been used as a weapon?
RD: No. Nothing like that. Is that where she was killed? Oh, man.

This writer notes that subject does cover his face with his hands.

HW: Did anyone see you walk home?
RD: Someone must have seen me. I wasn't hiding or anything.
HW: Who was at home when you got there?
RD: My mom was already asleep in her room. Her shift at the plant starts at five thirty in the morning, so she goes to bed early.
HW: Can anyone vouch for your whereabouts?
RD: Erica can. I called her as soon as I got home, around eight. You can check the phone records. We talked for hours.
HW: She had no idea you were supposed to be with Jessica?
RD: No. She still doesn't know. Unless you guys told her.
HW: Was Jessica jealous of Erica? Maybe Jessica wanted more than just a hook up from you.
RD: I know she really liked me. She called and texted me way more than I did her.
HW: Did she like you enough to try to get you and Erica to break up? Is it possible she confronted Erica? Maybe told her what was going on with you and her?
RD: No way. She was terrified Erica would find out. Shit, I was terrified Erica would find out.
HW: Did Jessica threaten you? Demand you break up with Erica?
RD: No. Jessica would never do that.
HW: Did you maybe meet up with her, argue with her

about Erica? Maybe Jessica wasn't happy you two were going to New York City.

RD: I told you, she never showed up! We made plans when I stopped by her stand and she was into it. I was pissed she left me standing there.

HW: Pissed enough to go and find her?

RD: What? No. I didn't go and find her. Are you saying I did this to Jessica?

HW: If I double check your story about being on the phone with Erica, would she back you up?

RD: She would because it's the truth.

HW: What if it wasn't the truth. Would Erica lie for you?

This writer notes that subject does stand up at this point.

RD: I don't want to talk to you no more. You said I was free to leave when I came in. Can I leave?

HW: You're free to go, but this is your chance to tell me your side of the story.

RD: What story? There is no story. Jessica never showed up at the rocks.

HW: Are you sure about that? Because we've been talking to people all day. We know Jessica left her stand to go meet you at the end of her shift.

RD: She never showed up. End of story! Period!

HW: You should be trying to help me figure this out. If you cared about her at all, you'd sit back down.

RD: You should be trying to find the person who actually killed Jessica instead of talking to me. I'm out of here.

HW: That's exactly what I am doing. If you think of anything else, here's my card. Please call me.

This writer notes that subject refuses to take interviewer's card, refuses to sign a written statement and does leave the room at 3:29 p.m. Interview ended.

****** Statement ended 3:29 p.m. *******

I understand that any false statements made herein are punishable as a class A misdemeanor, pursuant to section

210.45 of the New York State Penal Law, of the State of New York. Subscribed and verified under penalty of perjury.

Signed: ___Refused___
Witness: Tobias Lake

Sworn and Subscribed before Me

Henry Wiley
Commissioner of Deeds in and for
The City of Buffalo, New York,
County of Erie

It was times like this when Lauren really wished she could see how Raphael had reacted to the questions. Body language is key in any interview. She had no idea if Raphael had responded with anger, sadness or disdain from reading the words on the screen. Tobias Lake tried to slip in a couple of interpretations of Raphael's reactions, but that was exactly the problem, they were Tobias's interpretations.

Lauren clicked on the follow-up reports again. Detectives had subpoenaed the phone records between Raphael and Erica, but their call didn't start until 8:11 p.m. That was more than enough time for Raphael to kill Jessica and get home. Unless Erica left her brothers and somehow got a ride back to the park, it was hard to shake Erica's alibi. But Henry had hit on something in the interview: would Erica be willing to lie to protect Raphael? And now that their marriage seemed to be on the rocks, was she no longer willing to? Lauren pictured the title of that podcast: *I married my high school sweetheart, the cold-blooded killer*. Erica's ratings would skyrocket. People loved the whole idea of the man you'd slept next to peacefully for the last seventeen years being a murderer. They ate up the thought that the wife was blissfully unaware of the ticking time bomb and she could have been next. Raphael did say Erica loved drama, even back then. Tonight, Lauren had gotten a little glimpse of that drama in action.

Lauren put her phone on the nightstand and pulled the

deliciously warm, plush comforter up to her chin, letting her head sink down into the pillow. If Erica was telling the truth and she had read the file, then there was something in it that made her believe she knew who the killer was. Something Reese couldn't see. Something Lauren hadn't picked up on yet. Could it have been in her own husband's statement?

Or was it someone else's secret?

FOURTEEN

B*AM!*

BAM!

BAM!

Lauren sat straight up, blinking against the darkness, on high alert. Being woken up in the middle of the night was nothing new, her work phone rang at all hours of the morning, but someone banging on her door was always bad.

The pounding increased, along with her heart rate. She looked at the digital clock glowing on the nightstand. It read 2:06. From outside the sliding glass doors that led to her balcony the wind howled, and she could hear the sound of snow pelting the windows.

'Reese,' she called, throwing the heavy duvet cover off and swinging her legs over the side of the bed. 'This isn't funny. I'm not in the mood for this.'

Padding across the floor in her bare feet, the thumping didn't let up. She looked through the peephole. A huge bloodshot blue eye squinted back at her.

It wasn't Reese. It was Tyler.

Lauren threw the security bar back and opened the door a crack. 'I think you have the wrong room,' she told him.

The smell of alcohol hit her in the face in a hot gush of panting breath. 'Lauren,' he slurred, trying to lean against the door jamb to keep himself steady. 'How're you doing?' He tried peeking around her into the room. 'Is Shane in there?'

Lauren would've rolled her eyes if she wasn't so exhausted and now annoyed. She hated sloppy drunks more than mean ones. 'No, he's not. I'm tired. It's late. You better go back to your room and get some sleep.'

'All by myself?' Lauren could see a sheen of sweat on his lengthening forehead. The tufts of remaining hair over each ear were sticking straight out. One side of his rumpled button-down shirt had become untucked from his pants. 'Without any company?'

'Most definitely by yourself. Goodnight,' she told him, and tried to shut the door in his face.

He wedged himself in so it wouldn't close and exhaled an exasperated sigh so she could get the full effect of his rancid breath. 'Come on. You're here all alone, I'm here alone. No one is watching. Why not have a little fun?'

She had tried to be polite, but she was too old and had too much respect for herself to put up with these kinds of shenanigans. She took her hand, put it squarely over his sweaty face and pushed him backwards as hard as she could. He tripped over his feet and stumbled back into the hallway. Lucky for him, it was carpeted. He glared up at her, dazed and angry. 'What the hell did you do that for?' he demanded.

Lauren simply closed the door. Drunken louses weren't entitled to an explanation. She heard some shuffling outside as she made her way back to her still nicely warm bed, but no more pounding. She thought back to Chris's statement that Tyler had grabbed Jessica around the waist on the way to the concession stand on the day she went missing and told her she should've been grateful for it. Chris had warned Tyler to cut that shit out because if Jessica made a complaint, he'd lose his job and maybe his scholarship.

I'll have to read Tyler's original statement again in the morning, she thought, resting her head against the soft pillow, remembering Reese interrupted her just as she was reading it in the Homicide office. If only Marilyn hadn't had those two other files to scan into the Cloud ahead of hers, she wouldn't be playing catch up now. Lauren did remember him trying to distance himself and downplay what happened between him and Jessica though. And how he had no one to back up his claim he was home alone at the time of Jessica's murder.

Congratulations, asshole, she thought just before she drifted off. *You just tied Raphael as the number one person of interest in my investigation.*

FIFTEEN

Lauren woke to Reese knocking on her door. She knew this because she made sure to check the peephole before she answered. She wasn't about to deal with Tyler again. Nor should she have to. She should've left him standing in the hallway and called down to the front desk. She was done being courteous.

'You said to get you up for breakfast.' Reese was standing in the hallway in gray jogging pants, a blue baseball hat and a Buffalo Bills jersey. He looked rested and ready for the day. 'I'm going to run the stairs a couple of times. Chris told me the workout room is closed.'

Lauren rubbed the sleep out of her eye with one hand, keeping the door closed enough to cover her pajamas. 'Why don't you go outside? You love to run when it's cold out.' She usually ribbed on him for jogging in subzero weather, but with the view from the top of the hill it was sure to be spectacular.

He looked at her like she was crazy. 'Have you stuck your head out your balcony door? It's a whiteout.'

'Still?'

'Still.' He tried to look over her shoulder into her messy room. 'I'm thinking no one's going skiing any time soon. We got at least four feet of snow overnight, if not more and it's still coming down. Unless Chris has a hell of a plow somewhere and x-ray vision, we're stuck inside for a while.'

Lauren glanced behind her at the sliding doors leading to the balcony. A steady, violent stream of snow pelted the panes of glass. 'Go run on the stairs. I'll meet you down at breakfast.'

'OK, boss,' he said, giving her a two-finger salute.

'Hey,' she called to him as he turned away. 'Did you hear Tyler banging on my door last night?'

He paused mid-stride. 'Nope. Then again, I think Chris was telling the truth about these rooms being practically soundproof. The whole relaxation and rejuvenation idea.'

That made sense. 'You're probably right,' Lauren agreed. 'But he was really pounding on it.'

'So Tyler came a-knocking?' He shook his head. 'Some guys never grow up. Tyler has always been a pig. That's why we were never tight. Not like me and Chris.'

'I threw him out by his face.'

'I'm sure it wasn't the first time,' Reese said, but his voice had lost its playfulness. 'After all the drama at the bar last night, you would think he'd know better. I can't wait to have a talk with him about it downstairs. Maybe *my* fist will find his face.'

Lauren stiffened at the suggestion. She didn't want Reese punching out Tyler at breakfast. Not that he didn't deserve it. 'I can handle it myself.'

'You shouldn't have to,' he replied, frowning. 'You're my guest here. And that shit doesn't fly with me. I'll see you down there.'

Lauren groaned inwardly as she closed her door. Guys like Tyler didn't care if they got called out. He'd probably just blame her, say she overreacted, or that she should be flattered. She hated how she could literally be asleep and some stranger could come and insult her, make her forcibly remove him from her doorway, then try to play innocent. *If he does*, she thought bitterly, *he'll find out fast I am not the one to put up with it.*

Still, she wasn't about to let him ruin the day for her. That gave him too much power. She'd tell Chris because she thought he needed to know what Tyler had tried to pull. Now that she knew he'd had an incident with Jessica, he could be dangerous. She had an obligation to protect the rest of the women in the hotel.

What made it worse was that she'd been looking forward to going to the ski lodge in Ellicottville. It had a great bar on the second floor that overlooked the slopes and served fantastic hot chocolate. Yet she knew from experience there'd be no skiing this morning with these kinds of conditions. With the spa closed, she wondered what Chris would have planned to keep them all occupied.

Lauren rooted around her suitcase, which she hadn't unpacked yet, coming up with a sweatshirt and some lounge pants with lots of pockets. *Good enough*, she thought, walking into her massive bathroom. Lauren was all about being comfortable these days. She showered, making sure to sample the luxury spa products Chris had placed in the room, which was a nice touch.

I have to remember to jot down some notes later, she told herself as she toweled off. Even when she was supposed to be relaxing, she somehow managed to make everything a forensic examination. But Jessica's murder lingered in her mind. The way Erica had gone on the night before, she'd made it sound like she knew exactly who the killer was. If she could figure it out, so could Lauren.

Throwing on her clothes, her hair was just long enough to pull back into a messy ponytail. At least it was out of her eyes. She pulled her sneakers on and looked in the full-length mirror on the bathroom door.

That was as good as it was going to get. She was ready for the day.

Stepping into the hallway, she managed to catch a glimpse of Reese running full throttle up the stairs. Not sufficiently motivated to take that route, even though it was only one floor, she walked over to the elevator. She could hear her physical therapist yelling at her to take the stairs whenever possible. *I'm on vacation*, she told herself and hit the down button.

The elevator doors opened to the grand lobby, the rustic chandelier twinkling from its exposed wood beam, a fire already roaring in the stone hearth. No one was staffing the front desk, but someone had taken up residence on the couch in front of the fireplace. Raphael was stretched across the frame, arms crossed over his chest, still wearing last night's clothes, snoring loudly. The only thing different from the last time she'd seen him was the black and purple shiner encircling his left eye.

He snorted as she passed and shifted onto his shoulder.

She found the rest of the guests, minus Reese and Erica, already seated and being served breakfast by Mrs Brady with some help from Ward. Everyone looked up from their food when she walked in. 'Am I late?' she asked, heading toward the group who called their good mornings to her.

Chris had had the staff push three round tables together to set huge platters piled high with scrambled eggs, toast and bacon on them. The long table from dinner was now set for breakfast, two pitchers of orange juice replacing last night's wine bottles.

Lauren glanced at the big clock over the entranceway. It was five minutes to eight.

'Just in time,' Chris said as he got up from where he was sitting and pulled the chair out next to him. 'Have a seat. Would you like some coffee? Tea?'

Lauren slid into the chair and Chris helped push it in for her. 'Coffee. Black, please.'

'Very good,' Ward replied, and came around the table with the pot of piping hot coffee.

Lauren's eyes skipped around the table as he poured. Tyler looked haggard from his place on the end, slurping his coffee as he nursed a hangover. She hoped he remembered banging on her door in the middle of the night. She'd hate for him to forget her shoving him away from her room by his face. She wondered if Erica, after reading the same reports she had, dug around and found out something more about Tyler. That would explain the vicious comment she'd thrown his way last night.

Chris was in the middle of helping Mrs Brady serve breakfast. He wore his dark green Sloane Spa and Retreat polo shirt tucked into a pair of expensive-looking black pants. He was in full host mode. Lauren would pick her moment to take him aside and tell him what happened. She was sure Chris would ask Tyler to leave. She stole another glance at Tyler. He was rubbing his temples with his meaty fingers, sweat rolling down the side of his face. She couldn't wait to get back to her office after the weekend was over and dive deep into his background.

Seth looked bright-eyed, sipping a tall bloody Mary with a leafy stalk of celery sticking out of the glass. He raised it to

Lauren when their eyes met over the table. 'Hair of the dog,' he commented cheerfully.

'You're a better person than me,' Lauren commented. 'I try to never drink before noon.'

'Day drinking is the best way to relax when you're on vacation,' he said, and took another sip as Lauren spread her napkin over her lap. 'I once woke up in the Cayman Islands with a brand-new yacht after drinking all day. I don't even remember leaving the gaming convention I was attending in Grand Junction.'

'I'll take your word for it,' she said, catching a glimpse of Amanda and Owen sitting across from her. They sat side by side but seemed awkward and subdued. Lauren hoped that Erica's accusations and antics hadn't ruined their weekend. Amanda was pushing the scrambled eggs around her plate, occasionally taking a bite. Owen just stared over her shoulder out the window as he drank his coffee, seemingly mesmerized by the swirl of white snow.

'What time did you shut it down last night?' Lauren asked Seth.

He paused, thinking on it for a second. 'Shane left first, not too long after you. Then me. I started to develop a raging headache. Probably from the cheap rotgut Chris serves here.' Chris looked up from his serving platter and Seth winked at him. 'I don't know what time Chris and Tyler stayed out until.'

'I walked Tyler to the elevator around one in the morning,' Chris said, putting the platter of pancakes Ward had passed to him down on the table. 'Raphael was already on the couch, the poor bastard. I cleaned up a little in here and went to bed.'

'In your giant penthouse suite,' Tyler commented. His voice had a dry, gravely sound from drinking too much the night before. 'I grabbed a bottle of whiskey from behind the bar and took it to my room with me. You don't mind, do you, Chris? I've got about a quarter of it left if you want it back.'

Chris held up his hands. 'No thanks, brother. That's quite all right. Consider it my gift to you.'

'I can't believe this snow,' Owen chimed in, finally tearing his gaze away from the window. 'If we got an inch in Tampa everything would shut down for days. The power would be out, phones probably too.'

'That's where living in Western New York gets interesting. We've learned to adapt,' Chris said, taking a seat at the head of the table. 'If the power goes out, I have Guardian generators out back that automatically switch over to natural gas.'

'We had a freak November storm like this in 2014,' Lauren added. 'We got about seven feet of snow over forty-eight hours, and I was literally stuck in my house for four days with my daughters. We live in the middle of the city and it took that long for the plows to get to us. They actually had to call in the National Guard for help. But we never lost power, phone or Internet service. We just couldn't physically get out of the house. My next-door neighbor crawled out of his second story window and finally dug us out.'

'I don't miss the snow,' Seth agreed, swirling his drink around with the celery stalk. 'I haven't been back to Buffalo during the winter. Not once in seventeen years.' He looked out the window now and gave a shudder. 'I'll take the California sunshine any day.'

'We get snow in Cleveland, only it's not like this. I remember my parents calling me during the Snowvember storm. My dad managed to shovel out his driveway, but the streets weren't plowed so they couldn't go anywhere. I think they were stuck inside for at least three days,' Tyler said. Just the sound of his voice grated on Lauren's nerves.

'How much do you think has fallen?' Amanda asked.

Seth pulled out his phone, thumbed the screen, then read off: 'It says over three feet fell last night here in the Southern Tier. The city of Buffalo got pounded with over four feet of lake effect snow and wind gusts of forty miles per hour, with no signs of letting up until later today.'

'Nope.' Seth leaned back in his chair. 'I don't miss this at all.'

A shuffling noise from behind caught everyone's attention.

'Hey, Ward, can you make me another key card?' Raphael half staggered into the dining area from the lobby. Ward's head snapped over at the sound of his voice, but he didn't spill a drop of the coffee he was serving to Amanda. 'I lost my card and Erica has me locked out and she won't answer her phone.'

'Sorry about your face,' Tyler said with a snarky grin. 'Did Erica dot your eye?'

Raphael's hand reached up and gingerly touched the purple ringing his eye. 'No. She kicked me out and when she yanked the door open, it accidently hit me.'

Ward carefully set the coffee pot down on the polished wood of the long table. 'I'll ring your room. If she doesn't answer, I'll leave a message stating I'm making you a copy. However,' his thick grey eyebrow arched, 'if she has the security bar engaged, you won't be able to get in.'

Raphael ran the same hand he'd touched his face with through his already mussy black hair. 'Shit. I didn't think of that.'

Chris wiped his mouth with his cloth napkin, set it aside and stood up. 'Never mind, Ward. I'll follow Mr Diaz to his room. Mrs Diaz will open up for me. If she doesn't, then I'll use my master key.' He clapped Raphael on the back. 'She always liked me better than you anyway.'

'Very good, sir.' Ward looked to Mrs Brady. 'Will you be able to finish serving without me?'

Sliding a plate of scrambled eggs in front of Lauren, Brady gave her boss a pleasant smile. 'Of course.' Then she told Raphael, 'Please invite your wife to come down. I made enough food for an army.'

Amanda pushed back from the table as well. 'I'll come with you.'

'I don't think that's a good idea.' Lauren touched her arm before she got up. 'She didn't have a lot of kind words for you last night. Let me go. There's no history between us, no grudges.' Raphael hadn't admitted she'd punched him out, but he was sporting a hell of a shiner. And the 'accidently hit with a door' excuse was so common in domestic violence cases that Lauren had even said it herself when an ex of hers was using her as a punching bag.

'I think that would be better.' Raphael agreed, trying to smooth the same light blue button-down shirt he'd had on the night before. 'I'm sorry to drag all of you into our problems. She's been under a lot of stress with her podcast. There's a ton of pressure to actually solve one of the crimes she airs.

There's so much competition now, it's not enough to just report on the murders. The fans want to see results.'

'Vulture,' Amanda said under her breath, then sipped her tea, leaving a bright pink lipstick stain on the rim. Lauren wondered what time she had to get up to be able to come to eight o'clock breakfast with perfectly done corkscrew curls and full makeup, let alone the expensive cream-colored cashmere sweater set she wore. Lauren's own ponytail, lounge pants and sweatshirt must have seemed tacky to her. Supermoms like Amanda always made Lauren feel inadequate. Not that Amanda had been anything but sweet to her. It was Lauren's own insecurities that needed to be reined in, and maybe a hint of jealousy as well.

'Let's go,' Chris said, clapping his hands together. 'She might be experiencing the mother of all hangovers right now.'

'I'll come too,' Reese said, tossing down his napkin.

'No use making this a circus,' Lauren said, giving Reese a look. New York State had a pro-arrest policy for domestic violence, and even though Raphael hadn't stated Erica had hit him, depending on what she said when they got to the room, she might be looking at an arrest for domestic assault. Lauren didn't think Reese needed to be any part of that. Who knew how she'd twist the situation for her podcast listeners?

After the display she'd put on the night before, Lauren knew Erica was both vindictive and vicious. That made for a dangerous combination.

SIXTEEN

Lauren took one last sip of her coffee, then followed Chris and Raphael through the bar area back into the lobby toward the elevator. Outside, the wind howled, and snow beat relentlessly against the windows. The view from the glass doors in the lobby showed a solid sheet of white.

Chris speared the up button with the tip of his index finger, while Lauren and Raphael hung slightly behind him. The smell of stale booze was radiating off Raphael like an alcoholic cologne. Not only was his left eye almost completely closed shut, his right eye was watery and bloodshot. Sleeping on a hotel lobby couch was still sleeping on a couch, no matter how swanky the hotel.

The elevator doors slid open and they all stepped inside, Lauren and Chris visibly putting some space between themselves and Raphael.

'I'm so embarrassed,' he said again as they stepped off on the second floor. 'I can't believe she did this to me. In your new hotel.'

'No worries, brother,' Chris said, patting him on the back. 'You and Erica aren't the first couple I've had to broker a shaky peace treaty between, just the first here. Grab your stuff and you can come and stay in the bridal suite with me until the weather lets up, then we can figure out where you can go from there.' *If Erica ends up in the can for assault, maybe you'll get the room all to yourself*, Lauren thought. Having been on the receiving end of domestic violence, Lauren had no qualms about having a woman locked up if she was the perpetrator.

'OK,' he responded, sounding defeated as they passed Tyler's room and approached his own.

'Why don't you stand behind me,' Chris told Raphael quietly when they were squared up to his door. Hanging his head, Raphael stepped back and angled himself behind Lauren and Chris, out of view.

'Erica?' Chris leaned in close, his face inches from the peep hole so she could get a good look at who was outside. He rapped his knuckles lightly against the wood. No use banging if Raphael had already tried that move unsuccessfully. 'Please open the door. I'm out here with your husband and Detective Riley.'

It was so quiet in the hallway that all they could hear was the wind and the sound of their own breathing. Chris gave it a good twenty seconds before he tried again. 'I gave you fair warning. I'm going to open the door, and Raphael's going to grab his belongings. He'll be staying in my room with me on the third floor for now.'

Silence.

'Ready?' Chris asked in a whisper, pulling his master key card from his front pocket.

Raphael grunted, Lauren nodded, and Chris pressed the card to the lock.

A mechanical tumbling noise was followed by an audible click. The light above the door handle turned green. Chris grabbed the handle and twisted it down, pushing at the same time. He stepped in and immediately stopped, causing Lauren to run into the back of him.

The smell hit her before she could see what was on the bed in front of her. Whoever came up with the cliche that blood smells like pennies has never smelled real blood before. Not a lot of it all at once. Blood smells like blood. There's nothing to compare it to. And once you've smelled it in large quantities, especially in a confined area, you'd never mistake it or equate it with anything else.

Chris was frozen in place. Lauren shoved him aside and took one step forward. 'Raphael, stay outside the room!' she called.

Erica was face up on the bed in a twist of sheets so soaked in blood there was no telling what color they'd been before her throat was cut. The gash was wide and deep, her brown eyes were open, staring blankly at the ceiling. Her right hand was dangling off the edge of the bed, while the other was lodged above her head. That one had a deep incised wound across the palm. A defense wound.

'Erica?' Raphael's voice rasped from behind. 'Erica!'

Lauren spun around, grabbed Raphael by the front of his shirt and forcibly pushed him out the door.

'Erica! Erica!' He was screaming now, fighting against Lauren to get back into the room.

'Chris, help me with him!' she called, grappling with the hysterical man.

Chris stumbled out, the door slamming shut behind him. Lauren still had Raphael by the shirt, buttons popping off in all directions and bouncing on the floor as he tried to get past her. Chris came up behind his friend and put him in a headlock. 'What now?' he asked, looking to Lauren for direction.

'Get him downstairs. Call 911.'

'What about Erica? What the fuck is going on?' Raphael howled, straining against Chris.

'I need to go back in and check on her.' Gentler words than saying *I have to make sure she's dead*, but Lauren had been in Homicide long enough to tell when someone was gone. 'Give me your master key card.'

Chris was still twisted up with Raphael. 'Right front pants pocket,' he huffed.

Lauren reached past Raphael and extracted the card. 'I'll wait until you get him on the elevator.'

'What? No! No!' He struggled all the way to the doors. Chris managed to hit the down button with his elbow. Dragging Raphael backwards, the last thing Lauren saw was his tear-streaked face as the doors closed. In her haste to have the grieving husband removed from the scene, she had forgotten to tell Chris not to let anybody up to the second floor.

SEVENTEEN

Lauren put the key card against the lock. Pulling her sleeve over her fingers, she gingerly pulled down on the handle, trying to have as little contact with it as possible. Opening it just enough so she could get through, she slipped off her sneaker and used it to keep the door open so she wouldn't have to touch the inner handle when it was time to exit. Any possible fingerprints needed to be preserved.

She took a second to take in the scene in front of her. Nothing looked disturbed. There was no ransacking or tipped-over furniture. A line of fat, black blood drops started from the right side of the bed, trailing off about halfway to the door. Either the assailant cut themself or it was cast off from the murder weapon. The path to the bed on the left side was clear.

Lauren made her way over to Erica, watching her feet so she didn't step on any potential evidence. She came around to the left side of the bed and, leaning over, reached out and felt for a pulse on Erica's wrist. She noted the skin was cold to the touch and rigor mortis was present in the extremities. That meant she'd been dead more than two hours but less than twelve, roughly. Time of death was notoriously hard to pinpoint by just examining the body at the scene.

Dutifully, she counted to thirty as she pressed her fingers against the veins.

Nothing.

She reached into the pocket of her sweatshirt and pulled out her phone. Making sure the screen was black, she held it in front of Erica's mouth. Lauren noted no condensation on the glass. She then angled it under her nose, once again counting to thirty.

Nothing.

Erica was dead.

Lauren snapped into full homicide detective mode. Touching the screen to wake up her phone, she looked at the time: 8:37 a.m. She opened the notes section in her cell and began to document the scene.

Looking around the room again, she saw that the metal safety bar hadn't been engaged, meaning Erica hadn't set it when Raphael left or when she'd let the killer in.

Without moving from her spot, she started taking pictures. The body. She noted the presence of defense wounds on both of her hands, zooming in on the deep cuts across Erica's palms and fingers and the wide slash over her right forearm. One of the pillows, dotted with blood droplets, possibly cast off from the murder weapon, lay on the floor to the left side of the bed. The covers were a twisted crimson mess. A struggle had clearly taken place here.

She took a wide shot of the blood trail. The door. The nightstand. The balcony doors. The open suitcase on the floor next to the stone fireplace, clothes still neatly folded inside. The big sitting area that didn't look like it had been used. A glass half full of brown liquid on the dresser.

She squatted down. From that angle she could better see

the dark drops of the blood trail on the tan carpet. Four, that she could make out, heading toward the door in a wide line. Whoever had sliced Erica's throat had probably headed toward the door from the right side of the bed, bloody weapon hanging from his or her hand, dripping blood along the way, either Erica's or their own. The trail stopped abruptly though, from big spatters to nothing. Lauren pictured the scene in her head, the killer realizing they were covered in blood, literally dripping it from the murder weapon. If Reese was with her, they would've bounced questions off each other. Why does the trail stop like that? What would I do if I was the killer?

Lauren heard Reese's answer in her head as if he was standing next to her, *'I'd wipe the blade on my clothes.'*

It made sense.

Pinching her phone again, she zoomed in on the blood trail, photographing it. She looked back to Erica's body and then scanned the room. She'd have to check the bathroom, but so far she couldn't locate anything that could have been used to make the fatal wounds.

Walking into the bathroom, nothing was disturbed. The spa products were lined up in a silver tray against the mirror. Erica's makeup bag was on the marble countertop, zipped up next to Raphael's razor and a travel-sized can of shaving cream. Everything looked perfectly normal, except for the view of Erica's corpse from the doorway. She took photos anyway. When she checked, she saw that she had taken seventy-two. That was a good start for the State Police, who she assumed would have jurisdiction in an unincorporated town like Inverness.

As she left the bathroom, she caught a flash of something. Peeking out from under the dust ruffle on the right-hand side of the bed closest to her Lauren could see some paperwork. She bent over, trying to get a better look. Erica must have made her own file of Jessica's case. *Maybe she'd been looking at some of it when she'd gone to bed*, Lauren thought as she snapped more pictures. *Maybe she was tired and just stuffed them underneath her.*

A wedding picture of Owen and Amanda printed out from

a newspaper website sat underneath an article about an arrest Reese had made in a robbery before he got to the Cold Case unit. There were more pieces of paper under those two items, but Lauren couldn't move them to see what they were. She reached her hand out to pick them up, caught herself at the last instant, then straightened up. She couldn't disturb or alter the crime scene, especially with no gloves on. She needed to leave before her curiosity got the best of her.

Carefully, she made her way back to the entrance, photographing as she went, and slid through the opening, kicking her shoe along with her so the door would fall shut behind her.

Reese, Chris and Amanda were charging down the hall toward her. 'Reese!' She held out a hand, stopping all three in their tracks. 'Take them downstairs and sit everyone in the bar, separated, but where you can see them.'

'What did Raphael do to Erica?' Amanda demanded.

'Can you take them now?' Lauren urged Reese without looking at Amanda.

Reese nodded in understanding: locate, isolate and monitor the witnesses. It was standard homicide procedure. He knew Erica was dead without Lauren having to say it, just from her instructions.

'Come on, guys,' he said cupping his arms around Chris and Amanda, herding them back to the elevator.

'Is Erica OK?' Amanda called over her shoulder in a small voice. 'I'm a nurse practitioner. Maybe I can help.'

'Thank you, Amanda, but that's not necessary. I'll be down in a few minutes to talk to everyone.'

You can't undo rigor mortis, Lauren thought as she watched Reese ease Amanda into the elevator. An even more troubling thought bubbled up in her mind then: *And why was Erica looking at your pictures before she died?*

EIGHTEEN

As soon as she was alone in the hallway again, she switched over from camera to phone mode, punching in 911.

A female voice answered after three rings. '911, what is your emergency?'

'My name is Lauren Riley, I'm a detective with the Buffalo Police Department and I need to report a homicide at the Sloane Spa and Retreat in Inverness.'

Lauren heard the sounds of someone punching information into a keyboard. 'Ma'am? We've just gotten a similar call to that location. Can you tell me what's happening there?'

'There's a female, age approximately thirty-five, named Erica Diaz who is in room 203, deceased. The cause of death appears to be a homicide.'

The dispatcher's voice remained calm and even. 'And you can tell this how?'

Lauren realized she was pacing the hallway without her shoe on. 'I'm a homicide detective. I don't want to speculate on cause of death, but it definitely is not from natural causes.'

More typing in the background. 'Is there an imminent threat of danger? Does anyone there have a weapon or is threatening?'

'The victim has a neck wound that looks to be from a cutting instrument,' Lauren chose her words carefully. 'Aside from checking for a pulse, I did not touch the body. The rest of the guests are on the first floor right now. All I can say is none of them appeared to be armed.' She stuck her foot into her sneaker and squished it inside without undoing the laces, the tongue bending uncomfortably forward.

'Do you know who the perpetrator might be?'

'Not at this time.'

'Is the perpetrator still on the scene?'

'In all likelihood, yes.'

There was a long pause and she could hear the sound of more typing. 'Stay on the line with me, detective. I'm trying to get through to someone at the State Police barracks. A State of Emergency was declared overnight. Hundreds of people got caught on the thruway in the snowstorm. Emergency services are tied up with that right now.'

Lauren looked over to the window at the end of the hall. It was a sheet of pure white. 'I'll stay on the line.'

A State of Emergency. That was not good. Freak snowstorms were so common in Western New York that you could almost take the 'freak' out of the phrase. However, unlike in most TV shows and movies, a snow dump of four to eight feet overnight usually didn't mean the power went out or that you lost phone service or the Internet. In fact, if you did lose those things, they were the first things that got restored. It was mobility you could lose for days at a time. Even for an area that was used to regular, heavy snowfall, there was only so much equipment to go around and it had to be prioritized. Lauren thought of the secondary roads they'd had to use to get to the spa. And the almost three-quarters-of-a-mile-long private road you had to take to get to the doors. And the fact that it was still snowing, accompanied by high winds.

'Detective Riley?' The dispatcher's voice broke through her thoughts. 'I have State Police BCI Investigator Kevin Donovan on the line. Hold please and I'll put him through.'

A slight staticky sound and then: 'This is Investigator Donovan. To whom am I speaking?'

Lauren identified herself all over again and detailed the finding of the body. 'I've secured the room and I had my partner take everyone downstairs and separate them as best he can.'

'Is everyone else safe and accounted for? There is no imminent threat?'

Only a murderer among the guests downstairs, she thought. 'Everyone is accounted for.' She couldn't speak for everyone's safety, because she just didn't know. Whoever had done that to Erica was still in the building and obviously didn't want to get caught.

'Can you give me the victim's details, if you have them.'

Lauren repeated the information she'd given the dispatcher. 'Her name is Erica Diaz, age approximately thirty-five. She resides in Brooklyn with her husband, Raphael, who is on the first floor with the rest of the guests.'

'Is he the suspect?'

'Obviously, he'd be my first choice,' Lauren said. 'But there are others here that may have motive, so I wouldn't rule anyone out.'

She could hear the sound of a pen scratching out notes on the other end of the phone. 'You said you took pictures of the crime scene?'

'With my cell, after I checked for a pulse. I didn't search the room or touch anything.'

'Good. I'm going to call you at the number the dispatcher has listed for you. I want you to send me copies of those pictures as soon as I get on the line with you. Can you do that?'

'Yes.' Lauren clicked off the line and opened her photo app. She pulled up the pictures she'd taken in the short time she was in the room. Quickly, she put them into a single folder so she'd be able to send them to Investigator Donovan as soon as he called.

There was a good sixty-second lag before he called back. 'Detective Riley? Sorry about that. I'm updating my Major as we go. I'm trying to get him to break off at least two of our modified all-terrain vehicles to get me to your scene.'

She glanced at the locked door of Erica's room. 'And?'

'Right now, we have at least one hundred and sixty-seven people trapped on the New York State Thruway that we know of, including a bus carrying senior citizens, many of whom have health problems. It's worse than the situation we faced in November of 2014 because it's a holiday weekend. The thruway was loaded with people headed home from Thanksgiving get-togethers last night. Our priority is to get to the people stuck in their cars, many without food or water and running out of gas at this point.'

Lauren remembered the storm of 2014 vividly. 'What does that mean for us?' She put him on speaker phone and began sending the photos as he talked.

'I'm at least six to twelve hours from getting to the scene, if not more. The State Police are calling in everybody in this half of the state.'

'It's that bad outside?' She hit send, hoping the file wasn't too big.

'Six feet in some areas since eight o'clock last night and still snowing with high winds. I've been stuck in our barracks since yesterday. The visibility is poor to nonexistent in spots. We've actually got three State Troopers caught in their vehicles that we can't get to. Excuse my language, Detective, but it's a shitshow out there.'

The sheet of pure white still filled the window at the end of the hallway. 'So what do you want me to do?'

'Besides the husband, do you have any idea who might be the suspect?'

She paused for a second, trying to think how to word her response. 'Almost everyone here except me and the two staff members is on a kind of class reunion. There was an incident with the victim last night. She pretty much insulted or threatened all seven of the other guests.' *Including Reese*, she thought but didn't say out loud. 'At this moment they're all down in the bar area. I haven't spoken with any of them or questioned them about Erica or their movements last night.'

'Good. That's good. Where are you now?'

'I'm alone on the second floor, just outside the victim's room.'

There was a long silence, and then, 'Some of your photos just came through.' Lauren pictured him scrolling through the crime scene pictures. 'Someone cut her throat.' He was thinking out loud as he looked at the photos, the way she sometimes did. 'You didn't find the murder weapon in her room?'

'I didn't search it thoroughly, obviously, but it would have been a cutting implement of some kind. I didn't see one in the room.' Lauren thought back to the deep, bloody gash across Erica's throat. 'You'll also note in the photos she has defense wounds to both hands and her right arm.'

'At some point, after you make sure the witnesses are secured, I'm going to want you to check the common areas of the hotel, just to make sure there isn't a weapon laying around. Secure the premises. You mentioned some staff there?'

'Two. The general manager and the chef. The head of housekeeping left yesterday before the weather got bad.'

'Is there any reason to suspect either one of them?'

'I don't believe so, no.' She hesitated for a moment, then added, 'There's something else you should know.'

'I'm listening.'

'Seventeen years ago, one of their classmates was murdered in Memorial Park in the Old First Ward. A seventeen-year-old girl named Jessica Toakase. All the guests here, including the owner, were questioned about her murder at the time. It's still unsolved.'

She heard a low whistle on the other end of the phone. 'And everyone just happens to be at this hotel this weekend?'

'Yes. It was supposed to be a sort of class reunion. I got roped in because my partner graduated with them.'

'Your partner was questioned at the time of the first murder?'

'Yes,' she admitted. 'And last night Erica, the victim, threatened to reveal who Jessica's killer was on her podcast. She claimed to have figured it out. It got ugly before she went up to her room.'

'Do you know about that first case? Are you familiar with it?'

Lauren swallowed. She suddenly had a lump in her throat. 'I know the case. I have it uploaded and can access it through my phone. The file is large, so I'll have to see if Christopher Sloane, the owner, will let me use an in-house computer to send it to you.'

Outside, the wind let out a wicked howl. Lauren could hear Investigator Donovan on the other end of the line typing something. 'If you can send me that file, that'd be great.'

'I'll see what I can do,' she said, wishing her department didn't stick her with a five-year-old phone and antiquated technology so she could just send him a link to the file in the cloud.

There was another long pause. 'OK, I'm going to forward what I have so far to my Major. What I want you to do is make sure all the witnesses stay on the first floor and separated. Can you handle that?'

'Of course,' she responded.

'Do you think anyone else is in danger? I'm looking at these pictures and that's a hell of a lot of rage shown in that room.'

'I think keeping them all in the bar area where they can eyeball each other is the safest thing,' Lauren said. 'Especially if you're going to want to get search warrants for their individual rooms at some point.'

'I will want to do that.' Lauren heard the sound of shuffling paper in the background. 'Try to keep them off the floor of the crime scene and out of their rooms.'

'There are restrooms right off the lounge area. There's no reason for anyone to leave.'

'Good. Let me call my superiors and tell them exactly what's going on. You go downstairs and see if you can get everyone to cooperate. Text me the names of everyone in the hotel as soon as possible,' Donovan said, then added, 'I've driven by the sign for that place, but I didn't think it was open yet.'

'It's not. The owner invited us for a sneak peek. He's one of the suspects cooling his heels in the bar.'

'I think his rating on Tripadvisor just went down a star or two.'

'I think that's the least of his worries right now,' she replied.

He gave a grim-sounding laugh into the phone. 'I'll get back to you in a few minutes. Call me immediately if anything happens.'

He clicked off and Lauren turned and walked toward the door of her room. She needed to grab her notebook and pen.

At least our investigator has a proper cop's morbid sense of humor, Lauren thought bitterly as she waved her key card over her lock. *It would really suck looking for a homicidal psychopath with someone who can't take a joke.*

NINETEEN

Lauren emerged from the elevator with a knot in her gut. Now, as she crossed the lobby, she was mentally cataloging exits and entrances, placement of furniture, the position of the camera over the front desk. She looked up into it, a small, unobtrusive lens in the right-hand corner of the ceiling pointed down at the single computer screen mounted on the desk. In a hotel with only seven rooms, more than one computer would be a waste of technology. She wondered how far back into the lobby it captured. She'd need to see the footage from the night before right away.

Before heading into the lounge area, she walked over to the couch in front of the fireplace. A decorative throw pillow from one of the chairs sat scrunched at the far end. Given its position and the dent in the center of it, Lauren knew Raphael had used it to sleep on. Pulling out her phone again, she photographed it. From what she could see, without turning it over, there didn't appear to be any blood on it or the couch.

She turned around. Starting with the front doors she photographed the entire lobby, including the position of the security camera. When she was satisfied, she headed over to the entrance to the bar and dining area.

Reese had everyone spread out: Amanda at the long table, her husband on one of the bar chairs with Tyler at the other end. Raphael sat at one of the round tables, head cradled in his hands, shoulders heaving. Seth was seated at the table next to him, but on the far side, closer to the door. Chris sat perched on a stool behind the bar, his dreads loose around his shoulders, a look of anger mixed with despair etched on his face. Reese looked up from the leather chair he'd placed next to the entrance when she came in.

'Are the State Police on their way?' he asked, standing.

Chris got up from his stool. Ward and Diane Brady emerged

from the kitchen area to stand beside their boss. Everyone's eyes turned to her for answers, even Raphael's.

'I've just talked to an investigator from the State Police,' Lauren began. 'Right now, we are in a State of Emergency. The unexpected storm has stranded hundreds of people. What he wants from us right now is cooperation. I've locked up Erica and Raphael's room. There are restrooms right here in the bar area. Please stay in your seats for now. No one is to go to the second floor for any reason.'

'Wait, what?' Tyler asked. 'I've got medicine in my room I have to take before dinner.'

'If you need your medicine and the State Police aren't here yet, give me your key card, tell me where it is and I'll get it for you,' she replied.

'The hell you will,' he snapped back. 'Who put you in charge?'

'I did,' Chris replied. 'I'm putting Detective Riley in charge until the authorities arrive.'

Tyler muttered something under his breath, but Lauren didn't bother to address it. 'First and foremost is the safety of everyone in this building,' Lauren continued. 'I need to pat everyone down to make sure no one has a weapon on them.'

'Wait just a minute,' Owen said. 'You're not patting my wife down.'

'Who's going to pat you down, Detective?' Seth asked.

'Raphael, did Erica tell you who she thought Jessica's murderer was? We can end this right now,' Owen called over to him.

'No, she never said.' Raphael's voice was choked with grief. 'Don't you think I thought of that, asshole?'

Amanda put a hand up to her husband in a calming gesture. Tear tracks now marred her perfect makeup, and her eyes were rimmed in red. 'It's OK. She can pat me down. Someone killed Erica.' Her voice hitched a little. 'We have to let her.'

'Someone *murdered* my wife!' Raphael wailed, and pounded a fist on the table in front of him. '*Your* friend. Let her do what she needs to do. Let her pull the freaking place apart if she needs to!' He broke down into a fit of sobs, sinking into his arms, covering his face as his shoulders heaved.

'Mrs Brady can pat me down, if she's comfortable with it,' Lauren replied, hoping to ease the distraught husband and pacify the asshole, Tyler.

'I can do that,' the middle-aged chef responded, looking at the weeping husband. She was twisting the edge of her apron between her fingers so hard it looked like she might actually rip the starched white fabric.

'And I'm going to need you all to show me your hands.' She put her hands out in front of her, palms up, fingers splayed. 'Like this, please.'

'What is that for?' Seth asked.

'She's looking for cuts or wounds,' Reese responded grimly from his chair by the door.

One by one Lauren walked around to all the guests, patting them down and checking their hands and immediate areas for weapons. She could feel the awkwardness of it, but none of them resisted, not even Tyler, not after Raphael's plea. When she got to Chris, she slipped the key card he'd given her back into his pocket. She didn't want to mix it up with her own.

Lauren felt a tightness in her chest as she approached her partner. Reese held his arms straight out, looking to the side as she started on him. 'Never thought I'd see the day when you were treating me like a criminal,' he said in a low voice so only she could hear.

'You know I have to do this,' she replied, running her fingers along his waistband.

'I know,' was all he said in return, lowering his arms as she straightened up from patting down his legs. She had to treat Reese like everyone else. But he couldn't have done that to Erica. He'd put so much work into Jessica's case, trying to catch a break. But then the thought that maybe Reese kept such close tabs on the case because he really didn't want it solved.

Stop it, she commanded herself as the doubts crept in. *It's Reese.*

Lauren saved Ward and Mrs Brady for last, lifting the bar rail and coming back to them. Ward lifted his arms over his head easily, seemingly unshaken by the turn of events.

Mrs Brady, however, was stiff as a board as Lauren carefully started on one side and came down the other. Lauren stepped back from her when she was done and said gently, 'I'll talk you through it.'

Mrs Brady nodded and clumsily patted Lauren down for weapons. When she was finished, she exhaled and stepped away, putting a hand to her chest.

Lauren looked around the bar. 'Where's the knife you used to cut lemons, limes and oranges last night?' she asked. Chris had made a show of carefully slicing an orange with a large knife in front of his guests when Erica had ordered her muddled Old Fashioned. She'd seen him lay it on the rubber mat that lined the serving side.

Chris came off his stool and approached the bar. He went to reach for a drawer and Lauren shot out her hand, stopping it cold. 'In here?' she asked.

He nodded. 'It's full of barware.'

'Mind if I check?' She didn't have a warrant to search anything, so she needed Chris's permission.

'Go ahead.'

Using the pen she'd retrieved from her room, she hooked it into the handle and pulled the drawer open. It contained a strainer, a long spoon, bottle openers, corkscrews and several small paring knives.

But not the large knife Chris had used to slice the orange.

'I don't see it,' she said.

Chris's forehead crinkled as he stared into the drawer, then he looked up. 'Diane, did you take it and wash it?'

'I did and I put it right back where it belonged.'

'What time was that?' Lauren asked.

Her hand went back to her apron. A strand of gray hair came loose from the tight bun she wore and straggled down by her cheek. 'I gathered up and washed all the dirty implements before I went to bed, right before ten o'clock.'

'And the knife I'm talking about was in there?'

She nodded. 'I remember being careful with it because it's so new and very sharp.'

Lauren thought for a moment. 'OK. Chris, I'm going to need you to come out from behind the bar and go sit over there by the fire. Mrs Brady, Ward, I want you both to have a seat out there. Mrs Brady can still go back into the kitchen if anyone needs anything, but use the other entrance, not the one behind the bar. No one goes back there unless I say so.'

'So that's the way you secure a scene?' Tyler asked. 'With your say so?'

'I forgot my roll of crime scene tape when I was packing. Forgive me, please,' Lauren shot back. 'I have to make do with what's on hand.'

She followed thc three back out to the seating area. 'I'm going to come around and I want each of you to give me your name, date of birth and room number, so I can forward them to the BCI investigator.'

'The who?' Tyler asked, his arms crossed tightly in front of his checkered flannel shirt.

'Investigator Donovan from the State Police Bureau of Criminal Investigation,' Lauren replied. 'He's currently snowed in at his barracks. He asked me to gather this preliminary information for him.'

A collective buzz ran through the group, sort of a frightened and agitated exhale. They were cooperating for now, but Lauren knew she'd have to work quickly. Their horror for Erica and their sympathy for Raphael would only last so long.

'I'm going to put the news on, if you don't mind,' Chris said.

Lauren nodded. 'Good idea.' She needed to keep their minds busy, concentrated on the storm and not Erica lying dead one floor above them, her bed soaked in blood.

'Ward,' was all Chris had to say, and the tall, thin man stood, walked over to the polished bar and picked up the remote, turning the TV on.

Lauren walked from person to person as they sat transfixed on the images on the screen of cars, semi-trucks, buses and SUVs, all trapped bumper-to-bumper on the New York State Thruway. The reporter was walking against the wind down the line of vehicles with her camera operator following. The visibility was awful. At one point she turned and looked right into the camera as she battled to keep her hood up, snow caught in her hair. 'I just want our viewers to know that our truck has also been stuck about twenty vehicles back since last night. We'll continue to broadcast as long as we can . . .'

Lauren stopped in front of Reese. 'You know my date of birth,' he said dryly. 'And my room number.'

'And you know why you can't help me with this,' she replied.

He lowered his voice to almost a whisper. 'You think I killed Erica? Or Jessica for that matter?'

'You know it doesn't matter what I think,' she said. 'Right now, I have to preserve the integrity of the crime scene, keep all the witnesses separated and safe and try to locate that knife.'

'And I get to sit here on my ass and do nothing,' he added. The tops of his ears were flushed red, along with the apples of his cheeks.

'What you can do is watch everyone for me. You know this group better than anyone. Be my eyes for things I wouldn't pick up on.'

Lauren's phone vibrated in her pants pocket. She pulled it out and glanced at the screen. 'It's the BCI investigator. I have to take this.'

'Do what you have to do. I'll keep everyone in line here.'

Lauren found herself looking up at the clock above the doorway. It read 9:40. She stepped out into the lobby and swiped the screen. 'Lauren Riley.'

'Detective Riley? It's Investigator Donovan.'

'Why don't you just call me Riley and I'll call you Donovan. No need for the formalities.'

'Sounds good. How's everything over there?'

She looked behind her into the lounge. Everyone's eyes were glued to the flatscreen above the bar, except for Raphael, who was huddled on the table, breathing raggedly.

'About as well as can be expected,' she said, moving closer to the entrance doors and out of sight of the rest of the guests. 'I have everyone's information for you.'

'Good. Send it along. Is everyone cooperating?'

'For now,' Lauren said. 'But it only just happened. Who can say how they'll feel after an hour or three sitting down here.'

'We've got every available snowmobile, all-terrain vehicle and plow on the thruway right now. The wind isn't letting up, so it's slow going. The snowmobiles and ATVs are bringing more gas, food and water to the people trapped in their cars. Some people are experiencing medical emergencies. It's a nightmare.'

'No chance of you getting here any sooner then?'

'I'm still hours from getting there as of right now. But hell, I'll snowshoe in if a plow can get me close enough.'

'I do have a new piece of information.' Lauren automatically lowered her voice. 'A large carving knife is missing from the bar. The chef swears she washed it and put it in its proper drawer around ten o'clock. I kicked the owner and staff out from behind the counter to try to preserve any prints or DNA in or on the drawer area.'

'Did guests have access to the bar after ten?'

'The owner let everyone help themselves after the incident with Erica. Anyone could have grabbed it, but it was big. Not impossible to hide up a sleeve, but the blade was at least seven or eight inches long, not including the handle.'

'I want you to look in the common areas for that knife. There's not much we can do if the murder weapon is stashed in the killer's room until I can get search warrants written up. In the meantime, we have to assure everyone's safety. Can you do that?'

'I was thinking the same thing. Do you want me to get permission to search from the owner?'

'A verbal will do, as long as you audiotape it. Just make sure you add he has the right to revoke his permission at any time.'

'Got it.'

'Call me back when you've finished. I'm going to start running these names and typing up search warrants. And get me that file on the first victim ASAP.'

TWENTY

They hung up and Lauren walked back to the lounge area. Reese was still sitting sentry by the door, his face somber. He barely looked at Lauren as she passed. She could only imagine if the tables were turned and he had to investigate her and her friends while she was forced to sit idly by and watch.

Chris was sitting at one of the round tables, eyes trained on the flatscreen above the bar, a finger hooked in his mouth. He didn't look at her until she spoke to him in a low voice. 'Is there a business center here with a computer and printer?'

He dropped the finger and replied, 'I wanted to put one in, but my wife said no way. She wants to ban cell phones except in the rooms. She wants this place,' he lifted his arms and gestured around, 'to be an immersive experience. I guess peace and tranquility are out the window now.'

'What about in your office?' she pressed. 'Or behind the front desk?'

'I'll take you to the one in my office,' he said, starting to get up.

Lauren put her hand out. 'No. You have to stay here. Ward can take me. Just give me the password.'

He slumped back down in his seat, crossing his arms over his chest. 'I guess it doesn't matter. Take my password, my house key, my checkbook,' he said flatly. 'My dream spa isn't even open and it's already done for. Once word gets out a murder happened here, I imagine all the wedding parties and showers we booked for the spring and summer will be cancelled like that.' He snapped his fingers so loud that Seth turned around to look at him.

'Let's not worry about that now,' Lauren told him. A woman getting brutally killed in his retreat was sure to be bad for business, but Lauren was disgusted that that was what was first and foremost on his mind right then. Erica had been his friend. Or was she just another blank piece of paper he really couldn't be bothered with? 'We'll just take this step by step, OK?'

Calling Ward over, Chris instructed him to take Lauren to the desktop in his office. He scribbled his username and password in the notebook Lauren handed him. Clicking on her recording app, she asked him for permission to search the common areas of the hotel for weapons and for permission to enter his office and use his computer. The last thing she needed was a defense attorney coming at her a year from now saying she hadn't followed legal procedure.

'This keeps getting better and better,' Chris said, not even trying to conceal the anger creeping into his voice. 'Yes, I give you permission for both.'

When Lauren told him he could revoke that permission at any time, he just nodded dismissively, like he wanted her out of his sight as fast as possible. 'Ward will go with you when you look around. He has a master key, so you'll have full access. I'd do it myself, but apparently you're sequestering me.'

'It's standard procedure,' Lauren assured him.

'There's nothing standard about what happened to Erica,' he snapped back, then turned his eyes to the news.

'Follow me, Ms Riley,' Ward said in his formal tone.

Lauren walked a few paces behind him, watching the stiff way he carried himself, like he had a steel rod for a spine. Reese tipped his chin at her when she passed, not saying anything, and Lauren wondered if he'd been too far away to hear her conversation with Chris.

'Where do those doors lead to?' Lauren asked, gesturing to a pair of double doors to the right of the front desk.

'That's the main entrance to the spa,' he replied. 'The gym, massage therapy and treatment rooms are finished but the indoor/outdoor pool is still under construction, so it's off limits to guests right now. Mr Sloane has it locked due to all the construction equipment.'

Lauren followed him around the front desk to a plain door. He waved his key card over the lock and it clicked open. 'When the spa is fully functional, these key cards will be replaced with bracelets.' He held up his card. 'Mrs Sloane wants guests to be unencumbered by plastic squares.'

'That makes sense,' Lauren said, following him into the office. 'Who wants to keep track of their room key when they're supposed to be relaxing in the nude?'

Ward actually laughed at Lauren's attempt at spa humor. 'If you ever have the good fortune of working at a spa, you will find out just how many people love to be naked as much as possible.'

The office itself was large and sparsely furnished, but by the looks of it, filling up fast with all the equipment needed to run a business. Three large desks lined the back wall, each with a desktop perched on it. A large copy machine/printer sat in the corner, giving off a slight hum. Framed photographs of beautiful women lying on tables with flowers in their hair and serene smiles on their faces while a pair of hands rubbed their shoulders decorated the walls. In the far corner waiting to be unpacked, five huge cardboard boxes were stacked. The one on the very top had a large arrow and the words THIS WAY UP printed in red across the side.

Ward made his way over to the middle desk and sat down on the black-cushioned office chair. 'I'll get this one booted up,' he said, wiggling the mouse around.

Lauren noticed another small table in the opposite corner with a monitor on top of what looked like a DVD player. 'Is that for the security surveillance system?'

Ward looked over to where she was pointing. 'Yes. But it's not fully operational yet. Once again, there's some disagreement between Mr and Mrs Sloane about how much of the spa should be monitored on camera. Mr Sloane would like cameras on every floor and in all the hallways, but Mrs Sloane thinks that guests wouldn't be comfortable being surveilled their entire stay. Right now, only the front desk is monitored.'

'Would I be able to review the tape from last night?'

Ward stood up, smoothing the front of his black vest down with his long, thin fingers. 'Certainly. When you're done with the computer here, I'll pull up the footage.'

Lauren slipped into the seat that Ward had just vacated. She noticed him pick up a laptop case propped against the chair next to hers and move it to the top of the largest desk. 'Is that yours?' she asked.

'That's Mr Sloane's personal laptop,' he replied, turning back to her. 'The Wi-Fi on the third floor has been cutting out. The techs the service sends can't figure out why.' He shrugged his shoulders. 'Just another hiccup in trying to get this place in order before we officially open. There's always something that needs attention right away. Mr Sloane comes down here to work so he doesn't lose any correspondence. I'm surprised he left it here. It's his lifeline to this place when he's not on the premises.'

'I'm attached to my devices as well,' Lauren commiserated. 'I just need to log into my work account and send a large file from my Cloud to the State Police investigator.'

'You can't do it from your phone?' he asked, walking back over and hovering near her shoulder. 'Or just send a link?'

'I probably could if this particular model wasn't five years old and my department wasn't ten years behind in the technology department.' She logged into her work account and began pulling up the files she wanted to transfer. She realized as she was doing it, she hadn't called her captain yet to fill him in on what was going on. She wondered if the State Police had called the Buffalo Police Department to let them know that two of their detectives were involved in a homicide outside of their jurisdiction. Her mental list of things to do was getting longer by the minute.

'Ms Riley,' Ward said, his voice lowering a notch. 'I feel like I have to tell you something.'

Lauren stopped typing and looked up at him.

'Last night I made the rounds of the first-floor premises sometime after you retired to your room and Mr Sloane was still entertaining the rest of the guests at the bar. Mr Diaz was indeed asleep on the couch in the lobby. I reported it to Mr Sloane.'

'What did he say?'

'To leave him there. That Mrs Diaz would let him back in when she cooled off. Then Mr Owstrowski made a comment about women I'd rather not repeat. Mr Creehan and Mr Reese just shook their heads.'

'At Raphael sleeping in the lobby or Tyler's comment?'

Ward's frown deepened. 'Both, I think.'

'What time was this?'

'About eleven thirty, if I had to estimate.'

'What time did the party break up at the bar?'

Now Ward ticked the list of guests off on his fingers. 'Mr Reese left first, then Mr Creehan went up just a few minutes later, just after midnight. Mr Owstrowski and Mr Sloane had another drink together and followed shortly afterward. I tidied up, then retired to my room on the first floor in the staff quarters. I came out for one final check around one thirty in the morning and saw Mr Diaz still on the couch.'

'Did you notice if he had the black eye when you first saw him?'

'He did,' Ward confirmed. 'And I reported that to Mr Sloane when I first found him. That was part of the crude comment Mr Owstrowski made. But that's not what bothered me.'

Now she sat back in the chair to get a better view of him. 'What bothered you?'

'Mr Reese was back. He and Mrs Carter were at the bar, huddled together, talking. I saw them from the doorway, but they were so engrossed in their conversation with each other that I don't think they saw me.'

Reese hadn't mentioned a late-night meeting with Amanda this morning. 'What did you do next?' she prompted.

'I turned around and headed back into the lobby to use this door,' he pointed to a door on the far right wall marked STAFF, 'to get back to my room. You can access all the storage areas, the staff quarters wing and the kitchen from there.'

That was interesting. 'So theoretically you could bypass the security camera if you entered the kitchen from the bar then came in here?'

'Not theoretically, but actually,' he replied. 'However, only Mr Sloane and the staff have key card access that would allow us to do that.'

'Good to know,' Lauren said. This place was a nightmare for a homicide investigator. 'Go on with what you were saying.'

'As I was just about to walk into the office, I saw Mr Carter coming down the stairs into the lobby.'

'Did he see you?'

Ward's forehead wrinkled in questioning concern. 'That's

just it. I don't know. He appeared furious. I think he was looking for Mrs Carter.'

Lauren thought back to breakfast. Both Amanda and her husband had seemed very subdued. Lauren had assumed it was from the scene Erica had caused. Reese had made no mention of late-night drinks with Amanda or a confrontation with Owen Carter. 'Thank you, Ward. I'll be sure to ask them about what you saw.'

'Please don't mention my name, if you can help it. The staff here are supposed to work on the premise of discretion.'

Lauren assured the nervous manager she'd do what she could on that front. She finished choosing the files she wanted and hit SEND, then waited to make sure everything was successfully transferred. While she was waiting, she pulled out her notebook and jotted down the information Ward had just given her, making special note of the times. She also made a note to question Mrs Brady on anything she might have seen or heard the night before. As she was tucking the pad back into her pants pocket, her cell phone buzzed. It was Donovan.

'I just received your files. Thank you.'

'Any luck on hitchhiking a ride here?' she asked hopefully.

'Not yet. We've got every available vehicle taking water, food and gas from car to car stuck on the thruway, and every snowplow trying to carve a path at the on-and-off ramps, but it's slow going. Is everyone still sequestered on the first floor?'

'For now.' Lauren stood and walked about four feet away, turning her back to Ward and facing the wall. 'I was going to watch the front desk surveillance footage with the hotel manager here in the front office.'

'Do me a favor and check for the knife first. I'd feel better knowing the scene was secure.'

Lauren's eyes lit over to the computer monitor. She was used to running her own investigations, not taking instructions from someone else. Technically, it was his case and she was just a witness, but circumstances had propelled her into something more. She knew Reese would keep the rest of the guests in the dining area, at least long enough for her to fast-forward through the security tape and check the grounds. Yet she knew she had to put the shoe on the other foot and think what she would do if this was a hotel in the city and she had no way to get to it and had to control the situation from her office in police headquarters. She had to give up a measure of control, for now, at least. 'I'll do that next. I have to take the manager back with the others first.'

'Is he there with you, alone?' Donovan's voice lowered. 'How do we know he isn't a suspect?'

'We don't,' Lauren replied. 'But in my opinion, he and the chef are the least likely perpetrators at this point. They had no personal history with the victim. And the murder scene definitely felt personal.'

'Just be careful. Until I do a complete record search on all the names you gave me, every single person there could have committed this homicide, past connections or not.'

'Then that includes me,' she said.

'I'm going to have to trust that a seasoned police detective didn't get stuck in a hotel with a bunch of strangers overnight, snap, and go on a homicidal rampage.'

Lauren could hear the frustration bubbling over in his voice. 'I can tell you this – I was alone in my room from about ten forty last night until I came down to breakfast this morning. I was woken up at 2:06 by Tyler Owstrowski, pounding on my door. He was highly intoxicated. I made him leave and went back to bed.'

'Is that on the nose?'

'I looked at the digital clock on my nightstand when he woke me up.'

'Since I haven't read the original file yet and don't know what transpired with the victim last night, does that make this Tyler a likely suspect?'

'Most definitely. But the husband has a black eye, presumably from fighting with the victim. He claims that the door hit him in the face while she was kicking him out of the room around midnight. He also says he lost his key card. I know that the security bar was not engaged when I entered with the owner.'

An audible groan came over the phone. 'Two viable suspects with means and opportunity.'

'Do you want a brief recap of all the events up to now?' she asked, looking over her shoulder at Ward, who was waiting patiently by the door with his hands folded in front of him, politely staring at the screensaver on the computer monitor next to him, because eavesdropping would be rude, of course.

'Quickly. I need to know that there isn't a bloody razor-sharp knife laying in the middle of a stairwell.'

Lauren spoke in a low, measured voice, laying out the circumstances of Jessica Toakase's murder, her relationship to the guests at the spa and the subsequent events of the night before. When she was done speaking, Donovan let out a low whistle into the phone. 'This is worse than I thought. I'm really going to need you to step up for me until I get there.'

'I'll do what I can,' she assured him.

'Good. I'm going to check on those ATVs. In the meantime, look for that weapon, document everything, and call me back.'

'I'm on it,' she responded.

'And Detective Riley?'

'Yes?'

'You do remember the other name they had for the Snowvember storm, don't you? Because of the shape of the snowfall pattern?'

'Not off the top of my head,' she admitted.

'It was officially Winter Storm Knife. They called the storm The Knife.'

Lauren swallowed hard. She had forgotten that, maybe on purpose because so many people had died.

'Be careful,' Donavon told her.

I always am, she thought bitterly as she hung up, *and it's never helped me yet.*

TWENTY-ONE

Lauren walked Ward back to the rest of the group and had him sit at one of the tables. Reese didn't even turn his eyes away from the television when she came in.

Not a good sign, she knew. Chris asked if she needed anything and she told him no, she was going to take a look around the building. 'Can I have that master key card again?'

'Take it,' he said, handing it over. 'You know I would never have to steal Raphael's card, don't you?' Chris asked. 'I could just use mine or go behind the front desk and make myself a duplicate.'

Lauren pocketed the card. It was an odd and obvious statement to make to her. 'I'll be sure to keep that in mind,' she replied. Once again, Chris turned away from her and stared at the TV screen. The change in his personality was extreme and jarring.

People handle trauma in different ways, she reminded herself as she looked around the room until she spotted the chef. 'Mrs Brady, can I have a word?' she asked.

The older woman nodded, got up and followed Lauren into the ladies room, just off the dining area. She sank down onto a small, plush loveseat in the sitting area before the stalls began. She looked tired and frazzled. 'Do you mind if I have a rest?' she asked.

'Not at all,' Lauren said. She wished the seat was just a little bigger so she could sit next to her instead of towering over the lady, firing questions at her. 'Mrs Brady, I know you said you went to bed early last night. Is there anything else that happened that you think I should know about?'

Lauren watched as Mrs Brady's forehead wrinkled in thought. 'Nothing out of the ordinary, really. Mr Carter called and asked for extra towels at twelve thirty. Said he'd forgotten to call earlier. That's not an area I usually take care of, but Rhonda had to go home last night. She just moved into an apartment with her husband in Ellicottville and they've been having neighbor trouble – loud music, that sort of thing. Her husband is an older gentleman with heart problems, so she asked me last week when we were making preparations for your group's visit if I could cover for her. I told her it was no problem. If this were a hundred-room hotel I'd have refused, but with so few guests, it's really quite a pleasure to work here, even on the overnights. Mr Sloane set up the phones so if the guests called room service at night it would ring in my staff room and not Rhonda's.'

'Not many chefs would take over housekeeping duties,' Lauren observed.

'I worked with Mr Sloane in Colorado. He's a wonderful boss and I believe in what he's trying to build here. I brought the towels up.'

'Did you see Mrs Carter when you dropped the towels off?'

'No. He took them from me at the door, but the room was lit up, like he and his wife were still awake.'

'So you did not see Mrs Carter?'

Mrs Brady shook her head. 'No. Just the husband.'

'Then what happened?' Lauren prompted.

'Mr Creehan called down to ask for some aspirin and a water with lemon around one forty-five. I said I'd bring it up to him, but he said he'd come and get it. He came down to the front desk a couple of minutes later to pick it up. He said he had a headache from all that bourbon.'

'How did he seem?'

Her shoulders touched her ears. 'Tired. Maybe a little drunk.'

'Did you see Mrs Carter in the bar when you took the aspirin and water to Seth Creehan at the front desk? Or Mr Reese?'

'I did not. Only Mr Sloane as he came around the front desk and went to the computer.'

'Mr Sloane was in the lobby?'

'Oh yes. He and Mr Creehan must have just missed each other.'

'What was he doing on the computer at the front desk?'

She shook her head. 'I don't know. I just headed back to bed.'

Lauren inwardly groaned. Now she had Reese, Amanda, Owen, Tyler, Seth and Chris all wandering around the hotel. Not to mention Raphael on the couch. Which brought up a good question.

'Was Mr Diaz on the couch when you brought the water out to Mr Creehan?'

'I couldn't say. From the front desk all you can see is the back of the couch. As soon as I handed off the water and aspirin I turned around and went back to my room. I only caught Mr Sloane out of the corner of my eye. I did pass Mr Diaz on the way to deliver the towels to Mr Carter's room earlier though.'

Raphael could have slid off that couch and up to the second floor at any time during the night. She wished she could sit Seth and Chris down and question them, but she knew the BCI investigator would lose his mind if she overstepped her bounds. Questioning suspects would require Miranda warnings, video documentation, and if not done correctly might also trigger the utterance of those four words that killed an interrogation: 'I want a lawyer.' It was better to leave that to the State Police.

'One more thing, Mrs Brady. Do you have plastic gloves, like for food prep in the kitchen?'

She nodded. 'I do.'

'Would you be able to grab me a couple of pairs, some paper bags and a zip lock bag or two, if you have them?' When you didn't have access to an evidence collection kit, sometimes you had to make your own. There was no way she was going to leave a murder weapon out in the open with the suspect still in the hotel.

'I'll run and get them for you.'

Lauren waited in the ladies room for Mrs Brady to return. She knew as soon as she stepped back out that the rest of the guests would be restless.

'Thank you, Mrs Brady,' she told the woman, taking the large brown paper bag from her. Inside were thin, clear gloves, three other smaller paper bags and one quart-sized zip lock bag. DNA evidence had to be stored in the paper bags. The homemade collection kit was far from ideal, but she had to work with what was on hand. Folding the top of the bag and closing it shut, she told Mrs Brady, 'We can go and join the others again.'

As soon as they walked back into the dining area Lauren was peppered with questions.

'How much longer do we have to sit here?' Tyler called out.

'Lauren, I really need to use my laptop in my room,' Seth joined in. 'Can I pop up there?'

'What did the troopers say? Are they on the way?' Raphael asked.

'I'll be back soon,' Lauren said in reply as she crossed

through the dining area. She could sense the tension that had built since she'd left. The shock was starting to wear off. Once it did, Tyler and Seth would demand to go back to their rooms, Amanda would want to speak to her husband, and Chris would insist on getting back to running the hotel. She couldn't force them to sit downstairs, separated, forever. Knowing she had to make the most of the time she had left, she quickly departed, avoiding answering the questions that were being hurled at her.

Starting in the lobby, she carefully made her way around the room, photographing with her phone as she went. She decided to take the stairs to the second floor, where she walked up and down each side of the hallway, snapping shots of the door to each room. If the killer had cut him or herself, Lauren saw no signs of blood on the carpet. In her mind's eye she pictured the killer wiping the dripping blade on their clothing before exiting the room. Standing at the elevator doors, she studied the entire floor. The killer literally only had to cover a few feet without being seen, no matter which room they were staying in, unless it was Chris. Chris would have had to get back up to the third floor, either by the stairs at the far end or the elevator she was standing in front of.

She pictured who was staying in each room. On the left side, in room 201 was Seth, then next to him was the murder scene, room 203 with Erica and Raphael. Next to that, in room 205, was Tyler. Directly across from Tyler, in room 206, was Amanda and Owen. Then came Reese in room 204, then her in room 202.

Putting the paper bag on the floor next to her, Lauren took her pen and notebook out of her pocket and made a quick sketch by drawing six messy boxes, three across from another three and labeling them with names and numbers. Chris got his own page representing the third floor.

Tapping her pen to her lips, Lauren studied the notebook pages. She now knew that every single one of the other guests had been out of their rooms and moving about the hotel at some point last night. Every single one of them had had the chance to swipe the key card from Raphael while he was passed out on the couch in the lobby, if he hadn't used it himself. And every single one of them had had the opportunity to kill Jessica seventeen years before.

The only person from their graduating class who had a solid alibi for Jessica's murder was now lying behind a closed door down the hall with her throat cut.

Lauren didn't believe in coincidences and she hated books and movies where a seemingly unconnected person, like a chef or the hotel manager, turned out to be someone's long-lost twin or ex that had plastic surgery to hide their true identity. No, in real life the killer's name was most likely already in the file. In real life, the murderer was definitely still on the premises. And in real life, Erica had figured out who killed Jessica with her armchair detecting. Something Erica said or did last night had scared one of the guests enough to murder her before her big reveal.

Tucking her pen and notebook away, Lauren checked the ornate faux floral arrangement sitting on a long table next to the elevator, not that she really believed she'd be lucky enough that the killer had panicked and quickly stashed the murder weapon there for her to find. Once she was sure nothing was hidden in the silk leaves, she hit the up button. It was time to check out the third floor.

TWENTY-TWO

The elevator doors opened to an expansive, grand atrium, with floor-to-ceiling glass windows making up the entire west-facing wall. They curved up, over round tables set before another stone fireplace, so you could look up and see the stars, or on a day like today, an impenetrable blanket of white snow. The east wall was decorated with a rustic theme – old wooden sleds, skis, long tables with fall centerpieces. And smack in the middle was one door, with blue, green and pale-yellow stained-glass panels on either side. The grand bridal suite.

She now realized the two enormous mirrors on the east wall

facing the atrium were probably two-way to allow whoever had rented the suite to be able to enjoy the view as well.

There was a coffee and tea station set up in the far corner for guests to enjoy while they relaxed in the atrium. The white stoneware mugs sat stacked undisturbed on a serving tray. It looked like none of the guests had been up there before breakfast to pop one of the plastic pods into the machine. A tall, cylindrical vase with a carefully arranged assortment of fall flowers sat on the floor next to a waste bin. Even the garbage cans here were made to look elegant.

The round tables had matching votive candles surrounded by colorful silk leaves. Lauren imagined cozy fall evenings, watching the sunset in front of the fireplace, sipping herbal tea until the sky turned from pink to inky blue. It was perfectly designed to enjoy both the landscape and the stars. Almost immediately though, Lauren noticed something was off.

The fireplace wasn't on.

The fireplace in the lobby had been fully ablaze when she came down for breakfast. There were instructions in her room about turning hers on and off, or setting it to a timer. She'd left it off. Seeing this one, which was the focal point of the room besides the windows, not lit seemed wrong. She crossed through the tables and approached the darkened hearth.

It was very similar to the fireplace in the lobby, with rough stone that reached to the ceiling surrounding an ornate black metal grate. The mantel was decorated to perfection, with an elaborate set-up featuring mini pumpkins and gourds. Off to the right was a tall, slim glass cylinder filled with red-tipped matches. On the opposite side, to balance the display, was a pair of antique fireplace tongs and a matching shovel, standing in a wrought iron rack.

As soon as she was close enough, she knelt down and peered inside. She could see what the problem was. Someone had pried the protective grate away from the face. The decorative black metal was curled up in the right corner in a jagged lip. The fireplace was gas. The flames were real but the logs were not, so there shouldn't have been anything charred inside.

But there was.

Taking her cell phone out again, she leaned in and snapped a picture of the burnt object.

'Investigator Donovan? Did you get that last photo I just sent you?' she asked when he picked up on the first ring.

'I did. What is that?'

Lauren could just make out the title on the spine. The rest of it was charred beyond recognition, black ash and scorched pages scattered over the faux firewood.

'It's the victim's high school yearbook.'

TWENTY-THREE

Lauren explained to the investigator that Erica had brought the yearbook to dinner and drinks the night before and left it behind after making a scene.

'You're sure the manager took the book back up to the victim's room?'

'I saw him head toward the elevator with it. I'll have to confirm with Erica's husband if Ward delivered it and the exact time.'

'Careful with that. We don't want to run into Miranda problems. Raphael Diaz is a suspect at this point.'

She, of all people, knew that working with the State Police made her an agent of the state, and Miranda warnings would apply to questions she asked the guests. Any question specific to the murder would have to be predicated by her giving full Miranda warnings and memorializing it. For her to question any of them might jeopardize the investigation. At the very least, without giving the full warning, any incriminating statement made would be tossed out. Spontaneous utterances or statements made to her without asking were fair game, but she knew Investigator Donovan was going to want to sit down with each one of them as soon as he arrived and conduct by-the-book interviews. The only people she didn't consider suspects were Ward and Mrs Brady. She knew Donavon was just covering his ass by reminding her and she shouldn't take it personally, so she bit back her indignation. He didn't know her or how she operated.

'Sorry. I'll talk to the manager. I know when I went to bed it was right around eleven o'clock and he was back downstairs without the book. Also, I heard Erica and Raphael arguing in their room as I passed by.'

That definitely interested him. 'You're certain you heard both voices?' he asked.

'One hundred percent certain. Erica was in radio and Raphael is an actor. Both of their voices are distinctive and project.' Lauren found herself nodding, even though the investigator couldn't see it and a thought came to her. 'I'm going to call you on FaceTime, to show you what I'm seeing.'

'Now I feel a little foolish for not suggesting that myself,' he admitted.

'I think it's safe to say both of us are in uncharted territory right now,' she assured him.

When he laughed in reply, Lauren hung up, hit the redial and called him back using the FaceTime option. With a name like Kevin Donovan, she was expecting to see a twenty-something, red-headed, freckled Irish cop, since she knew exactly three Kevin Donovans – none of them related – from the neighborhood in South Buffalo where she grew up. Donovan was such a common surname that there used to be a local joke – throw a rock and you'll hit a Donovan.

But instead of a sun-starved ginger, a raven-haired, dark-eyed, olive-skinned middle-aged man was looking back at her.

'This is much better,' he said. He was sitting at a desk in an office, not unlike her own. In the background behind him she could make out a picture of the New York State Police's superintendent on the wall. Lauren really liked Barbara Bennett, the Buffalo Police Commissioner, but she would have felt a little freaked out if Bennett was literally looking over her shoulder every day at work. 'It's nice to meet you sort of face to face.'

'Same,' Lauren replied, then turned the phone around. 'This is the fireplace.'

'OK, OK, OK,' he said, more to himself than to her. She

held the phone steady for a good minute, then turned it back toward herself.

His eyes were cast down for a second before he looked up into the camera at her. She suspected he was jotting notes. 'What does the spine say? Can you make it out?'

'It says "Buffalo Public School 91". The rest is charred. Erica, the victim, brought it with her from home. The other guests were passing it around at the bar last night.'

'You're sure it's the same yearbook?'

'No one else said they brought one and it's their junior yearbook.' She turned the phone back around so he could look at it again.

'Do you think the husband cut the wife's throat, burned the yearbook, then passed out on the couch in a drunken stupor?'

Lauren turned the phone to face the screen so she could answer. 'It normally would be the most likely scenario,' she admitted. Lauren had worked in the Buffalo Police's Special Victims Unit before coming to Homicide and she'd handled a lot of domestic violence cases. Too many. And long before that, she herself had been in a physically abusive relationship. She had no doubt in her mind that her ex could have been capable of killing her. But likely scenarios weren't facts. She had to follow the evidence. 'Except where did all the blood go? Raphael is wearing the same clothes he had on last night. If he murdered Erica like that, he'd be covered in dried blood. And the killer didn't clean up in their bathroom. I didn't see any traces of evidence on or near the sink, and the droplet trail headed toward the door.'

'If it wasn't the husband, then the murderer would have had to get in the room, kill the victim, and leave with the yearbook and the murder weapon. There's no knife anywhere in that fireplace, is there?'

Lauren double-checked, but she knew the answer. 'No.'

'Any blood on the yearbook?'

'It's hard to say, it's burned up pretty good. I'm sure once it's in the lab they'll be able to find any trace evidence.'

'Can you secure the area around the fireplace?' Kevin's camera bounced as he leaned over and typed something into a computer off-screen with one hand.

Lauren glanced around the atrium. 'Right now, we have evidence on all three floors of this building that needs to be collected and processed. I'll do my best, but I can't physically restrain the guests if they decide to move around the building, and I can't be in two places at once. And last I checked, everyone was getting restless.'

'They've known each other since they were teenagers, you'd think they'd want to cooperate to find out who killed their friend.'

'They've been acting like a bunch of kids since last night. It's like they've all regressed into their high school selves.' She'd seen petty rivalries, jealousy and accusations that had been brewing for seventeen years all rear their ugly heads already.

'Then you're going to have to work fast for me.'

'The spa section is closed off due to construction. I still have to check the kitchen, and after that I was thinking I should watch the surveillance video in the office.'

A look of hope crossed his face. 'Please tell me they have cameras on every floor.'

Lauren shook her head. 'Have you ever worked a homicide that was so easy? The only camera faces the check-in desk in the lobby.'

'It figures. We'll fast-forward through the video together. Call me when you've got it queued up. Try to keep everyone off the third floor.'

'There's only one room up here and it's the owner's. He's been cooperative, so far. Hopefully, I can keep the rest of the guests contained in the dining room for a little while longer.'

'Sounds like a plan. Call me back.'

They hung up and Lauren found herself staring at what was left of the burned yearbook. Someone had gone to a lot of trouble to pry up the grate. She looked at the decorative fireplace hardware. The killer could definitely have used the wrought iron shovel, then hung it back in its stand. She made a note in her phone to remind the trooper's evidence techs to grab it for prints and DNA. Unless the killer had worn gloves.

She hadn't thought again about what the killer had worn

until she'd just had that conversation with Investigator Donovan. The murderer would have had a large knife, bloody clothes, Raphael's key card and the yearbook to dispose of. Where were those other items? Anyone with half a brain who watched television knew the first thing the State Police investigators were going to do was get search warrants for every guest room. If the killer had worn gloves, those would have had to be disposed of too.

Lauren's head whipped around. A nasty gust of wind howled, continuing to pelt the panels of the atrium with ice and snow. It coursed like a river of white sand across glass. A shiver ran down her spine. It had been snowing heavily when she'd gone to bed, but she had no idea when it had turned into blizzard conditions.

Standing up, she shifted her weight from foot to foot. Her left leg had fallen asleep while she knelt in front of the fireplace. She slapped it, trying to restore circulation. She had to get back down to the office and watch that footage. *This day just keeps getting better and better*, she thought, limping away from the fireplace, legs tingling as the circulation returned.

TWENTY-FOUR

Forsaking the elevator for the staircase, Lauren made her way slowly from landing to landing, taking pictures as she went. She zoomed in on the handrails, the steps, the walls, searching for blood smears and droplets. If the killer had used the stairs, she could find no trace of evidence.

As she was making her way from the second to the first floor, she heard a dull, thumping noise behind her.

She froze in place, phone in hand, fully aware she was unarmed. She could hear her heart beating in her chest as she strained to listen for the source of the noise. It definitely sounded like it had come from the second floor.

Lauren retraced her steps to the second-floor landing.

Using the tips of her fingers, she pulled the door toward her and looked down the second-floor hallway.

Empty.

Whatever or whoever had made that noise was gone.

Lauren waited a full minute, just listening, before letting the door fall closed behind her and continuing back down the staircase. She couldn't shake the feeling that someone had been on the second floor just then. She needed to check on the rest of the guests.

She made her way down the stairs slowly, listening to the sound of her own footsteps, body tense and ready to spring into action. Against what or who, she had no idea yet.

She made it to the first-floor landing, eyes immediately going to the display above the elevator doors to make sure no one was in the process of using it. Satisfied it was empty, she stepped off the last carpeted stair onto the hardwood floor.

Crossing the empty lobby, Lauren entered the lounge where everyone was watching a young female newscaster bundled from head to toe in winter weather gear struggle to be heard over the relentless wind. She was yelling into a microphone clutched in her gloved hand, trying to keep her balance at the same time. Whatever she was standing in front of was obscured by the snow.

Taking a quick head count, everyone was accounted for.

Maybe a chunk of ice had fallen from the roof or someone's bag in their room had slid off their dresser and hit the floor. Maybe she was being paranoid. *It's not like I'm trapped in a half-finished resort with a dead body and seven potential suspects, with no weapon and no back up*, she thought bitterly. *Oh, that's right, actually I am.*

Lauren spotted Ward leaning against the far wall, eyes to the screen, with his hands folded neatly in front of him, ready to spring into action at Chris's call. She saw Reese's attention fall on her as she approached the manager, but he said nothing. Lauren felt a tug in her chest as her eyes met his. She hated that she had to sit him out. And from the look on his face, the feeling was mutual.

'Can I have a word with you in private?' she asked Ward, who straightened up as she came near.

'We can step into the kitchen,' he replied, motioning to the door behind the bar. His voice's usual steady monotone faltered a little. The stress of the situation was wearing on him as well.

Still holding her paper bag, Lauren followed him behind the bar and then through a door marked STAFF ONLY in small gold letters. It led to an expansive kitchen that was so new it seemed like it had never been used. There was nothing to indicate Mrs Brady had made a huge breakfast that morning. She'd already put all her tools and utensils away. Every pot and pan was hung in place. Every surface had been wiped down so that not a single crumb remained. The industrial oven gleamed under the fluorescent ceiling lights.

'Is this open to guests at night?' she asked.

'Mrs Brady locks that door we came through when she goes to bed. She still has access to the kitchen from that door.' He pointed to the left back corner. 'That leads to the staff quarters, so if someone rings room service in the middle of the night, Mrs Brady can get up and take care of their needs.'

'And that one?' Lauren indicated the back right-hand corner.

'That leads outside to the dumpsters.'

Lauren walked to the door and pressed the crash bar as hard as she could. 'Is it locked?' she asked.

'Only from the outside, it also serves as an emergency exit.' Ward came over and the two of them pushed. He double-checked the mechanism, making sure it was unlocked. 'The snow must be blocking the door.'

Lauren stepped back. She knew it would be the same with the rest of the doors on the ground floor. She needed to see those dumpsters. But she had to handle one thing at a time. 'Did you deliver that yearbook to Erica and Raphael's room last night?'

The older man's mouth turned down in the corners in a slight frown. 'I went up there straight away. When I knocked on the door, Mrs Diaz answered it.'

'Was Raphael in the room?'

'He was standing by the balcony doors with his arms crossed.

She snatched the book from my hands and practically slammed the door in my face.'

'How did they seem?'

'You saw how they exited last night. They both seemed furious. I believe I interrupted a continuation of the argument.'

'Was Raphael wearing the clothes he has on now?'

Ward didn't even have to think about that. 'Yes. Those are the same clothes he had on. The same ones he went to dinner in and the same ones I saw him wearing this morning when I spotted him sleeping on the couch.'

'You're sure?'

'His dress shirt is a brand I favor very much. I have the same one in forest green. The pants, I can't say for certain, but they appear to be the same ones.'

'What did you do after you dropped the book off?'

'I came right back downstairs. I believe you saw me. I'm not off the clock until Mr Sloane goes to bed.'

'But you were still up and about later last night?'

He nodded. 'Because we're short-staffed, practically no-staffed, I have to make the late-night rounds myself. When we're fully operational, I'll have employees who'll have that responsibility.'

Lauren studied the manager's serious face. Deep lines were etched in his forehead and along the corners of his mouth. His hair was still neatly combed, not a strand out of place, despite all the chaos of the morning. She could see why Chris had hired him. 'I wanted to ask you about the fireplace in the atrium. It was off when I just went upstairs.'

His eyebrows drew together in a questioning V. 'That's odd. It's on a timer. It should come on at 6:30 a.m. and automatically go off for the night at 2:00 a.m.'

'It looks like the metal grate in front was tampered with,' she said, not wanting to give him too much information.

'That makes sense then. That's a safety feature. It won't light if the metal grate isn't in place.'

'Will it continue to burn if someone pried it open?'

He considered this for a moment. 'It's a gas fireplace. The safety feature should have kicked in right away.'

Lauren pictured the killer taking the yearbook up to the third floor, prying open the grate, probably with the wrought iron fireplace tools, and watching the flames sputter out. It wouldn't have taken much to set the yearbook on fire. Lauren thought back to the glass canister on the mantel containing the matches. Even though they were meant for decoration, Lauren was sure they'd light just fine if you ran one of the tips over the rough stone. That would explain why the spine survived but not the inside pages. The killer must have stuffed the book into the hearth, lit it, and left. She made another note in her phone to have the State Police evidence techs, when they showed up, collect the glass canister for prints and DNA.

It occurred to Lauren that if the killer had pried the grate open, the fire must have still been on. In the immediate flight from the crime, yearbook in hand, the killer would have wanted to dispose of it right away. The safety feature kicking in must have thrown him or her for a loop for a moment. That put the time of the murder sometime before the timer would have shut the fireplace off automatically.

If her assumption was correct, the murder had to have occurred between 11:00 p.m. and 2:00 a.m.

'One more thing,' she said. 'Has anyone left this room at all?'

Ward thought on that for a moment. 'A few people got up to use the bathroom. I suppose someone could have slipped out the entrance. We were all glued to the news shows, trying to get an idea of when the authorities will be able to get to us. It's possible someone snuck out and back in.'

'Thank you, Ward. That's all I needed to ask you,' she told him, and he seemed to visibly relax. 'Let's go join the others.' Lauren gathered up her paper bag and let Ward lead the way. She needed to see that footage on the security system. Hopefully, it was time stamped. That way, she'd be able to get a better timeline of at least some of the guests' whereabouts the night before. And maybe catch a glimpse of whoever might have decided to go up to the second floor.

TWENTY-FIVE

Before they even reached the door to get back into the lounge, the sound of raised voices sprang from the dining area. Lauren pushed past Ward and entered first. Tyler was standing by the door to the men's bathroom holding his phone up to Chris and Reese. Everyone else was staring at the trio from their seats.

'What's going on?' Lauren demanded.

'I'll tell you what's going on,' Tyler said, shaking his phone at her. 'I just got done talking to my lawyer who said unless you arrest me, you have no right to keep me here.'

Lauren folded her arms across her chest, paper bag dangling from her fingertips. 'Your lawyer is correct. However, the State Police are preparing search warrants for everyone's rooms, so none of you can go back to them and none of you can take anything out of them. We can legally keep them off limits until the warrants are served. I found evidence on the third floor, so I'm holding that as a crime scene. The spa section is locked up and closed to visitors. Besides here and the lobby, where are you going to go?'

Tyler's face took on an explosive shade of red. Mashing his lips together he slumped down in the nearest chair and glared at Lauren. That was OK with her; she hadn't expected to be voted Miss Popularity at this reunion.

'Any other grievances?' she asked, looking around, studying each face looking back at her. 'Everyone here is free to leave the hotel. However, it makes sense that if the New York State Police can't get to us with all of their resources, none of us will get very far. Chris, I take it you don't have a plow in the garages out behind the parking lot?'

He shook his head. 'I contracted with a local company. They're based out of Ellicottville. I've been trying to reach them all morning, but I just keep getting their voicemail. I imagine they're plowing their clients in town and working their way out toward us.'

'So unless anyone plans to cross country ski twenty miles to Ellicottville in blizzard conditions, it's safe to say we're all stuck here for a while,' Lauren told them.

'This is insane,' Seth said, just as another wicked howl of wind smacked snow against the windows. Lauren noticed that someone had drawn the heavy blinds on the two big picture windows that framed the fireplace. It was a good idea. Sitting there, staring at the undulating white blanket was mesmerizing, but it was probably also demoralizing. 'Can we get a deck of cards? Monopoly? Something?' he asked.

'I have decks of cards in my office,' Chris responded. 'There's also a decorative chess set that was meant to go in the spa lounge I can bring out.'

'You really want to play games right now?' Raphael asked in disbelief as he lifted his head from the table he'd been slumped over. 'My wife is dead. Dead. One of you murdered her and you want to have a game of freaking gin rummy?'

'We all just want to keep our minds occupied,' Owen said. 'Nobody meant to offend you.'

'Offend me?' Raphael snorted. 'You threatened to throttle my wife last night. Everyone heard it. You'd do anything to protect your wife, just like I'd do anything for mine.'

'I have nothing to protect her from,' Owen said defensively. 'She didn't do anything.'

'Can anyone say where you were when Erica was killed?' Raphael challenged, turning to Amanda. 'Did you and your husband ever leave each other's side after you said you were going to bed last night?'

Amanda's hand flew to her mouth and she looked over at Reese.

'You know what, Raph?' Tyler asked, taking a step toward him. 'What if the twist is that there is no twist? Everyone knows it's always the husband.' He turned at the waist slightly so he could focus his venom on Lauren. 'He was the number one suspect in Jessica's death back in the day. We need to stop pretending he walked into a damn door, and you have to put some handcuffs on him already. For all of our safety.'

'Was I?' Raphael snapped back. 'Because the police checked and double-checked my alibi and couldn't shake it. What about yours?'

'Your alibi was your dead wife,' he snorted. 'How convenient.'

'Your alibi is nonexistent.' Spittle flew from Raphael's mouth.

Lauren put a hand up in a calming gesture. 'Let's wait for the troopers to get here before—'

'Your side piece gets offed and then your big mouth wife.' Tyler was almost face to face with Raphael now, a vein bulging on his shiny forehead as he cut Lauren off mid-sentence. 'Who's next on your hit list, Raph?'

Raphael launched himself at Tyler, knocking him over the table Amanda was sitting at and crashing to the floor in a heap. Amanda leapt back in shock as they grappled, fists flying, Tyler getting the worst of it from the distraught Raphael. Amanda started to scream as Chris, Reese, Seth and her husband joined the scrum, wrestling the two combatants away from each other. Ward rushed over to Mrs Brady near the ladies room and pulled her as far from the fight as possible.

'She said she had something on you, Tyler,' Raphael spit out as Seth and Reese held him back, knocking another chair over in the process. The pocket on the front of his shirt was ripped and hanging by threads. An angry red scratch beaded with blood now graced his forehead. 'You attacked Jessica the day she was murdered. You had the most to lose with her death – a job and a scholarship.'

'I didn't attack Jessica, I didn't kill her, and I certainly didn't kill your wife,' he yelled in return, Chris and Owen hauling him to the far side of the room. He got one arm free and dragged it across his nose, his sleeve coming back bloody.

'Cut that shit out,' Reese yelled, losing his temper. 'You two claim you're innocent, and now you're going to leave your DNA all over to muck up the crime scene. Sit your ass in that chair, Tyler. And both of you shut your mouths.'

'Everybody just calm down,' Lauren commanded. 'This isn't helping.' She was dealing with a bunch of scared, stressed people whose friend was just murdered, and who were trapped by a storm. She knew tempers were going to flare and all she could do was try to keep some kind of order.

Tyler yanked his other arm free. 'I'm going to wait in the lobby, watch the front doors, and if there's even the slightest break in the weather, I'm driving my car right out of here.'

'I'll sit with him,' Seth volunteered as he and Reese deposited Raphael in one of the leather chairs by the fireplace where they'd been drinking bourbon the night before. He was panting and gripping the armrests so hard his knuckles were white. Reese was bending down, talking quietly in his ear, trying to calm the distraught man.

'That's a good idea,' Lauren said. 'No one goes upstairs. Not to the second floor, not to the third,' she warned, looking right at Tyler.

Not bothering to respond, Tyler marched off toward the lobby with Seth at his heels. Exhaling a breath, Lauren looked around at the remaining guests, finding Chris. 'I've got to go back in the office. I need to check the front desk surveillance video.'

Chris was bent forward with his hands on his knees, panting a little from the struggle. He nodded his head, sending a shower of dreadlocks forward, grazing the hardwood floor. Suddenly he stiffened and Lauren followed his gaze.

Laying there, exactly where all the men had converged to pry Tyler and Raphael apart, was a plastic key card.

TWENTY-SIX

'Whose key is that?' Lauren asked, pointing to the little rectangle of plastic sitting on the polished wood amid the wreckage of the table.

For a long moment, everyone just stared at the white card with SLOANE SPA AND RETREAT printed across the front in green lettering.

'It must have fallen out of someone's pocket during the scuffle,' Reese said. 'Everybody show your room card.'

Reaching into the front pocket of his shirt, he pulled his out and slowly swiveled as he held it up so that everyone could see he still had his.

One by one, everyone produced their room key and showed it, except for Raphael, who was patting his pockets furiously for something he knew wasn't there, and Chris because Lauren still had his.

'Ward,' she called behind her to the general manager, who was still comforting Mrs Brady by the bathroom door, 'could you please go ask Tyler and Seth to show you their key cards?'

Ward exited into the lobby under the big clock, which now read 11:45.

Lauren put her paper bag down on the table next to her, then quickly snapped a few photos of the card. Putting her phone back in her pocket, she opened up the bag and pulled a plastic glove onto each hand. Everyone in the room was silent, watching her. The only noise was the wind blasting against the windows and the ticking of the big clock over the doorway until the sound of Ward's returning footsteps broke the uneasy quiet.

'They both had their room cards,' he reported from the doorway.

Amanda audibly sucked in a breath. Someone had dropped that key card during the fight. Lauren carefully pinched it up by one corner and deposited it in the paper bag but didn't seal it.

'Is that Raphael's?' Owen asked. He'd moved over to his wife and had an arm around her shoulder, hugging her to him. Her face had gone a ghastly pale.

'You can run it through the reader at the front desk to find out,' Ward offered.

'No,' she replied. *Down the road, running it through the reader could be construed as tampering with it*, she thought. 'I'm going to check it against Erica's door. Ward, I want you to come with me. Everybody else, please stay put.' She looked at Amanda and her husband. 'And try to stay separated.'

The window is getting narrower. Neither Ward nor Mrs Brady had been anywhere near the scuffle, she thought. If the key card belonged to Raphael's room, in Lauren's mind, that took them out of the suspect pool altogether. But that still left all seven of the other potential killers.

Even Reese.

TWENTY-SEVEN

Lauren called Investigator Donovan on FaceTime as she and Ward were on the way to the elevator and explained what had just happened.

'We're about to go to the second floor now,' Lauren told him. 'Ward was nowhere near the fight, so he couldn't have been the one to drop the key card, and I want a witness with me as I take it straight from the lounge to Erica's door.'

'Smart thinking,' he agreed.

The elevator doors opened with a pleasant *bong* and she and Ward stepped out into the second-floor hallway.

'Can you record this?' she asked. 'I'm just going to walk over and wave it over the locking mechanism.'

'Give me a second,' he said. She could see him fiddling with his phone, his face getting up close and then far away and back again. 'All set.'

Lauren carefully made her way over to Erica's door, mindful of not stepping on any trace evidence she might have missed. Ward was right on her heels, almost up against her back. She stopped short, took another plastic glove out of the larger paper bag, and proceeded to extract the key card from the smaller bag using just the tips of her fingers to grasp the very edge.

She realized she was holding her breath as she slowly brought it across the black plastic reader.

The lock made a tumbling sound as it disengaged and a light on the panel turned green.

The door was open. This was Raphael or Erica's card. Either way, the killer had dropped it.

She didn't say it out loud, because at the last instant she

remembered she was on camera, but the saying she and Reese used whenever they made a puzzling observation popped into her head: *Son of a bitch.*

TWENTY-EIGHT

'Seal that card in the bag,' Donovan told her when she put her phone back up to her ear. 'Do you have a safe in your room where you can secure it for now?'

'I do,' Lauren replied.

'Let's get that stowed away, then I want you to check that surveillance video.'

Lauren kept Donovan on the line, but Ward waited outside her door as she went into her room and found the small safe in the closet. She read the directions twice, then deposited the bag that now contained two smaller bags – one with the card inside and one with the gloves she'd used to touch it. She closed the door and committed the digital code to unlock it to memory, Gabe's birthday. 'All set,' she told Donovan.

'Call me when you're in the office and we can look at the surveillance tape together.'

'Will do,' she replied, as she stepped back from the safe. She was just about to tuck the phone back in her pocket when she looked up and scanned her suite. The thought popped into her head that it was the same layout as Erica's. In her mind, she visualized the victim laying face up on the enormous bed, soaked in blood. Then she found herself picturing the killer, knife in hand, walking away from the victim.

She pulled up the crime scene photos again on her screen. She zoomed in on the fat drops of blood that headed toward the door, then stopped. The killer had the key card, the knife, bloody clothes on and the yearbook to take with them. Once again, the visual of the killer wiping the bloody knife across their chest came to mind. But then what?

She walked to where the last blood drop would be in Erica's room and slowly turned in a circle. A half turn left her directly facing the balcony doors. Lauren stepped forward, pulled the latch up, and with all her strength, slid the glass door to the side with her right hand. She was immediately assaulted by the vicious wind and snow as it pelted her cheeks in stinging blows. She could step out onto the windswept balcony, but didn't, choosing to pull the door closed again. She studied the position of her grip on the long, rectangular handle.

Had the killer thrown the knife and possibly bloody clothes off Erica's balcony? And if they did, why didn't they throw the yearbook and key card too?

Letting go of the handle, she scrolled through the wide shots of Erica's room. Finding a shot of the crime scene's balcony doors, Lauren pinched the screen, then pinched it some more, zeroing in on the handle. Lauren stared hard at the screen. Sure enough, she saw a small dark shadow on the top left corner. Was it blood?

She reached out and gripped her own matching handle again, flexing her fingers. She tried using her other hand. If it was a blood smear, it was in the right position, no matter which hand the killer used.

She had Raphael's card. She could just go in and look, but every time you entered a crime scene you risked contamination.

The knife was heavy. Even if the killer had tried to throw it, with the momentum of the wind, it wouldn't have gone too far from the hotel. And maybe the killer wrapped the blood-spattered clothes around the knife. That got the evidence outside of the hotel, enabling the perpetrator to walk around unarmed and unbloody. Maybe the idea was to retrieve the items later last night and permanently dispose of them, when the killer realized there was no way anyone could venture out in the dark during blizzard conditions.

Once again, she came to the question of why would the killer toss the knife and possibly the clothes, but burn the yearbook and keep the key card?

She tucked her phone back in her pocket, wishing she could bounce these questions off Reese. Whenever the two of them got stuck on a case they'd go over all the evidence, talk it through, work the problem. Now Reese was sitting on the sidelines in the lounge, and she still hadn't found a single piece of evidence that pulled him out of the suspect pool. That twist in her gut came back. She'd worked with Reese for years now, lived in the same house with him, they'd nursed each other through life-threatening injuries and seen each other at their most vulnerable, and yet the events of the last week had her doubting the one person she literally trusted with her life.

A troubling notion rose to her mind with an even more problematic solution. *Reese is not going to like this*, she thought as she headed into the bathroom and switched out her glasses for a pair of rarely used contacts. *Not one bit.* Blinking until her vision cleared, she looked at herself in the vanity mirror. Sometimes she felt like she was hiding behind those thick-framed black glasses. Like if she wore them, people wouldn't be able to see her anymore. She'd never been comfortable with her looks until she lost them. The idea that people assumed she got where she was on the police department because she was beautiful used to drive her crazy. Time and injury had worn away her looks and she'd been grateful for it. No one could accuse her of using sex appeal to get what she wanted now, even without the glasses. She was forty-something, too tall, too gaunt, too pasty. She rifled through her drawers and took out the pair of jeans and thermal underwear she'd planned on wearing to the ski lodge. She quickly swapped out her lounge pants for them, then added a thermal top under her sweatshirt, thinking, *Nope, Reese is going to try and talk me out of this.*

And that's fine with me, she concluded, while she scooped up her winter coat, hat and gloves. Sliding her sneakers off, she stuffed her feet into the winter boots she had lined up next to her closet. She dumped her things on the floor for a second to tighten the laces and tie them.

We all wear different faces when we need to. Walking toward the door to meet up with Ward, the last thing that popped into her head was: *What if I never really knew Reese at all?*

TWENTY-NINE

'Ward, how many ways are there to get out of the building?' Lauren asked after she made sure the door to her room had locked behind her.

'If you look right here, Ms Riley,' Ward motioned to a framed map on the wall next to the elevator, 'this shows all the emergency exits.'

Lauren walked over, still hugging her parka, and studied the map. 'Can you get back inside from all of these exits?'

'If you have a key card you can access the main doors and side door in the lobby at any time from the outside. These doors here and here,' he pointed to multiple exits in the lounge and spa, 'are exit-only from eleven to six in the morning.'

'What about the kitchen, office and other staff areas?'

'All those can be opened from both inside and out twenty-four hours a day with a staff key card.'

Lauren thought on that for a moment. Fire regulations called for numerous exits, but getting back in undetected would be a problem. Unless you were staff. Or the owner.

'Are you planning to go outside?' he asked, eyeing her cold weather gear, a hint of concern in his voice.

'Maybe,' she replied, hitting the down button for the elevator. 'But I'd like to check the surveillance camera first. You said it only shows the front desk? You can't see the front doors at all?'

He shook his head as the elevator doors opened. 'No, the camera is angled so as to capture the guest's face and the employee helping them. It's a very narrow view by design. Once again, Mr and Mrs Sloane have a difference of opinion on cameras being used in a spa. If it was up to her, there'd be none.'

They stepped into the carriage and Ward hit the lobby button.

'I think this incident might change her mind on that subject. If there were cameras in every hallway this investigation would be over.' Lauren had barely gotten the words out when the doors slid open revealing Reese and Owen Carter grappling in the lobby, with Amanda trying to get in between them.

'Hey! Hey!' Lauren yelled, tossing her clothes to the ground and rushing forward. Owen had Reese's shirt clutched in both hands, while Reese had backed him against a wall, bouncing him against it.

'Get off me!' He slammed Owen hard by the shoulders into the drywall, but it didn't loosen Owen's grip.

Lauren pushed past Amanda and wedged herself between the two men. 'What the hell is going on here?' she demanded.

Owen let go, face crimson. Reese backed up, Lauren's hands planted against his chest to keep him from going after Owen again.

'I want to know what these two were doing up at two in the morning alone together in the bar?' Owen said, shoulders heaving from the adrenaline rushing through him.

'We were just talking!' Amanda insisted.

'You snuck out of our bed in the middle of the night to meet up with your old boyfriend just to talk? I'm supposed to believe that?'

'It's the truth,' Reese snapped, trying to straighten out his shirt, now warped from Owen's grip.

'We were talking about Jessica,' Amanda said. 'I wanted to know what he knew about the case. She was my best friend.'

Owen wasn't buying it. 'And you both conveniently wandered into the lounge at the same time?'

'No,' she said, her voice tinted in shame. 'We arranged it at dinner when you went to the bathroom. I should have told you. I'm so sorry, Owen, but I didn't want you to be upset.'

'Why would I be upset.' He threw his hands in the air. 'Because my wife snuck around behind my back?'

'It wasn't like that!' she insisted. 'I only wanted to ask him about Jessica. That's all.'

'We only spoke for a few minutes,' Reese told him. 'Unfortunately, I didn't have much to say.' Lauren could feel Reese's heart thumping in his chest as she kept her hands pressed against him, still holding him back.

'You're lucky I caught up with her alone while you were still at the bar,' Owen said, pointing his finger at Reese's face.

'Or what?' Reese challenged. Amanda jerked her husband's arm down, positioning herself between the two men as tears flowed over her cheeks.

'Stop! Stop! Stop!' Lauren commanded fiercely. Reese took another step back and blinked, shocked out of his anger by Lauren's voice. 'Erica Diaz is dead upstairs and you two are down here having a pissing contest in the lobby.'

Lauren's eyes bounced from Reese to Owen, then to Amanda. All three suddenly seemed contrite but Lauren didn't care. She didn't have time for a teenage love triangle being played out by three grown-ass adults. These high school distractions were getting them nowhere.

'Where are Seth and Tyler?' Lauren asked, noticing their absence from the lobby for the first time.

'I think they went back in the lounge when we started arguing,' Reese said.

Lauren's felt her blood pressure spike. 'I go to the second floor for fifteen minutes and everyone decides it's a free-for-all. Great.'

'I'm sorry, Lauren,' Reese said, face falling as he looked around.

Of all the people she needed to keep their shit together right then, it was Reese. And now she knew for certain he'd met up with Amanda the night before, keeping him and both the Carters out of their rooms and roaming the hotel halls when the homicide occurred. Before she could respond to his apology, her phone vibrated in her pocket. She held up a finger as Owen opened his mouth to say something, cutting him off. His mouth snapped shut as she answered. 'Detective Riley.'

The three of them just stood there like cattle, staring at her, unsure of what to do next. They were waiting for her to tell them, even Reese.

'It's me, Donovan. Have you watched the surveillance tapes yet?'

'I'm just about to do that. I had to handle a situation in the lobby.'

'What kind of a situation?' he asked.

Her eyes narrowed at the three offenders. 'Some of the guests decided to move about the premises instead of staying put. I'm herding them back into the lounge now.'

'Try to keep a lid on things. I just got a call that some of our modified ATVs may be available for me in a couple of hours.'

'Modified?'

'They have treads instead of tires, like tanks. They're amazing in the snow. They can get through just about anything. They really saved the day in 2014.'

Lauren felt a wave of relief wash over her. 'Good. That's good news.' She couldn't wait to turn the reins of this investigation over to him.

'Handle the lobby situation, then FaceTime me when you're ready to watch the video and we'll go over it together.'

Lauren agreed and clicked off. Turning her attention back to the warring trio, she told them, 'Investigator Donovan says he might be here sooner rather than later. I want the three of you to get back in the lounge and settle down. Hopefully, the troopers will get here and expedite things.'

Owen hooked his arm through Amanda's and headed back toward the lounge without a word. Lauren didn't try to stop them. Instead, she caught Reese by the wrist before he could retreat. 'Can we talk, please?'

Ward cleared his throat behind her. 'I'll cue up the security video.'

In all the chaos she'd forgotten Ward was there. She nodded to him. 'I'll be there in a minute, thank you.'

Ward disappeared into the office, leaving Lauren and Reese alone in the lobby. She dropped her hand from his and her anger bubbled to the surface. 'What the hell are you doing? Getting into fists fights in the middle of a murder investigation?'

He slumped against the lobby wall, eyes closed. 'I know. I messed up.'

'Why would you meet with Amanda in the middle of the night?'

Reese opened his eyes as he let out a stuttering breath. 'At dinner last night when Owen went to the bathroom, Amanda and I agreed to come down to the bar to talk after everyone went to bed.'

'You don't think that sounds suspicious?'

Reese let out a deep breath. 'After Jessica's body was found, she and I just, disintegrated, I guess. I only saw her in person one more time. The night after it happened all of us met up behind our high school. Erica's mom came looking for her because she snuck out. She made everyone go home before we had a chance to really talk about the murder. All of our parents kept us apart during the investigation. I think they all believed that one of us killed her, but not their kid.' Giving a bitter laugh, he said, 'By the end of August, the case was cold and everyone was off to college. I enlisted in the army and was gone by Christmas.'

'This was the first chance you've had to talk to Amanda about Jessica in all these years?' Lauren said.

Reese picked up his baseball hat and ran his hand over his bald head, over the scars that crisscrossed it. 'Raph and Erica, me and Amanda were just kids who thought we were in love.' He pulled his cap back in place. 'I guess Erica and Raphael really were in love because they got married. But Chris and Seth and Tyler were just guys who wanted to work in the park and hang out. And Jessica was just a girl who had nobody and didn't deserve to die like that. All the people I most wanted to talk about the murder with were cut off from me.'

The anger faded from Lauren. She couldn't let her emotions overwhelm her objectivity. She had to keep it together as well. 'I get it, Reese. I do. But it complicates things.'

'I wish Owen could get it in his head that even if we were both single, totally unattached, Amanda and I could never be involved again.' Now he inhaled sharply, like he couldn't catch his breath. 'It's like Jessica's ghost is haunting us all, keeping us apart. I thought if I investigated the case when I became a cop, I could bust it open. I wanted to know for sure what happened to her. And finally, we'd all be able to move on.'

'You mean you and Amanda,' Lauren clarified.

Reese shrugged. 'Jessica meant a lot to Amanda. And Amanda meant a lot to me at the time.'

'You both lied to the police.' It wasn't a question, but a statement of fact.

His mouth dropped open, and for a second, Lauren thought he was going to deny it.

'I should have known you'd be the one to figure that out.'

'I know you didn't just walk her to her car.' Lauren knew Reese well enough to know that if he and Amanda had been in a long-term relationship, a quick peck on the cheek at the car door wasn't his style. He was always respectful of boundaries, but they were a serious couple at the time. 'In your statement you said you held her car door open and kissed her on the cheek. In hers, she said you went to your car and she went to hers. You're expressing physical closeness and she's distancing herself from you.'

Lauren knew more about verbal cues than anyone in the Homicide office. What was left out of a statement was sometimes more significant than what was said. She knew she was right when his eyes dropped to the floor. 'We made love for the first time that night.'

She gave him a second, then asked, 'Is that why you never told me about the case? Because you lied to the police?'

His voice dropped as he glanced toward the lounge, making sure no one was within earshot. 'How could I tell those old men in the Homicide office that the first time I ever had sex was when Jessica was getting murdered? I couldn't put Amanda out there like that for the whole world to see, especially her mother and racist hillbilly father. Who knows what that asshole would have done?'

'You could have trusted me.'

He went on as if Lauren hadn't spoken. 'It happened inside the concession stand after Jessica stormed off. It was the first time for both of us. And it was awkward and awesome and emotional.' He shrugged his shoulders helplessly. 'It was supposed to be the best night of my life. I laid in bed all night, staring at the ceiling, heart pounding, replaying everything over and over in my head. I thought that was love. I couldn't wait to see her the next day. And the day after that. And the day after that.'

'Then the police came to your house in the morning,' Lauren prompted.

She saw the tough façade he wore crumble as the memories came flooding back to him. 'And everything fell apart. I knew I drove home around eight thirty. Amanda pulled out of the parking lot the same time I did. After talking with the detectives, instead of replaying what happened inside the concession stand, I kept asking myself, did she circle around and go back? And I didn't know for sure, because Jessica did threaten to tell Amanda's father about us.'

'And that made her a suspect.'

His smile was sad and his eyes far away. 'Just like it made me one.'

Lauren waited in silence as Reese took a moment to sort through all the long-lost emotions. For once some witty banter between them wouldn't make everything better.

'All of you suspected one another,' Lauren said. 'None of you believed Jessica was murdered by a stranger.'

'We were right.' His eyes turned to hers now. 'We've all been pointing the finger at each other for seventeen years in our heads. It was hard to come here, but I knew everyone would show up because we wanted answers, and unfortunately for Erica, one of us has them.'

'So you and Amanda met together to try to hash things out and get some closure for your relationship?'

He shook his head. 'We were already going in different directions before the murder. I was tired of hiding our relationship from her father. It wasn't my job as an eighteen-year-old kid to have to deal with her family's issues. I vowed after we broke up I'd never get involved with anyone who wasn't willing to accept me, one hundred percent, as I am. We met to try to figure out who killed Jessica. That's all.'

Lauren explored the anguished look he wore. She knew every contour, every line and shadow of Shane Reese's face. Lauren knew when he spoke about being involved, he was talking about her. Because they were involved, in some strange way that had changed and grown over the years. They had gone from work partners to something else, something deeper. They'd come close to crossing the line, then Gabe had come along, and all of their energy had been diverted to caring for him. But even that they were doing together. She wanted to reach out and touch her fingers to his cheek, brush her thumb along his jaw while she swam in his beautiful green eyes. She wanted to ease the pain he was experiencing because that was what they did, care for each other.

She felt her hands curling into fists at her sides as she

tamped down those feelings. There was no happily ever after for her and Reese, just what they had here and now. If she wanted to keep that, she needed to trust him. *If he is a suspect, he's still innocent until proven guilty, right?* she told herself. *How would I treat him if I didn't know him?* If this was a homicide in a downtown hotel involving a high school reunion of complete strangers, she'd be cautious, meticulous and by the book.

But she did know him. At least, she'd convinced herself over the years she did. Then the image of the wedding picture and Reese's newspaper article popped into her head again.

'You have to do this without me,' he said, his voice catching a little in his throat as he practically read her mind. 'I want you to treat me like you would any person caught up in a situation like this. And I know you know in your heart I didn't do this, but I need you to find out who did.' He put his hand on his chest, like he was about to recite the pledge of allegiance. 'I can't stand the doubt in your eyes. I saw that same doubt in Amanda's eyes after Jessica's murder and she saw it in mine.'

'Go back in the lounge,' Lauren said, hoping it didn't sound as pleading as it felt. 'I'll do what I can.'

He studied her face for a second, searching it the way she'd searched his just a few moments earlier, then gave a tight nod and a simple, 'OK,' before turning on his heel and walking away from her. The knot stayed tight in the pit of her stomach. *I may not really know Shane Reese*, she thought, just before heading to the office to meet up with Ward, *but he sure knows me.*

THIRTY

Alone behind the front desk, Lauren rapped on the office door with her knuckle. Ward must have been waiting right next to it because it opened immediately. He stood aside so she could enter and she saw he had the security camera's computer monitor paused on a still frame of the front desk. He had been kind enough to pull two chairs up to the little desk so they could watch together. Lauren recognized the brand name of the security system. She'd dealt with them many times before. Businesses loved them. There were no video tapes or discs to deal with, the daily digital recordings were stored off-site and easy to retrieve. It was a boon for law enforcement because even if someone attempted to alter the footage, the master copy was tamper-proof.

'I recalled all the footage from yesterday,' Ward told her, moving the mouse around on a white and green Sloane Spa and Retreat mouse pad.

'Let me call Investigator Donovan. He wants to watch it as well.'

With that, she FaceTimed the State Police detective and held her phone facing the screen. 'Can you fast-forward?' he asked. 'I'll tell you when to stop. Detective Riley, please narrate and tell me who I'm seeing.'

'I have to say, officers, that I've never seen this done on any of the true crime shows I watch,' Ward said as the screen suddenly came to life with one click of his finger.

'I think that's probably good, because I've never had to do this before,' Lauren said.

'Working a homicide remotely during a blizzard? I'd have to Google that, but I know this is a first for me too,' Donovan concurred.

'I queued it up to six a.m. yesterday,' Ward said.

'Might as well start from the beginning,' Donovan said and Ward clicked the video into life.

They fast-forwarded until the time stamp read ten o'clock yesterday morning. That was the first appearance of Ward. 'This is our hotel manager and technical advisor you've been hearing in the background. Say hello, Ward.'

'Good afternoon, Investigator.'

'Same to you,' Donovan responded. 'Given the circumstances.'

After a few back and forths behind the counter, Chris came walking into the frame. 'Pause it,' Lauren said. Ward clicked the mouse and she put a finger on the screen. 'This is Christopher Sloane, the owner.'

'My analysts are running his financials as we speak,'

Donovan's voice replied. With the screen facing forward, all Lauren could see was the back of her dark blue phone case. 'It's looking like he received the vast majority of his money from a single source.'

'Got a name?'

'Working on it. You have to peel back a lot of company layers to get to the actual investor.'

For the next two hours of fast-forwarded footage there was just a lot of Ward and Chris going back and forth from the office to the front desk then out to the lobby and back again, preparing for their guests to arrive.

Lauren watched as Ward clicked through all the guests' arrivals, pausing and announcing to Donovan who each person was. There was a long stretch of video of just the empty desk, presumably when everyone went to their rooms to get ready for the dinner that Ward and Mrs Brady were preparing with Rhonda's help. Lauren suddenly wondered if Rhonda had made it home all right after she left for the night, or if she was one of the people stuck in their cars. She'd have to follow up on that.

The camera didn't catch people coming out of the elevator or emerging from the staircase, it stayed trained on the lone front desk computer monitor and keyboard. The clock on the bottom left-hand side of the screen raced ahead, the only sign the footage was still rolling. Six o'clock came and went. Eight o'clock passed without a soul being seen. Nine, ten, eleven. Just when Lauren was starting to think the tape was going to be of little value, Mrs Brady suddenly appeared from the right. 'Slow it down,' Lauren told Ward, checking the time. It was 1:47 a.m. This must have been when Mrs Brady brought Seth his aspirin.

Sure enough, he appeared, and she handed him a tall glass of water with lemon slices floating in it. She then put two foil packets in his outstretched palm. He made a thank you gesture and turned and walked away from the desk. Mrs Brady watched for a moment, then moved out of the frame. Just then, Chris appeared and came around the desk.

He'd changed his clothes from what he had on at dinner. He was wearing gray pull-on sweatpants with a matching sweatshirt and sneakers. He walked over to the computer, tickled the mouse to wake it up, then tapped something into the keyboard. Even though the camera faced the screen, Chris's body blocked the view of what he was looking at. He circled the mouse a few more times, then clicked off. As he turned to grab the door handle for the office, Lauren noticed he was holding his laptop case by its handle down by his side. When he appeared five minutes later and exited back out into the lobby, he was empty-handed. 'Pause it,' she said.

'That was the owner again?' Donovan confirmed.

'It was,' Lauren replied, swiveling around in her chair. Her eyes swept the office. The laptop, which had been sitting in plain view when she was in there last, was now gone.

'Can you fast-forward this?' she asked. Someone had come into the office and taken Chris's laptop since she and Ward had last been in there.

She watched as time flew by.

1:47.

2:39.

3:03.

Then at 4:48 something caught her eye. 'Stop. Go back,' she told Ward.

'Did you see that?' Donovan asked.

'You saw it too,' she replied as Ward backtracked frame-by-frame. She kept her screen facing the monitor, propping her elbow on the desk to keep her hand steady. 'Good.'

If you weren't paying attention, you would miss it – a quick ruffling of the neatly placed brochures in their rack on the front desk.

'There!' Donovan said, and Ward stopped on the image. 'Someone opened the main lobby doors at 4:48 this morning.'

Lauren leaned in to get a better look. Reaching over, she took the mouse from Ward with her free hand and clicked through the sequence twice before she spoke. 'Someone tried to leave,' she declared. 'They opened the inner door, crossed the breezeway then tried to exit the outer doors. When they got hit in the face with the storm, they rushed back in and both doors were open for just a moment.'

'That would make sense,' Ward said in agreement. 'They would have had to use the manual buttons to open the doors after eleven. They don't close very fast. We wouldn't want a door sliding shut on one of our guests because they're not spry enough.'

'Go forward,' Donovan said. 'Let's see if anyone tried to leave again.'

Lauren continued to fast-forward. She kept going until she saw her and Ward entering and leaving, then entering again at supersonic speed.

'Stop there,' Donovan said, and Lauren hit the pause button. She thumbed the frame-by-frame button on the remote again. They watched Christopher Sloane walk into the office empty-handed and come out with his laptop in slow motion. Lauren glanced at the timer in the lower right-hand corner. He'd exited less than ten minutes ago.

'Son of a b—' she started to whisper when a panicked shout from the lounge cut her off.

'What was that? What's going on?' Donovan asked as Lauren jumped up from her chair.

'I'll call you back,' she said, clicking off the phone and heading for the door. 'Ward, come with me.'

She raced out of the office with Ward at her heels. A chorus of noise greeted her as they crossed into the lounge area. She spotted Mrs Brady at one of the round tables, hands covering her eyes as her shoulders racked up and down with sobs. In the far corner, Raphael was propping the door open to the men's bathroom with his body. She could see people clustered inside.

'What's going on?' she demanded as she approached.

Tyler stuck his shiny, balding head out. 'It's Chris. Someone bashed him in the melon in the john. He's out cold.'

Lauren pushed past him into the cramped room. Chris lay on his back on the tile floor. Blue and green ceramic shards from a decorative vase lay scattered across the floor. 'I found him in the last stall,' Reese said. He and Amanda were kneeling over him, trying to administer first aid. 'I saw his foot when I came in to use the urinal. It was turned at a weird angle and when he didn't respond to me, I pushed the door open. Whoever did it hit him with the vase from behind, propped him up on the toilet, and left him.'

'Is he breathing?' Lauren asked. Chris's polo shirt, so perfectly ironed this morning, was now soaked in blood. His drenched dreadlocks fanned out around his head as his friends tended to him. Owen stood behind Reese and his wife, wringing his hands, forehead creased in a concerned V.

'He is,' Amanda said. 'I think he has a concussion. Maybe worse. He needs medical attention right away.' Quickly swiping a curl that had come loose from her updo out of her eye, Amanda deposited a crimson smear across her cheek. She was so intent on her patient, she either didn't notice or didn't care, just returned her hand to Chris to keep him steady. All the emotional weepiness she'd shown over the last twenty-four hours had disappeared. Like Lauren morphing into detective mode, Amanda switched into her healer persona, laser focused on her patient.

'Where's all the blood coming from?' Lauren could hear Mrs Brady outside in the lounge, crying loudly.

'He's got a small cut to the top left side of his head,' Reese replied. 'But that's not the worst of it. You know how much even a small head wound bleeds.'

'How long was Chris missing before Reese found him?' Lauren asked.

'I don't think any of us noticed he was gone,' Seth admitted. He was backed up to the row of sinks, hands gripping the white porcelain behind him, propping himself against them. 'Everyone was moving around.'

'That's my fault,' Reese said. Lauren could hear the disgust in his voice. 'I should have made everyone stay put.'

Of course he would blame himself, Lauren thought. *Just like I'm blaming myself for not controlling the situation.*

'Now what do we do?' Tyler asked from behind her.

'We can't move him,' Amanda said. She'd tilted Chris's head back to make sure his airway was open and had both hands on either side to keep it aligned with his spine. Reese had a towel pressed against the top of his skull. Lauren could see red blood starting to seep through the plush white terry cloth.

'Tyler, go get some cushions from the chairs and couch,' Reese told him. Tyler seemed flustered for a second, then rushed off. 'If we can't move him, we have to keep him stable.'

Ward knelt down next to his boss, his face awash with concern. 'What can I do?'

'Get ready to relieve me when my arms get tired. And Lauren, get that investigator on the line and tell him we need medical help for a traumatic head injury,' Amanda replied.

'I'm on it,' Lauren said, pulling her cell phone out. She glanced down at Chris's handsome face as she hit redial. Expressive and full of life this morning, it was now ashen and slack, his mouth hanging slightly open.

Looking away, her eyes combed the bathroom, searching for some sort of explanation for what had happened to Chris. Donovan picked up on the other end with a hasty hello, but Lauren's voice was suddenly caught in her throat. Just inside the last stall, smashed to pieces and scattered across the tile floor, she spotted something.

It was Chris's laptop.

THIRTY-ONE

'Hello? Hello?' Donovan's voice echoed through the crowded bathroom from her cell phone. She'd called him back right away, but everyone was talking at once.

'Give me a second,' Lauren replied, putting the phone to her ear as she walked out into the lounge. There was nothing she could do for Chris that Reese and Amanda weren't already handling. She knew Reese would keep anyone from going near the stall.

She positioned herself near the bar where she could keep an eye on the bathroom door and still be far enough away from the wailing Mrs Brady to hear Donovan. She got back on the line with him and laid out the latest twist of events.

'My Major will demand a rescue crew break off,' he said once she was done. 'They've given your situation priority status already, and this just upped the ante. One thing before I click off to call him. My analyst gave me a preliminary report on Mr Sloane. This is what she found out.'

He gave her a quick rundown. Lauren exhaled. 'I think it fits with what I suspect, but I'm going to need you to have your analyst look something up for me.' She relayed her own request for information to him. He made her repeat it twice, just so he was clear on what she was asking for. When she was certain they were on the same page, she added, 'Just get here as fast as you can. I don't know how badly Chris is injured.'

'I can put your nurse practitioner through to the doctor at the command center, that way we'll know what medical supplies to bring.'

'Send me the contact number as soon as you can. He got bashed in the head pretty good.'

'Is he safe?' Donovan asked. She could hear other voices in the background, possibly the support staff that was running the records and looking up information.

'He won't be alone. They're keeping him stabilized. I doubt the killer will try anything with everyone in the room.' She gave a bitter laugh. 'But I thought that before, right?'

'You're doing everything you can,' Donovan assured her. 'Just hang on a little longer.' With that he clicked off.

Lauren watched the assembled guests clustered in and around the bathroom. Guests that were all also suspects. She ticked off the list in her head: there was a jealous husband and a regretful trophy wife, a failed actor who was abused by his deceased spouse, a disgusting louse of a man who treated women like garbage, an insecure millionaire who'd do anything to impress his friends, a spa owner who obviously had secrets, and Reese.

Reese, who may or may not be the person she thought he was.

I just have one more thing to do, she thought, eyes turning to the entrance, cognizant of the huge ticking clock above the doorway. *If Donovan can come through with the information I need and I can find what I'm looking for, maybe I can tie this whole thing up.*

THIRTY-TWO

Lauren marched back to where Amanda was tending to Chris, along with the rest of the guests. She pulled up the contact number Donovan had just texted her and told Amanda to touch base with the doctor at the command center because the State Police were on their way. Amanda punched the number into her phone and made the call. While she was talking to the doctor, Lauren bent down and said quietly in Reese's ear, 'Can I have a moment with you?'

He gave a nod and followed her out of the bathroom, forcing Tyler to take his place holding a fresh towel to Chris's head. She motioned him past the bar, under the ticking clock, and back out into the lobby, out of earshot of the others. When she stopped with her back to the stone fireplace, he leaned against the wall near the couch, rubbing at the blood on his finger. It wouldn't come off. 'I can't believe this,' he said, still rubbing, still trying to get the red stains off his fingertips. 'Just when I think this situation can't get any more bizarre, something even worse happens.'

'I need to go outside.'

'What?' His head actually jerked a little, as if the idea was so ridiculous, he had to recoil from its very suggestion.

'The knife and bloody clothes are still missing. I doubt the killer stashed them in their room for the police to find. Someone tried to leave last night. I need to check the perimeter, under the balconies, and look in everyone's car windows.'

'That's crazy. It's a blizzard outside. The knife will be buried under a foot of snow and the clothes will have blown away.'

'The wind is blowing the snow into drifts on the eastern side of the building. The western side should be better and I can dig down to look into the car windows. I doubt the killer wore gloves and I know the clothes will have both the killer's and Erica's DNA on them. That's why they tried to retrieve them in the middle of the night, but the storm turned them back.' Behind her she heard the snapping and crackling of the lobby's fireplace. The heat radiated to her back, warming it despite the howl of the wind coming from the main entrance doors. 'If the evidence is out there now, it's frozen. And any DNA on it is frozen with it. If we have to wait for a thaw to find the knife or clothes, any DNA evidence might melt away with it. And every second it's out there exposed to the elements we risk losing more. You know that.'

'You'll freeze,' Reese said, his eyes following hers to the double doors. 'It's a whiteout outside. You won't be able to see a thing.'

'Come on, Reese. We've had to dig people out when we were on patrol, directing traffic for hours in snowstorms. Not one cop ever froze to death in Buffalo doing their job. Chris said yesterday they had recreational equipment on hand. I'll borrow a pair of ski goggles.' She realized her parka and winter wear were still scattered across the lobby floor from her having to drop them to break up Reese and Owen's fight. She bent down and began to gather up her stuff, putting on each item as she picked it up.

'You can't go alone,' he insisted with finality, folding his arms across his chest.

'I can't take anyone with me,' she shot back, pulling her orange knit hat down over her ears. 'Having you with me could contaminate the secondary crime scene, if I do find something. I need you to stay here, keep an eye on everyone, because if I can find that evidence, I'll be able to prove once and for all you didn't kill anyone. And be able to nail the real murderer.'

Lauren knew Reese understood the rules of evidence as well as she did. While she was the one who always seemed to go rogue, Reese was the cop who followed the protocols to the letter. She was counting on his need for procedure, because his body language and tone were telling her he wasn't convinced this was necessary. 'You really think you know who killed Jessica and Erica? In a couple of hours you figured out what a squad of detectives and I couldn't in seventeen years?'

'Listen, it's a hunch. I won't know for sure until Investigator Donovan does some homework for me. He did confirm a nagging suspicion I had about someone.' She wound her black fleece scarf around her neck. 'I believe Erica figured it out, or at least she thought she did. She was going to make an accusation on air without proof and it got her killed. That's why I need to find this evidence. I need actual proof.'

'Can you at least tell me who it is?'

Lauren pulled on a thick black glove. 'You already know. I think you caught the same thing I did when you went over those files, but you just couldn't figure a motive.'

Now Reese's eyes went wide. 'What did Donovan say to you?'

Lauren straightened up as she plunged her arm into the sleeve of the parka. 'What you've suspected all along. Let's go back to the group so Ward can find me some goggles.' Now almost fully dressed to brave the weather, Lauren looked one last time at the sliding glass doors, a sea of solid white pelting them. 'And I'm going to need you to do one thing while I'm gone to keep everyone safe.'

'Anything.'

Her eyes narrowed at the thought of the killer in the other room, acting like a victim in all this, playing the same role for seventeen years, secretly happy they'd gotten away with everything for so long. Her voice was as cold as the biting, bitter wind.

'Watch them.'

THIRTY-THREE

There was a general protest when Lauren announced she was going outside. It was half-hearted, as the guests were still huddled in the bathroom, their focus on Chris and his injury, and their suspicions of each other.

'I don't understand why you have to go out in this weather,' Seth said. He'd boosted himself up onto the vanity that encased the sinks. 'Just wait for the State Police if they're on their way.'

'I have to check the perimeter,' she repeated. She fell back on the old standard line cops used when people questioned what they were doing. 'It's standard procedure.'

'I'll go get you the goggles,' Ward said.

'Owen, you go with him,' Lauren instructed, and added before he could protest, 'Nobody goes anywhere by themselves. Not even to use the other bathroom.'

Tyler and Raphael had propped open the door to the bathroom. Pulling chairs from one of the tables and setting them facing the doorway, they could keep an eye on Chris without adding to the already crowded space inside. Mrs Brady had finally come in and was now holding a fresh towel to the top of Chris's head. Next to her, on the floor, was a pile of its discarded, bloody companions. The one she was holding was still mostly unstained, which was a good sign. They'd gotten the bleeding to slow down at least. Amanda had used couch cushions on either side to keep Chris stable. 'One of the troopers they're sending is an EMT,' she told Lauren. 'The doctor says she can't come with them, they have to secure the scene first, but she'll be sending medical supplies and the EMT can help me keep him stabilized until they can get a plow up here for an ambulance.'

Chris's face, which had taken on a gray, ashy pallor, his lips a bluish tinge, now appeared to be gaining some color. 'That's good news,' Lauren said. The knowledge that help was actually on the way seemed to lift the mood of most of the group a little. Except for Raphael. He looked sick and gaunt, dark purple circles now ringing both of his hollow-looking eyes.

An awkward hush fell over the group as they waited for Ward and Owen to return. Now that the State Police actually had a plan to get to the hotel, everyone seemed to be holding their breath. The silence was broken only by the howl of the wind, which seemed to be dying down, and the ticking of the clock over the doorway. Lauren found herself staring at the second hand sweeping around the face, counting the seconds until Ward and Owen came back. In the back of her mind, the possibility of Owen being the killer raised its ugly head. If Amanda had killed Jessica, would he have killed Erica to cover it up? But if Amanda had been involved in Jessica's death, then so had Reese.

Which was why she needed to get outside as quickly as possible before the State Police came and took over.

Finally, they appeared with green and white plastic ski goggles and a pair of ski poles. 'I thought you could use them to help navigate the drifts,' Ward said as they stopped next to Raphael by the bathroom door. Owen looked past Lauren to check on his wife. Lauren could tell he didn't like how close Reese was to her in the cramped space.

'I hope these fit,' Ward said, holding out the goggles. He, too, was looking worn out.

Lauren took them in her gloved hand and thanked him, then grabbed the poles as well. She turned and addressed the group clustered in and around the bathroom with Chris. 'I won't be long,' she said, pulling the goggles over her head and letting them dangle around her neck.

'How are you going to get out of the building?' Mrs Brady asked. 'All of the doors open outward. There's over four feet of snow holding them shut.'

'Except for the sliding glass doors on the front of the building,' Lauren said. 'The wind is sweeping the snow right past them. There's only a few inches right outside them. I'm sure their motion sensors have a weather feature that's keeping the doors closed right now. I'll hit the wall button and exit.'

'Whoever did this to Chris and Erica is still here!' Seth said. 'This is not the time to go on a scavenger hunt in a blizzard.'

Lauren could see the frustration and worry in Seth's face, along with the others. She'd been a cop for almost two decades and had never been in a situation like this. Reese knew she was improvising as she went along, but the others had to have confidence she was handling things. 'I tried leaving all of you on your best behavior and Chris still got ambushed. I don't know what else to do, aside from sitting you in a circle and watching you like toddlers. The State Police will be here soon, sooner than they had first told me. All I need from you is to stay here until I come back. Nobody goes anywhere alone.'

After stuffing two paper bags in her left front parka pocket and her phone on the right side so she'd have easy access to it, she was ready to go. 'I'll walk you out,' Ward said.

'I'm coming too.' Reese walked toward Lauren. 'Everyone goes in pairs, right?'

She nodded and the three of them passed under that damned loud clock on their way to the lobby. The time read 1:10 p.m. *Has it really only been a few hours since this whole thing started?* Lauren thought to herself as they walked by the couch in front of the fireplace where she'd seen Raphael sleeping that morning. *It feels like time is standing still. Like we're stuck in a snow globe and the only thing moving is the fake plastic flakes swirling around us.*

They got to the first set of double doors and Ward hit the blue square metal wall button. They slid open easily. Crossing into the heated breezeway, the howl of the wind was even louder. Lauren could see the snow being whipped along the glass. With nothing solid to stop it, it was just being swept away on this side of the building, facing south. The north side, where the cars were parked, was sure to be a different story.

Ward opened a door that Lauren hadn't noticed on the way in. It was a shallow closet, but inside were two rakes, a wide push broom and two snow shovels. He grabbed one. 'Will you be needing this?'

She shook her head. 'Unless I could strap it to my back, I don't have enough hands to carry it. You don't happen to have any snowshoes around, do you?'

'There's some on the walls near the bar,' Reese said, hopefully.

'Purely decorative, I assure you,' Ward said, closing the closet but leaning the heavy shovel against the wall. 'We don't have any functioning snowshoes on the premises.'

Reese stood with a fist on each hip, looking Riley up and down. 'Are you sure you want to do this?' he asked.

She looked into his eyes and zipped her parka up past her chin. 'I have to.' *I have to do this for the victims, but I also have to do this for you*, she wanted to say, biting back the words. She and Reese weren't sappy like that.

'Listen to me.' He grabbed onto both of her shoulders, his fingers digging into the padding of the parka. 'If you can't find anything, just come back in. Don't be wandering all over.

You know how easy it is to get turned around in a snowstorm.'

'I wish we had some rope on hand, like they always do in the movies, so you could tie it around my waist and pull me back when I'm done.' Lauren tried to make her voice sound lighter as she tugged the hood of her parka up over her head, brushing Reese's hands away in the process. Pulling up extra material from the black fleece scarf around her neck, she covered her mouth and nose.

'No ropes, no snowshoes,' Reese said with a bleak smile. 'You're wearing jeans instead of snow pants. This is a shitshow. Let's call it off.'

'I wouldn't fit into anyone else's snow pants. Too tall and skinny, remember? The last thing I need is trying to keep my pants up and my ankles warm.' Shaking her head, she gestured back toward the lobby with one of the ski poles. 'Stay inside and watch everyone.' With the scarf over her lips, she sounded muffled. 'I need *you* to keep them safe.'

Her saying that cemented the fact she didn't believe he was the killer anymore. His face, taut with worry, softened and, for a second, Lauren thought he was going to pull her into a hug. He caught himself though and actually took a step backwards. 'Get out there and get back in. I'll be waiting right here for you.'

You always are, she thought, reaching over to hit the button on the wall. *You always have been.*

THIRTY-FOUR

The door slid open, unleashing a torrent of swirling snow and cold that hit her in the face like a thousand tiny icepicks. She'd forgotten to pull the goggles over her eyes and now struggled to get them in place, battling to pull back the scarf she'd wound around her head, while six-inch drifts of snow that had built up along the bottom of the doorway caved inward and piled onto the black rubberized entrance mat. She stood blinking, blinking, blinking, eyes watering, on the brink of the entryway until she could finally focus. She inhaled a deep, stabbing breath of ice-cold air, recoiled her scarf around her face and head, then stepped out into the storm.

Immediately she felt a dagger of pain in her side where she'd been stabbed and her lung had collapsed. She was still in physical therapy for the injury, which flared up at the most inopportune times, like when confronted with ice cubes in a drink. She pondered that for just a moment, then gritted her teeth, pushed down the pain and moved forward.

Underneath the awning, most of the snow was being swept away by the constant wind. It wasn't until it hit the shrubbery lining the pavement that huge snowdrifts had formed. She knew if she went left and around, she'd be underneath her own balcony. If she went right, it'd take her underneath Erica's, and if she kept going, to the parking lot around the back of the hotel. Unfortunately, that was also the way the wind was blowing, so the drifts against the building would be huge.

She leaned into the wind and started to make her way in the direction of Erica's room. The walkway was icy underneath the snow, so she used the ski poles to give her leverage and help propel her forward. She could feel the tips of the poles hit the ice-covered cement with every stride. It was that little layer of ice, piled with the accumulation, that was keeping all the doors from opening outward.

Snow continued to batter her. Each flake felt like a needle hitting the exposed skin of her cheeks just below her goggles. It was the wind, she knew, that stole your warmth. Every blast of wind robbed more of her body heat.

Thankfully, it was afternoon and not night-time or she'd have been completely blind in the whiteout. As it was, she could make out the dark shape of the building and the trees closest to the hotel through the blowing snow. The yellow light coming from the windows she passed looked warm and inviting but she only paused for a few seconds at a time to get her bearings. Ahead of her she could see the overhang of the balconies on the second floor. The snow was deep, but loose. Lauren could shuffle her legs through it, like wading through a shallow lake. She had to keep moving. That was the key.

Looking up, she could make out the underside of the three balconies. Each was its own box with a space of about five feet separating them. Positioning herself under the middle one, she stepped out and away from the building, pushing herself through the almost thigh-deep snow until she was where she judged the railing would be above her. The rooms overlooked the woods that crept up the hill. Lauren lifted the right ski pole and tried to judge its weight. It was much longer, but roughly the same weight as the missing knife. Taking a deep, biting breath she heaved it over her head. It immediately disappeared in the snow.

The wind and snow masked the sound of the pole landing. Lauren imagined the wind must have carried it a little to the left. Keeping that trajectory in mind, she walked toward the tree line, sweeping the other pole through the snow in front of her in a wide arc.

Snow angels, she thought, sweeping the pole again, briefly leaving an imprint like half of an angel she'd made with her sister as kids in their backyard. They'd lie on the ground in their snowmobile suits and flap their arms and legs while soft flakes fell from the sky and landed on their outstretched tongues. The winter was beautiful then, cold and clean and magical, a fairy tale of frozen wonder in the eyes of a ten-year-old.

But fairy tales always have a dark side to them, don't they?

She counted her steps: eight, nine, ten. Still no pole.

Fifteen, sixteen, seventeen.

She realized she was shivering. Shivering so hard the pole in her hand was trembling.

She felt metal hit metal. Bending down, and feeling around with her gloved hand, she retrieved the pole and stuck it straight up in the snow until she felt the tip pierce the not-yet-frozen ground. If it had been January instead of November, she'd have been in trouble. This was the first snow of the year and the ground wasn't frozen yet, even with the mounds of accumulation on top.

Shoving it in hard, Lauren continued her sweep with the

other pole, using its mate as a reference point. She decided to go twenty paces forward and to the left, then return. She was at six paces when her pole hit something again. This was deeper. Looking down, all she could see was the accumulated snow, white and windswept. Using the pole for guidance, she sank down on her knees and plunged her hand into the snow.

Her gloved fingertips traced the outline of the knife. Lauren debated what to do. She could gather the knife, put it in the paper bag she had tucked in her parka and risk contaminating a vital piece of evidence, or she could try to mark the spot and wait for the troopers to show up and properly collect it.

Her lips quivered against the fabric of her scarf as she made up her mind.

No one was coming out into this mess from the hotel. She couldn't stop the other guests from wandering around, but now that she knew where the knife was, she could damn well sit by the front doors and make sure no one could get at it.

Using both hands, she raised the pole and brought it down with every ounce of strength she had. The tip sank in until the round guard stopped it. Lauren packed snow around it to keep the wind from toppling it. Even if the pole did blow away, she'd still have a pretty good idea of where the knife was. All they'd need was a metal detector once the storm died down.

Lauren tried to stand without the pole for support and almost fell. Catching herself at the last second, she realized she couldn't feel her feet. *They're there*, she told herself, *walk. Just because you can't feel them doesn't mean they don't work.*

The weather was getting to her. Having lived and worked in Buffalo her whole life, she knew the signs of hypothermia. She had to get back inside the hotel right away. She knew there was no way she'd make it to the parking lot out back. She had to turn around and head for the front doors.

The wind seemed to lessen a bit, maybe the storm was waning, but it didn't seem to matter as Lauren trudged toward the building. It was still ripping through her layers, taking her body heat with it.

She somehow made her way back to the first pole and yanked it out. At least now she'd have that for some added leverage. It was definitely clearer underneath the balconies. Lifting one leg at a time she took wide strides in the snow, purposely placing each foot and making sure it was planted before taking another step.

She could hear the crunch of the snow underneath her boots now. The wind, while still biting, wasn't as strong as when she'd first come outside. Her visibility was getting better as she crept along the side of the hotel.

Out of the corner of her eye, she caught a flash of red.

Wiping the snow from her goggles she looked toward the tree line. Something was caught in the lower branches of one of the skeletal trees. The wind would pull it vertically, edges flapping violently with each gust, then it would fall straight only to be ripped sideways again.

How far was it? Lauren knew that the cold and snow had a way of playing tricks on your mind with distance. If it was a clear day, she could probably jog over to the tree and back to the hotel in under a minute. It was that close. Or so it appeared.

You're not thinking clearly, she reminded herself. *Confusion is a sign of hypothermia.*

But if it was what she thought it was, she needed to get it. She couldn't mark it with a ski pole. It was barely hanging on. One really good blast of wind and it would be gone and lost forever. *It's toward the front of the hotel*, she told herself, *just farther right. I need to go forward and to the right, grab it, then turn around and head for the double doors. Piece of cake.*

Using the pole for support, she shuffled off the snow-covered sidewalk next to the hotel and began crossing what would have been open, empty lawn a week ago toward the trees. She started counting steps again.

Twelve, thirteen, fourteen.

You're doing this for Reese, she told herself. *He needs to know. He had one secret from you all these years because he didn't want you to look at him differently.*

Twenty-one. Twenty-two. Twenty-three.

Her skin was prickling all over. She was having a hard time keeping her grip on the pole. *Maybe if I take my gloves off*

– she shook that thought out of her head. Taking off one's clothes was a sure sign of hypothermia. Rescue teams often found victims in the woods naked, or nearly so, when campers got caught in snowstorms and tried to walk out on their own.

Thirty. Thirty-one. Thirty-two.

She was almost there. Now that she was closer, she could see that it was a piece of clothing. It was snagged by a thick brown branch, but it was barely hanging on. She squinted up, wiping her goggles with her gloved hand for a better view. It looked like a shirt. She could see it snap with each new gust of wind, tugging precariously on the end of the limb.

She trudged closer until she was underneath it. Using the ski pole, Lauren poked upward, trying to spear the fabric with the pointy end. Just when she thought she had the tip hooked around the cloth, another blast of wind hit it, ripping the fabric away. Planting her feet wide, she gripped the pole with both hands, her left covering and steadying her right, and tried fishing the cloth out again. With a grunt, she stabbed upward, into the tree branch, then scraped back, snagging the item. Carefully she lowered it.

She was about to pull it off the end when another gale of wind kicked up and yanked the fabric off and away. Lauren dropped the pole and dove for the shirt. Facedown in the snow, she lifted her head to see it clamped between her gloved hands. A cough racked her body. She gripped harder, afraid the fabric was going to slip from her fingers.

Carefully, she pressed the shirt down into the snow and pushed herself up on her knees at the same time. Despite being frosted with ice, she could now see that it was a deep red and brown plaid flannel with dark, almost black stains all over it. Dried or frozen blood, depending how quickly the killer threw it off the balcony. Keeping the shirt pinned, she used her other hand to fish out the paper bag she'd stuck in her front parka pocket. She shook it open. Not bothering to brush the snow away, she scooped the shirt into the bag and rolled it shut as best she could.

Still clutching the bag, Lauren struggled to her feet. She was afraid if she reached for the ski pole, she'd lose her grip on the shirt altogether. She couldn't stuff the bag into her parka. She didn't want to take the chance of what little body heat she had unfreezing the evidence.

With no feeling in her feet, it felt like she was walking on stilts – wobbly and unsteady. *I can see the window lights of the hotel*, she told herself, willing her body toward the front entrance as another hacking cough ran through her. *I just have to make it that far.*

But from where she was, that seemed an impossible distance to cross.

She tripped over her own boot and fell forward.

Her goggles were covered in snow. Lauren tried to sit up but couldn't. She tried taking a deep breath, but it was too painful, and she coughed out what little air she had. She felt herself taking little gasping breaths. She used one arm to keep the bag pinned to her chest, and the other to prop herself up. *Of all the things I've faced over the years – getting stabbed, strangled, cut, shot at – I can't believe the thing that's going to do me in is the freaking weather.*

She couldn't see. If she lifted her hand to wipe her goggles, she'd tumble back into the snow. Her scarf was crusted with ice from her breath. *Let go of the bag or you're going to die*, she commanded herself. *Let go, get up and move toward the hotel.*

She struggled to push herself into a sitting position. *You can't catch Erica's killer and prove Reese innocent if you freeze to death.* Her thoughts were jagged and scattered. It was hard to concentrate. She finally managed to push herself onto her knees. Her feet were like great useless blocks of ice at the ends of her legs. She wiped the snow from her goggles. The hotel looked miles away. *Maybe if I take my goggles off, I could see better.*

All around her, the wind and snow seemed to be ebbing. It was the cold that wasn't letting up. In her addled brain she knew it was still November, and the temperature was likely in the low teens, but the wind chill factor was making it feel like minus temperatures. Lauren knew that even if it was twenty degrees Fahrenheit, which seemed positively balmy compared to the temperatures in the winter months, hypothermia could still kill you if you were outside in it long enough.

Get up! Get up! Get up!

Lauren slid the bag in front of her and willed herself to crawl toward the yellow light coming from the windows. Maybe if she could just get to the side of the hotel, she could bang on one. Maybe they'd hear her over the wind.

Her life depended on maybes.

But she was so tired. She needed to rest a while. Lay down and take a nap. She couldn't remember if she had plans for the rest of the afternoon. The snow had put everything on hold. She felt so peaceful, lying there. She didn't even feel cold anymore. *I could just stretch out*, she thought, *and shut my eyes for a couple of minutes . . .*

THIRTY-FIVE

'Get up!' Hands gripped under both of her armpits, hauling her forward. 'Don't fall asleep! Come on!'

Startled, Lauren swiped at her goggles with one useless hand. Reese was pinning her to his side, crushing the bag between them, dragging her toward the hotel.

'What are you doing out here?' She could hear the dull confusion in her voice, barely audible above the wind. She was a dead weight, falling back onto her knees.

'I'm not going to let you die,' he replied, scooping her up in his arms and carrying her.

With her extra weight and the wind, even Reese, as strong as he was, staggered through the knee-deep snow toward the safety of the building.

'I got it,' Lauren told him, rustling the bag she was still clutching. 'I found the proof that you're innocent.'

He didn't respond, just slogged through the snow, with no hat or scarf, carrying her like getting her inside was the most important thing on the earth right now.

The details of the hotel came into focus as they got closer. She could see the lights in the windows and the outlines of shapes within as her body spasmed with another round of wracking coughs. The wind really did seem to be letting up, causing the steady sheet of white to break apart. Even in Lauren's confused state she could tell the visibility had gotten better.

After what seemed like a hundred-mile trek, which in reality was much less than a hundred yards, Reese stumbled under the awning above the entrance. The double doors slid open and Ward was standing there with a blanket, which he immediately draped over Lauren. Reese whisked past him, carrying her through the second set of double doors into the lobby, and gently laid her on the couch in front of the fireplace.

'Let's get these off,' Reese said to Lauren, pulling off her scarf, then goggles, then her gloves. The tips of her fingers were red and puffy.

'Ward, go get Amanda, find a cooler and some hot tea,' Reese told him. Ward hesitated, mouth open as if he was going to say something, then nodded and disappeared into the lounge area.

'You came and got me,' Lauren rasped out. 'Why did you do that?'

Reese reached over and yanked the knit hat off her head and held it up. 'We saw you struggling to walk and then it looked like you went down. I started to panic, but then I spotted this stupid orange pumpkin hat through the snow. It was like a fucking beacon. And it wasn't moving.'

'You shouldn't have come and gotten me.'

Reese snorted out a laugh. 'Like you wouldn't have done the same thing. I just hope it was worth it.'

'I found the evidence to exonerate you,' she said, pulling the bag out from under the blanket. It was hard to talk, she could hear the slurring of her own words. 'We need to get this into a freezer.'

'How does that,' he gestured to the brown paper bag, 'prove to you that I'm innocent?'

'Because I know every piece of clothing you own,' she replied. 'The bloody men's shirt in here is not yours. But it's loaded with the real killer's DNA mixed with Erica's blood. I have to keep it safe.'

'Just put it on the floor next to you. I'll pack some snow

from your boots around it for now. I'm sure Ward has a cooler around here somewhere. No one will touch it.' Reese was trying to get her boots unlaced and warm her up and she was worried about chain of custody issues and the integrity of the DNA. The only thing that could make her turn off being a cop for one minute was to worry about Reese.

'You don't have a coat on,' she said, letting the bag slip to the ground next to her. 'Or boots.'

He glanced down at his snow-covered sneakers. 'I was only outside for three or four minutes, tops. Just long enough to haul you in. I thought you were never coming back. I didn't think, I just did it.'

'You've done a lot of crazy things but going out into a snowstorm without a coat and wearing sneakers takes the cake,' she said, trying to get her ice-cold lips to form a smile. Even the muscles in her face felt frozen.

'You were out there so long. I thought I'd lost you. Then I finally spotted that orange hat. Ward and I saw you fall down and not get back up,' he was talking quickly, repeating himself, as he knelt next to the couch while he worked at taking her parka off so the heat of the fireplace could get to her. Lauren knew when Reese was frazzled, he tended to babble. 'I thought, am I so crazy that I just let the most important person in my life risk herself in a snowstorm for me? I ran out there. I had to get to you.'

'Second most,' she corrected, meaning Gabe, then added, 'And I did it for Jessica and Erica and Chris too.'

'I know you.' He leaned in, until their foreheads were touching, melting snow causing little rivulets of water to run down from his scarred, bald head. 'I know who you did this for. And I can't lose you,' he whispered, taking her numb hands into his. She could feel the heat surround her frozen fingers. 'I can't.'

'Is my nose still on my face?' she asked. Even in her addled state she was acutely aware of how close his mouth was to hers. She could feel each breath wash over her face, see the concern in his eyes. She could smell the scent of the hotel soap he'd used that morning, now mixed with sweat from having to carry her.

'Your lips are blue, your nose is red, but I don't think you have frostbite.' Gently, he smoothed her hair away from her forehead. 'Amanda will look you over, just relax.'

'I can't relax. I have to see this through.'

'What are we doing, Riley?' he asked, his face still close to hers.

'We're solving a homicide,' she replied, as if that was the most obvious thing in the world.

The resigned look on his face told Lauren he was talking about something else. Something they danced around every single day. 'No. You're solving a homicide. What are *we* doing?'

It was a question that kept her up at night lately. They lived in the same house. She was helping him raise his newborn son. They went grocery shopping and rode to work together. They were partners in every sense of the word. But they'd never shared one kiss, let alone a bed.

'I don't think this is exactly the right time for this conversation,' she told him. Truth be told, she was more afraid of having that conversation than braving the elements or facing a murderer.

'There'll never be a right time for us,' he said. 'But we both need more than this. Hell, after all we've been through, we deserve more than this.'

She heard the clatter of people approaching and Reese pulled away from her to look. 'She was out there for twenty minutes,' he called over his shoulder. Amanda suddenly came into view, with Ward and Owen right behind her. Owen was carrying a steaming teacup, which he put on the oval table in front of the fireplace.

'You got her boots and gloves off, that's good. Let the heat get to her.' Amanda crouched down next to Reese and started to examine Lauren.

Ward set a small white cooler with a beer logo on it next to the couch. 'One of our distributers left this behind the bar last week when he was setting up the kegs. I wanted to put it in storage, but Mr Sloane thought it might come in handy.' He pressed the red button on the side and the top slid open. 'Once again, he was right.'

Before Reese could touch it, Lauren grabbed the bag, put it in the cooler and snapped it shut. She realized that feeling was coming back into her extremities.

'That was good. Good manipulation,' Amanda told her, taking her hand and splaying Lauren's fingers out, looking at the tips. 'No frostbite. Let's get a look at those toes.'

While Amanda examined her feet, Reese picked up the teacup and brought it to Lauren's lips. 'Careful,' he warned, as she leaned in to take a sip. 'It's hot.'

'I wouldn't want to burn myself,' Lauren half-heartedly joked. The herbal tea tasted like heaven, warming her mouth and throat as it went down. She still had her hand on the handle of the cooler. There was no way she was letting it out of her sight after she almost lost her life for the evidence inside. At least the cooler seemed to be of good quality. She had to keep the paper bag from disintegrating. Ideally, she would get the cooler into a freezer as soon as possible, but then she would be stuck in the kitchen, babysitting it. *Chain of custody is a bitch*, she thought.

It was easier to concentrate on the evidence rather than on her and Reese.

'I'd say she has a mild to moderate case of hypothermia,' Amanda announced, rocking back to sit on her heels. 'More on the mild side as it seems her color and motor skills are coming back rather quickly. It's a good thing you went out there when you did,' she told Reese.

'What do we do now?' he asked, still holding the delicate teacup in his large hands.

'Let her warm up,' she said simply, rearranging the blanket covering Lauren. Owen placed his hand on her shoulder and she reached over and put hers over it, giving it a squeeze. Amanda was a strong, beautiful, confident woman married to a man who constantly needed to be reminded he was good enough. His possessiveness bothered Lauren. She remembered the feeling of always having to reassure your partner that they were number one in your life. It was exhausting.

'How's Chris?' Lauren asked.

'He's starting to come around,' Amanda said. 'He's awake and talking, which is a good sign. I won't let him move though.'

'Did he say who hit him?' Lauren asked, then let out a string of hacking coughs. The pain in her side flared up again. She reached around and pressed a hand over the scar where she'd gotten stabbed. *It's been over two years now since it happened*, she thought as another round seized her, *and I'm still not better.* All she could do was hope the freezing air hadn't damaged her lungs even further.

Amanda waited until Lauren's coughing fit was over before she answered. 'He doesn't even remember going into the bathroom.'

'Can you get my phone out of my parka pocket?' Lauren asked her, glad Owen had taken a seat in one of the chairs and his hand off his wife.

'We need to get these jeans off,' Amanda said, eyeing what Lauren had on. She reached back, grabbed the coat and searched Lauren's parka for the phone. 'They're all wet. And the sweatshirt.'

'I can get one of the robes from the spa,' Ward piped up. 'They're very plush and warm.'

Owen looked uncertainly from Amanda to Reese and back again, then said, 'I'll go with him.'

'Perfect,' Amanda replied shortly, pulling out Lauren's cell and handing it to her. 'That'll do the trick.'

'I've got to call Donovan.' Lauren fumbled with the phone, trying to press her finger on the button to unlock it.

'Don't bother,' Amanda told her. 'They're on their way. The doctor called me when they were packing the ATVs. She said it should take them about an hour once they got moving. That was fifteen minutes ago.'

Still, Lauren rubbed her thumb on the blanket, then pressed it against the button again. Her phone unlocked. She had four unanswered voice messages from her daughters left throughout the morning and one message from Investigator Donovan that was twenty-one minutes old. She hit play and put the phone to her ear.

A grim smile crept to her lips. He'd found out the answer to the question she'd put to him before she'd gone outside and had sent her the pictures to prove it. She now had everything she needed.

'What?' Reese asked, seeing the look on her face transform. 'What did he tell you?'

Lauren turned the phone off and put it face down on the oval table before reaching for the steaming cup of herbal tea. Cradling it in both hands, she took another warming sip. She felt a wave of nausea and dizziness wash over her. It was all she could do to manage, 'That it sucks being right. We now have one hell of a motive to go with our means and opportunity,' before Reese grabbed the mug out of her shaking hands and she fell back into the cushions.

THIRTY-SIX

Amanda decided not to move Lauren from the couch until the EMT arrived and checked her over, even though she was the more qualified medical expert being a nurse practitioner. They had her stretched out on the couch, boots, socks and jacket off, lying underneath a fleece blanket with a green and red chevron pattern on it. With Amanda's help, Mrs Brady had managed to pull Lauren's jeans and sweatshirt off, while shielding her from view by a blanket Reese was holding up. Amanda had helped her slip on the white robe Ward had brought. Even in her semi-conscious state, one hand rested on her chest, while the other dangled over the side, touching the handle to the cooler. She hadn't gone to all that trouble of retrieving the evidence just to let it literally slip from her fingers right before the State Police came. She'd wanted to jump up and finish this once and for all, but her body would not cooperate.

Reese sat on the end of the couch, watching Lauren while she drifted in and out of a sort of hazy sleep. Amanda left her to go check on Chris, taking Ward and Owen with her. Lauren slowly became aware of her surroundings again. She let the sound of the crackling fireplace soothe her, and chase away her racing, muddled thoughts, knowing that Reese was keeping watch over her.

She was safe, for a few minutes anyway. *But there's no rest for the weary*, she thought as she finally felt herself becoming coherent again. She and Reese had work to do.

'How are you feeling?' he asked when she opened her eyes and blinked against the light of the chandelier shining down on her.

'Better. I can feel my toes again.' She gave the plastic cooler's handle a squeeze to make sure it was still there and did her best to smile at him.

He nodded, satisfied with that answer. 'Good. How about we try to get you to sit up.'

'How long was I asleep?' Lauren struggled to pull herself into a sitting position with Reese's help, then asked, 'What time is it?'

Flipping his phone over on the table next to him, he read off the screen. 'It's 2:01. You got somewhere to be?' he joked.

Craning her head, she looked out through the two sets of double doors. The wind had indeed let up. The snow was still falling, but in huge, fat flakes, not the icy projectiles that had stung her face. They had roughly a half-hour to do what needed to be done. 'Help me up.'

Reese propped a pillow against her back. 'You needed the rest.'

Lauren swung her bare legs over the couch, planting her feet on the floor, and pulled the French terry cloth robe tight around her. 'I have to get my clothes on,' she said, struggling to stand up.

Someone – maybe Reese, maybe Amanda – had taken her wet clothes and hung them over the backs of two of the wing chairs on either side of the fireplace to dry. From the looks of it, none of the items were quite there yet.

'Whoa.' Reese grabbed her arm to steady her. 'What do you think you're doing?'

'We can't wait for the troopers to get here.' She glanced back toward the double doors. 'We don't have much time. I'm going to need your help.'

He slid his arm around her waist. She had the cooler by the handle. 'I don't think this is a good idea. You need to rest.'

'We're only going to have one shot at this,' she told him, leaning into his chest. 'And Donovan will never go along with what I have in mind.'

'What's that?'

She steered him toward the elevator. 'We're going to expose the killer, old school.'

'What the hell does that mean?' Reese asked as he pressed the button for the second floor for her.

'You get to be the Watson to my Holmes,' she said, 'or the Hastings to my Poirot. I know you've gotten pissed in the past about being called my sidekick, but I'm going to need you to play that role for me today.'

'I'm liking the sound of this less and less,' Reese said. With his eyebrows pulled tight into the V of a frown, he helped Lauren into the elevator.

THIRTY-SEVEN

On the ride up to the second floor, she explained what Donovan had sent her in his latest email, its significance and what she wanted to do. They continued strategizing about their next move all the way to her room, and he now wore a look of admiration and amazement. 'You're a freaking genius,' he told her, stopping in front of her door.

'Sometimes when you're looking at something too closely, you have to take a step back,' she said, repeating what she'd told him in the Cold Case office. She wanted to say the answer had been right in front of him the whole time but didn't want to add insult to injury. There was a reason they didn't let detectives work on cases they were personally involved in. 'And sometimes you get lucky and the technology catches up to the crime. But you figured out who it was. You just didn't want to believe it.'

'No, I could believe it,' he replied. 'I just couldn't prove it. It didn't make sense. Until now.'

'Just like the original investigators,' Lauren reassured him.

Reese made her wait outside her room while he checked it. Under normal circumstances she would have told him she was a big girl and could clear her own room, but she knew she was close to helpless right then. Once he'd given her the OK, he waited outside, while she quickly discarded the spa robe and threw on a pair of jeans and a chunky mint green sweater. Sitting on the corner of her bed, she slowed herself down and bent at the waist to carefully pull a dry sock over each foot. The thought of stuffing her tingling toes into her sneakers made her stomach clench. She tossed them into the corner. She was just getting the feeling back in her feet, there was no way she was going to impede that by lacing up running shoes.

Leaving her sneakers behind, Lauren met up with Reese in the hallway.

'Are you ready to tell your old classmates what happened?' she asked as they waited for the elevator. Lauren was still a little shocked that he'd agreed to go along with her plan. The State Police were notoriously by the book, but she'd pointed out to Reese, as Donovan had said earlier, they were sailing in uncharted waters. Donovan had seemed receptive to her and her ideas the entire day, but there was no way the straitlaced trooper higher-ups would go for what she was planning, so they had to be quick.

'I'm afraid my classmates won't believe us. Hell, I barely believe us,' Reese said.

'It's been seventeen years,' she replied, stepping inside. 'I think they deserve to finally know the truth, whether they want to believe it or not.'

'Are you going to tell everyone about me and Amanda?'

She shook her head. 'Not today. It'll come out if this ever goes to trial, but I'd rather have Amanda tell Owen herself.'

A look of relief passed over his face. 'Thank you.'

'Don't thank me. It really doesn't give either of you an alibi. It's just the evidence I have against the killer is so overwhelming, it's irrelevant now.'

'We have to be careful that this doesn't turn into a "Christmas burial" speech,' he said, pushing the button for the first floor. He was referring to the Supreme Court case that said police officers who told a suspect in the backseat of their patrol car that giving his victim a decent Christian burial at Christmas time amounted to interrogation – even though no questions were asked – because it was intended to elicit a response. The two key prongs of giving Miranda warnings have always been custody and interrogation. Interrogation was to be assumed. It was custody she was worried about. A defense attorney could argue that even though no one was under arrest, no one in the hotel was free to leave because of the weather.

'Are we going to Mirandize everyone first?' she confirmed.

'Of course. And get it on video.' He held up his cell phone. 'I'm all set. I even made sure I still had a Miranda card tucked in my wallet.'

'We have to be certain they're all seated far apart. I don't want a hostage situation,' she added. What they were about to do was risky enough.

Reese nodded in agreement as they reached the first floor. Lauren had thought the elevator in the old police headquarters was the world's slowest. This one actually seemed designed to be. There would be no rushing to your room at the Sloane Spa and Retreat. Even the elevator ride with its tinkling new age music was meant to induce relaxation. 'I'll stand behind our suspect and put the cuffs on them as soon as you're done.' The doors slid open and they walked into the lobby.

'We could just secure them now. Ward might have some zip ties around here somewhere,' she said, still uncertain that letting the killer sit among the others was a good idea. In fact, she knew it was a terrible idea. In the movies the murderer always launched into a big diatribe when they were revealed to be the culprit, and was then taken grumbling, but peacefully, into custody after explaining themselves. She didn't think that was going to be the case here. Strangely enough, the person they needed the explanation from was not the suspect. If they allowed the guests to leave once the troopers got there without this confrontation, all they were doing was allowing the witness time to get coerced into concocting a cover story for the killer.

Reese shook his head. 'Let's just stick to the script. If he moves a muscle, I'll grab him. I'm not taking any more chances than I have to.'

'I'm walking into a room full of homicide suspects in my socks,' she countered.

He glanced at her stocking feet as they passed under the huge clock. It read 2:37. 'Point taken,' he said.

Lauren took in the lounge area. Everyone had done as Ward asked, sitting apart from each other again. She thought maybe Chris getting attacked had been enough to scare them into behaving for a little while longer and stop acting like spoiled teenagers.

For his part, Chris was sitting in one of the chairs, his polo shirt stained with blood, holding a towel to the top of his head. He was awake, definitely alert, and looked pissed. Amanda was sitting close by, monitoring his every move.

All eight pairs of eyes glued themselves to Reese, who'd chosen to stand in the middle of the room. Lauren stood next to and slightly behind him. It was his show now. The room smelled of old coffee, burning wood and the lemon-scented disinfectant Ward had used to clean up after Raphael went for Tyler. Everyone watched him, waiting for him to tell them what came next.

Lauren saw Reese swipe open the phone in his right hand and hit the record video button without even looking at it. Setting it on the table next to him, he casually rotated the camera so it was facing the group. If anyone noticed, no one said anything. 'Hello, everybody. I know this is unconventional, but Detective Riley here asked me to help her out a little.'

'Now she's Detective Riley,' Tyler said. 'This just keeps getting better and better. Are you the Chief of Inverness Police now because you saved her from the elements?'

'When are the troopers coming to evacuate us?' Seth demanded before Tyler even got his last word out.

Reese stuffed his hands into his pants pockets and rocked back and forth on his heels before he answered. Lauren could tell he wasn't about to be rushed into doing or saying anything. 'Riley is still in contact with the State Police, who should be here any time now. Investigator Donovan told her that plows are making their way to our location. The weather is finally letting up, but please remember that the plows have to be able to put the snow somewhere. It's an exhausting process that's been going on since last night. The troopers still have people stuck on the thruway, keep that in mind.'

'We need to get Chris to a hospital,' Amanda said. One of the round tables separated her from her husband, who was gripping a water glass so hard Lauren was afraid he might actually shatter it.

'I'm fine,' Chris complained from his spot near the bar. 'My head aches a little, but I'm all right. I'd really appreciate it if you'd let me have a drink of something. Anything.'

'Not a chance,' Amanda told him. 'You need tests done at a hospital for traumatic brain injury.'

'Traumatic brain injury, my ass,' he shot back. 'I know my name, the date, who the president is and what I had for breakfast yesterday morning. The only reason I don't know who hit me is because I don't have eyes in the back of my head.'

'That's good, Chris, because I'm going to need you to listen very carefully to me and then Detective Riley for the next couple of minutes. All of you were read your rights seventeen years ago when we were first questioned in Jessica Toakase's murder. I'm going to read them again and ask you all individually if you understand them, and if you wish to talk to us now. Understand, it's your absolute right not to say a word. Got it?'

'I don't get it,' Owen said, clapping a hand to his chest. 'Am *I* a suspect?'

'Just listen to the rights and answer the questions and then Detective Riley here is going to explain everything to you.'

'So you aren't a suspect anymore and we still are? How did that happen?' Chris asked.

'I want the real police here,' Raphael called out, his voice rising in anger. 'My wife was murdered. I don't want to hear a speech. I need to know which one of you assholes butchered her. This is such bullshit.'

'That's what we're about to tell you,' Reese assured him.

'I can tell you right now,' Tyler piped up, crossing his arms in front of his chest and slumping down in his seat, 'I know this is not standard procedure.'

'You're right, Tyler,' Reese replied. 'So bear with us.'

He produced a little white card from the leather wallet in his back pocket and began to recite the Miranda warning word for word. When he was done, he flipped it over and asked each person in the room, including Mrs Brady and Ward, if they understood their rights and if they wished to speak to them now. Everyone said yes to both except Tyler, who was now glaring at the two of them. 'I understand my rights and I'm not saying a word to either one of you.'

'Fair enough,' Reese said, tucking the card away. 'Just sit there and listen.'

Reese melted back as Lauren stepped forward, still holding the white cooler. While everyone watched silently, she bent at the waist and set it at her feet, making a show of it. She wanted every single person in the room wondering, *What's in there?*

She cleared her throat and for a second thought she was going to launch into another coughing attack. She took as deep a breath as she could without doubling over in pain and began. 'You need three things to commit a homicide.' Her eyes bounced from face to face. 'And you need to be able to prove those three things in a court of law to convict someone of a homicide.

'Means, motive and opportunity.' There was no reaction to that statement and no protest, so she went on. 'Jessica's murder provided the motive for Erica's. Erica claimed to be about to out Jessica's killer on her podcast. Every single one of you, with the exception of Owen, Ward and Mrs Brady, obviously, had the means and opportunity seventeen years ago to kill Jessica. And after digging around today, I now know that every one of you had the means and opportunity to kill Erica last night. So it comes down to motive. Who killed Jessica Toakase, for what reason, and what would they do to keep it secret now?'

Some murmurs rose from the group. She was hitting a nerve, throwing everyone off balance.

'It all circles back to Jessica. I look around this room and everybody had a reason to want Erica dead, if only to protect the identity of the killer.'

'That's the most obvious thing in the world, Miss Marple,' Tyler said. 'The detectives back then couldn't figure it out. There's no way you did in a couple of hours.'

Lauren wagged a finger in his direction. 'That's where you're wrong. Erica figured it out. She requested the files under the Freedom of Information Act and pored over them, same as Reese did when he got to Cold Case. She ran into the same walls he did. Until she got the invitation to come here this weekend. That opened up a whole new avenue of investigation for her, one that Reese didn't know about when he was investigating Jessica's murder, because the connection didn't exist yet.'

'What are you babbling about?' Chris asked. 'I just wanted to invite my friends up for a nice weekend.'

'Did you?' Lauren asked. 'Then why isn't Tonya here? She and Erica were best friends. She lives less than three hours away in Toronto. She could have left her house at nine in the morning and been here by noon. When we ran into you at the restaurant you never said you actually invited her, just that she was in Canada.'

'I figured she was done with us,' Chris protested. 'She didn't keep in contact—'

'None of you really kept in contact,' Lauren pointed out. 'After Jessica's murder you all went your separate ways. The only thing different about Tonya was that she was the only one of your group that had a rock-solid alibi for Jessica's murder. She was literally out of the country.'

'What does my being lazy about inviting her have to do with any of this?' Chris asked.

'Because I don't think you were being lazy. I think someone else gave you the guest list and she wasn't on it because she'd have nothing to contribute.'

'What the hell does that mean?' Chris sat up straight in his chair, eyes wide.

Lauren picked up the cooler and started to wander off to the left. *Use the whole stage*, she told herself, then said, 'Do you remember what we talked about last night? About why anyone would ever willingly talk to the police, especially if they did it? To gather information. To see what we already knew. Everyone claimed to never have caught one of her shows, but that was a lie. Someone here listened to Erica's podcast two months ago where she said she was going to unveil the truth about that night, and they wanted each one of you at this Spa to find out exactly who knew what.'

'This is ridiculous.' Chris tried to stand up too quickly, wobbled a little, then sat back down, still clutching the towel to his head. 'You're just making this up as you go along.'

'I know you're scared, Chris.' Lauren came and stood in front of him. 'You had no idea what the killer was up to. I really believe that. But I also believe running into Reese was no accident, either. You weren't being lazy by not inviting Tonya, because you tried like hell to get ahold of Reese. It wasn't a coincidence that you just happened to be at Amichi's when we were there. You didn't realize you'd been used until you went and got your laptop out of your office. You might not have seen who hit you, but you know who did it.'

Chris mashed his lips together. Lauren scanned the room, making sure Reese was right where he was supposed to be.

'Erica threw out a lot of allegations last night. Hinted at things. But the one thing she didn't dance around was actually bringing your high school yearbook. She was playing her own game as well. She specifically brought your junior yearbook to see how one of you would react. Maybe she never believed the killer would do it again. Jessica's murder, you see, was a crime of opportunity.'

Lauren locked eyes with Reese, who gave her the slightest of nods. 'Opportunity is the key word here. The killer has proved to be someone who takes advantage of their opportunities. They're smart. They adapt to the situation at hand. They knew from the yearbook that Erica wasn't bluffing, and they reacted to the opportunity put in front of them to silence her. When Ward announced that Raphael was passed out on the couch in the lobby, the killer saw an opportunity. They knew Erica was alone and probably passed out drunk in her room. All they needed to do was slip the bar knife up their sleeve and swipe Raphael's key card from his pocket as they passed by him on the way to the elevator.'

'Your theory is shit. How would the killer have known the safety bar wouldn't be engaged?' Tyler called out. His face was twisted in a look somewhere between incredulity and annoyance.

'I worked in our Domestic Violence Unit for a very long time,' Lauren replied coolly. 'She hit Raphael.' Raphael made a move to respond but Lauren shot her free hand out, shushing him. 'Abusers often feel remorse. She would have left the bar off for him to come back into the room. Besides, our killer is an opportunist. If they couldn't get to her last night, they now had a key card to her room and a weapon. The murderer had all weekend to get in and take care of her. As it happened, she hadn't engaged the safety bar and they were able to slip into her room, and from what I saw of the scene, probably while she was asleep.'

Raphael made a choking sound from his seat and covered his face with his hands.

'All this is great information,' Owen said. 'But you still haven't said one thing that proves who did it.'

'Let's go back to Chris and who really wanted everyone here. Was the killer blackmailing Chris somehow? No. Chris had no clue who killed Jessica. But the killer did have a lot of sway over Chris because he's his number one investor in this business venture.'

'I swear,' Chris said, a note of desperation in his voice, 'I had no idea this was going to happen.'

'Don't say another word,' Seth snarled at him from his seat. He started to rise and Reese clamped a hand on his shoulder, preventing him from standing. Seth looked back, startled to see that Reese had somehow managed to get behind him while Lauren was speaking.

Lauren went on. 'I believe you, Chris. I think Seth Creehan approached you at some point, I don't know when. Those are details that were probably spelled out in your now smashed laptop. He had a business proposition for you. Six months ago, when you were about to go belly-up, he invested millions of dollars in this place. Investigator Donovan confirmed that for me over the phone. Seth used his software company's investment arm. It's public record, if you know where to look. He lied about never listening to Erica's podcast. He'd heard her podcast about getting the files via the Freedom of Information Act two years ago, and then again two months ago, when she teased she was getting close to revealing the killer.'

'Why would he pay that much attention to Erica?' Tyler asked.

'Seth Crechan has been keeping tabs on every single one of you for a very long time. He had the time, money and resources to do it. He proposed this get-together, even suggested who to invite. Am I right, Chris?'

Chris gave a single nod in affirmation.

'That makes no sense,' Amanda said. 'That would mean Seth killed Jessica. He had no reason to.'

'He had hundreds of millions of reasons to,' Lauren replied, turning to face her. 'They were in the computer club together. She started to develop a game, a really great game, and shared it with Seth – probably to get his opinion on it as she built the world line by line on her computer. Seth knew it was groundbreaking, something special. He waited for his opportunity, and it almost passed him by. She was getting ready to take it to college with her. It finally came that night in the park.'

She paused and took a deep breath before going on. 'It was all in the original statements you gave to the police seventeen years ago. I read Seth's statement. He was the only one Raphael had told exactly where Jessica was going to be and at what time. All Seth had to do was get there ahead of him. He used what was on hand, a garden stake. Then he went home and waited to talk to the cops so he could throw suspicion on Tyler and Raphael. Then he took her rough copy of the game, reworked it over his freshman year of college, and passed it off as his own, making millions in the process.'

'You killed my wife over a video game?' Raphael jumped from his seat. Tyler caught him around the waist as he passed and pinned him to the ground before he could get to Seth, who sat still as a stone, listening to every word Lauren said with an impassive look on his face.

'Not just any video game,' Lauren continued once Tyler had managed to get Raphael seated, standing next to him so he wouldn't try to get at Seth again. '*Random Mutual Destruction*, which went on to become Video Game of the Year. Seth Creehan claimed in a *Fresh Gamer's Weekly* article that the idea for the game came to him in his freshman dorm one night when he was studying for his mid-terms. Which would be plausible, if not for this.' She held up her cell phone and slowly walked around the room, showing the enhanced picture she had pulled up on her screen to each and every one of them. She stopped at Seth, holding it an inch from his face, forcing him to look at it.

'Investigator Donovan had his analysts pull up your junior yearbook on highschoolmemories.com. I had them look for the picture of Jessica sitting in front of her computer that we were all looking at last night. They zoomed in and enhanced the screen. See that? That's the code for *Random Mutual Destruction*. Notice the little back slashes there? That's for notes she embedded to remind her to switch the lead character's hair color from brown to red because she'd changed the name to Rusty Misrandino.'

Seth stared at the picture silently. Finally, Lauren pulled it away from his face. 'Rusty Misrandino is the name of the main character in the game you marketed, Seth. How could she have known a full two years before the idea came to you what your main character's name would be and what color hair he'd have?' Seth's hands were flat on the table in front of him, palms down, but his fingertips were turning white from pressing against the wood. Still, he kept his mouth clamped shut.

'How did Erica figure it out?' Owen asked. 'If all those detectives and Shane couldn't solve Jessica's murder, how did Erica do it?'

'She wasn't the first person to realize that Seth was the only person who knew where Jessica was going to be. The original detectives made a note of it in the file. Our friend, Shane Reese here, followed up on that. He suspected Seth, but once again couldn't find a motive or evidence. Without those things, it still could have been any one of you.'

'Including him,' Owen pointed out. 'Your theory still doesn't answer the question of how Erica would think Seth was a suspect over everyone else.'

Lauren looked straight at him when she answered. '*Random Mutual Destruction* is often referred to by gamers as "RMD". Raphael's full name is Raphael Martinez Diaz. Of course Erica would recognize her own husband's initials, especially since she was well aware of Jessica and Raphael's relationship.'

'I told Erica about me and Jessica the day her body was found,' Raphael said. 'I thought the cops were going to tell her. I wanted it to come from me.' He ground the heels of his hands into his red-rimmed eyes. 'I've played that stupid game a thousand times and it never occurred to me that Jessica used my initials.'

'But it would occur to your admittedly jealous wife. And she dove deep into the case, Seth and Jessica. She found that picture in your junior yearbook, which is proof the game Seth singlehandedly took credit for was actually designed by Jessica two years earlier.' Lauren held up her phone. 'You don't need any special equipment to enhance the screen, just a cell phone with a camera that can zoom. When I found the burned yearbook, I remembered that she said at dinner last night that she'd brought the junior one because it was more interesting. I knew there must have been something in there the killer didn't want anyone to see. I had the State Police analysts pull up the yearbook and look for pictures of all of you, but specifically of Jessica.'

Lauren turned back to Seth. 'The fact that Erica brought that yearbook here told you she knew what you'd done. And she was waiting for you to confront her. She rattled everyone up after dinner on purpose. I believe Erica wanted to get it all on audiotape for her show, along with everyone else's denials, so she could do a big reveal.'

'Like you're doing now?' Seth's voice was cold, colder than the storm she'd just survived. His eyes were narrowed into slits behind his glasses.

Lauren pressed her advantage now that she'd managed to get a rise out of him. 'You took the knife and the key, went into your room and put on a dark flannel button-down. You wouldn't want to ruin the expensive shirt you had on last night, would you? Then you went into Erica's room, killed her, wrapped your bloody flannel around the weapon and threw them off the balcony. You took the yearbook, went back to your room and changed the rest of your clothes. You must have realized you'd smeared some blood from your hands on something in your room after you cleaned up, so you called down to room service for water with lemon and aspirin, both of which are used to get rid of blood stains. A simple Google search will tell you that.' She took another step closer to Seth, closing the gap between them. 'You saw Erica's file and planted the photo of Amanda and Owen and the article about Reese on top and put it by the side of the bed to muddy the investigation. Then you took the yearbook up to the third floor and burned it. After everyone was done wandering around for the evening, you tried to get outside to properly dispose of the knife and shirt, but you didn't figure on a blizzard popping up. You opened the front door and got pushed back by the wind and snow. You were forced to wait out the storm and hope to get the chance to snag the evidence and get the hell out of here at some point later.'

'What about the key?' Chris asked.

'Insurance. He kept the key card to frame Raphael. If it showed up again suddenly in his vicinity, the trooper's eyes would definitely focus on him.' She tilted her head a little. 'Because it's always the husband, right?'

Seth Creehan didn't answer, just sat glaring at her.

'And now here we are. I have the bloody shirt, no doubt covered in your epithelial cells.' She held up the cooler again. 'And your window of opportunity to get the hell out of this hotel and out of the country, like I think you planned even before we were snowed in, has just been closed. I think you probably put a nice nest egg in some offshore accounts before you came this weekend, just in case. I bet you thought come Monday morning you'd be at a villa in some non-extraditable island, sipping Bloody Marys and crowing about how you managed to put one over on everyone. I mean, you did it once when you were just a teenager, why couldn't you do it again?'

'I swear I didn't put it together until I got hit with that vase and my laptop was smashed,' Chris repeated. 'And even then, I wasn't sure exactly what was going on.'

Lauren nodded sympathetically. 'If you'd have known Seth had killed Jessica you wouldn't have waited until now to hit him up for cash. You would've blackmailed him long ago, if that was your angle. You filed for bankruptcy for the first time twelve years ago when the restaurant you opened in Denver failed. It took a long time for you to pay off those debts and rebuild your credit.'

'Public record,' Chris muttered under his breath.

'It is. And I'm sure, somewhere in your laptop, there's an email from Seth suggesting you two meet and talk about a collaboration. He mentioned being in Grand Junction this morning at breakfast.'

'He did email me,' Chris confirmed. 'Nothing specific. It was just a note saying he was in Colorado and he wanted to get together. He sprang the silent partnership on me over dinner one night. But it's all gone now.'

'I once had to call an FBI friend of mine who works in their Computer Crimes Squad for a stalking case I was working on,' Lauren said. 'I asked him if there was ever a computer they couldn't retrieve information from eventually. He told me just one, and that was because the suspect had blasted the hard drive with a shotgun. I'm sure our computer genius Seth has all kinds of safeguards for his personal and business accounts, making them untraceable, but he didn't trust that you did and he didn't have time to try to hack into your laptop to see what you had in there connecting him to the planning of this weekend. When he saw you carrying the laptop he followed you into the bathroom, knocked you out and just destroyed it. I'm sure all the information is stored in the Cloud, but he just needed to buy a little time to get out of here and then out of the country. I think he was hoping he hit you hard enough that you wouldn't wake up anytime soon. Good thing the computer genius doesn't know how hard the human skull is.'

'You son of a bitch,' Chris snarled at him. 'You murdered our friends. You set me up. You tried to frame Raphael . . .' He trailed off as words failed and his anger overtook him. He began to try to get up again and Amanda rushed over, knelt down on one knee next to him and slung an arm around his shoulder, restraining him. There was nothing Lauren could do to stop the separation rule from being broken again for the umpteenth time that day.

Amanda twisted her face away from Chris to look at Seth over his shoulder. 'For almost twenty years we've all had to deal with Jessica's death, while you sat in your mansion making money off of her and her game. Then when Erica figures it out, you just take her out. Like we're all garbage for you to throw away.' Tears were flowing freely down her cheeks. Chris took a deep breath and gave her a squeeze to show he had himself under control. She got up and went over to her husband and buried her face in his chest. 'I can't believe this. I can't,' she sobbed from the folds of Owen's shirt.

'I'll destroy you for this,' Seth told Lauren in a voice so low she wouldn't have heard him if she hadn't been standing right in front of him. Reese was the only other person within earshot.

Lauren bent forward, putting one hand on the table so she could lean in until their noses almost touched. 'Get in line, Mr Creehan,' she said softly, and a look of rage washed over his face for an instant before settling back into its impassive mask. 'Get. In. Line.'

Lauren straightened up and walked back toward the bar, the cooler full of damning evidence dangling from her fingertips.

'So what do we do with Seth?' Raphael asked. The despair in his voice had been replaced with a scary calm as he sat alone in the corner, regarding Seth with the intensity of a lion stalking a gazelle.

'We wait here until the State Police come,' Reese said, hand still on Seth's shoulder.

'I want to wait with Seth,' Raphael said, getting up. 'I want him to sit here and look me in the eye.'

When Seth continued to stare straight ahead, Raphael took a step closer and pointed to his own face. 'Look at me!'

Seth's eyes snapped to his. The two men stared at each other for a long, tense moment. Raphael took another step toward him. 'You've taken the most important person in my life from me. You took Jessica from all of us, too. I want a seat in the front row, watching as every single good thing you have gets taken away from you,' he said, refusing to break eye contact.

Raphael came slowly forward until he was standing right in front of Seth. His chest was heaving under his shirt, threads sticking out where the buttons should be, his hands trembling. Lauren could tell it was taking every ounce of his control not to reach across the table and throttle Seth. Seth began to shrink into his seat.

Raphael grabbed a chair and swung it around so he could sit facing Seth. 'I want to see you go down. And I want you to know I'll be there every step of the way, you bastard.'

As Lauren turned and walked toward the bar, a faint rumble came from outside the windows.

Reese called over to Lauren, who'd picked up an open bottle of red wine someone had left on the bar and was pouring some into one of the glasses she'd snagged from the overhead rack, 'I think your friends are here.'

She raised the glass to her lips and took a sip. It was bitter and terrible. 'Cheers,' she said, then polished off the rest in one swallow.

THIRTY-EIGHT

Lauren, Reese, Tyler and Mrs Brady broke off from the rest of the group and made their way to the front lobby. As the noise got louder, Lauren and Reese moved closer to the doors, while the other two hung back. 'Well done, back there,' Reese said, watching three separate beams of light pierce the gloom underneath the awning out front.

'Do you think Seth will try something stupid?' Lauren asked.

'Not a chance with Raphael watching him,' Reese replied as the three sleek, black ATVs pulled in one after the other outside the main entrance.

The troopers used modified all-terrain vehicles with treads

instead of wheels for snow emergencies. Lauren and Reese watched as the four helmeted riders dismounted their ATVs and began unloading equipment bags off the back. Lauren noticed two of the vehicles were hauling what looked like black plastic clamshells, like the kind you put on top of your car to store things in. Two of the troopers unhooked them and began to drag them toward the doors. As they worked quickly in the snow out front, other guests began to emerge from the lounge area, drawn by the rumble of the vehicles.

'Does this mean we can leave?' Mrs Brady asked, squinting at the sliding glass doors. 'I just want to go home.' Lauren held back from telling her that they were all a long way from going home. Every single one of them had hours of questioning ahead of them, most likely at the State Police barracks. No use in traumatizing the poor woman further.

'How the hell are they going to get all of us out of here on just three of those things?' Tyler asked as the troopers entered through the outer set of double doors. The four State Troopers paused in the space between the sets of doors, two of them setting down what looked like a huge duffle bag, while the other two parked their storage pods and removed their helmets.

Lauren recognized Investigator Donovan right away. His sweaty hair was plastered to his forehead. Stomping the snow off his boots, Donovan tucked the helmet under his arm then strode through the interior sliding glass doors into the lobby with his colleagues.

'I'm BCI Investigator Donovan. I'm looking for Detective Lauren Riley,' he announced, looking at the assembled guests who'd filtered into the lobby, trying to pin her down.

'I'm Riley,' she said, acutely aware that she was still in her socks. *Not my finest moment*, she thought as the four sets of eyes settled on her, *but far from my worst either*.

'Glad to meet you in person.' Striding forward, he pulled off his gloves and stuck his hand out for her to shake. His hand felt like it was on fire compared to hers, but she could feel it, and that was what mattered. He looked her up and down, taking in her stocking feet, then the clothes drying in front of the fire. 'My major had a county snowplow break off from the thruway. We followed him all the way from the State Police barracks.'

'Is the plow still out there?' she asked, squinting out the doors.

'It stopped at the top of the drive. He's going to plow in the vicinity as much as he can while he's waiting on us. The visibility is better, but it's still coming down.' Donavon scanned the lobby. 'Is the suspect secure?'

'Trust me,' Lauren said. 'Seth Creehan isn't going anywhere. This is my partner, Shane Reese.' She motioned to Reese, who leaned over and shook Donovan's hand as well.

Donovan's eyes fell on the clothes drying in front of the fireplace. 'Did you go outside?' The shock and surprise in his voice was evident.

'I recovered the physical evidence you're going to need to convict Seth Creehan of Erica Diaz's murder,' Lauren responded.

He wasn't about to be deterred by her diversion tactics. 'I asked if you went outside.'

Lauren saw Mrs Brady and Tyler watching her from near the front desk. 'I'd rather fill you in on all the details in private.'

Donovan took the cue from the tone of her voice. 'Where's Mr Sloane?' he asked. 'We brought a neck brace to help stabilize him.'

'He's right through there,' Lauren told him, pointing to the entrance to the lounge. 'Sitting up and complaining.'

One of the troopers immediately grabbed the strap to one of the clamshells. 'Where?' he asked. He was short, with a tight buzz cut and his voice was unusually deep. Lauren pegged him for ex-military.

'Right this way,' Mrs Brady said, motioning for him to follow her. The trooper dragged the clamshell behind him as he followed the tiny chef.

'Only he's not in the bathroom anymore,' Tyler said. Being exonerated had emboldened him and he stood in the middle of the lobby with his meaty hands on his hips. 'He came to and insisted on getting up. Amanda managed to convince him to sit in one of the chairs. I'm surprised he didn't come charging out here.'

'Sir, why don't you join the rest of the guests where

Detective Riley had you sitting? That would be a huge help while my team locates the evidence and secures the scene.'

Tyler opened his mouth to say something, realized Investigator Donovan wasn't in the mood to entertain his whining, and snapped it shut. He spun around and marched off without another word.

Donovan's fellow troopers were busy unpacking their gear. 'I hate to do this to you, Detective Reese, but from what Detective Riley—'

'Lauren,' she interrupted.

'Lauren,' he continued, 'has told me, you are one of the original suspects in Jessica Toakase's murder. I'm going to need you to join the others.'

Reese nodded, knowing it was up to Lauren to fill him in on the events of the last half-hour. 'I'll be right in there if you need me,' he told Lauren, then walked away.

He hadn't even passed all the way through the lounge's entrance before Donovan asked, 'You two went outside?'

'I needed to find that missing evidence we'd discussed. The storm got to me. I went down about sixty feet from the front doors and Reese had to come out and get me.'

'That was incredibly stupid,' he said, crossing his arms in front of his chest, the nylon fabric of his parka making an angry *rshhh* sound, his helmet dangling from his fingertips. 'Especially since you knew we were on our way here. I also see you've done a bang-up job of keeping the witnesses separated.'

'I'm one person telling a bunch of distraught, stranded people under an incredible amount of stress what to do. How did you think that was going to work out for me?' she snapped.

'Unprecedented circumstances,' he muttered, as if trying to convince himself.

Lauren knew from the beginning she'd have to defend the choices she'd made. 'Because as soon as the storm lifted, as soon as you could get people out of here, Seth Creehan would have been gone. I explained to everyone how he murdered Jessica and orchestrated this whole weekend. I believed Seth would get to Chris and blackmail him into silence if I didn't confront him with the evidence in front of everyone. Without Chris Sloane's corroboration and cooperation, the case against Creehan could be picked apart by any good defense attorney.'

'So, you went ahead and told all of our witnesses your theory of events?'

'I found the murder weapon,' she said, ignoring the disapproval in his voice. 'It's the bar knife. I marked its location outside with a ski pole. Creehan threw it and his bloody clothes off Erica Diaz's balcony. I found the stained shirt caught in a tree branch. I couldn't leave that for you to collect because the wind was about to take it.' She touched the cooler with the tip of her toe. 'It's in here. I suggest you have one of your troopers put it in the hotel freezer. I couldn't do it without taking eyes off it. Chain of custody and all that.'

The shirt was the most important piece of evidence and chain of custody had to be maintained. Now she could hand it over to one of the troopers, who could put it in one of the freezers and sit on it until their evidence collection techs could come and properly collect and store it. Even with her head fuzzy and muddled from the cold, she'd still managed to safeguard the key to the whole case.

Donovan turned to the trooper unpacking to his left and told her, 'Perrin, start a chain of custody sheet. Then take this cooler to the first freezer you can find and make yourself comfortable.'

'Yes, sir,' she replied, and rifled through the clamshell she was unloading for the proper paperwork.

Donovan dropped his helmet on the couch and sat on the arm. Lauren took the hint and sat down next to him. He lowered his voice. 'My analysts did exactly what you wanted, but I still don't know what all this means.' Pulling a phone out from the folds of his parka he brought up a series of pictures. 'Show me,' he said, and held it out to her. Lauren took the cell from his hand and began to scroll through the photos.

She stopped on one and pinched the screen, zooming in. 'This one.'

'Tell me everything you told all of them.'

Lauren stared down at the enhanced photograph that had broken the case open for her. She lowered her voice to match his and explained her theory of the homicides, weaving in the evidence she and he had both gathered, at the hotel and from his analysts at the State Police. Then she described the trip outside and Reese's rescue of her. By the time she got to the reveal in the lounge, his mouth was hanging open. When she finished, Donovan let out a low whistle. 'When the DNA comes back on that shirt, Creehan is done for. I can't believe the way you shook this case out.'

'Would your superiors have approved of my methods?' she asked.

The skin around his eyes crinkled as he shook his head and smiled. 'No way in hell. You'll never be a trooper, I can tell you that.'

'I definitely haven't made many friends this weekend.' She looked toward the lounge entrance. 'Ready to meet Seth Creehan?'

THIRTY-NINE

Donovan's hand pushed back his parka from his hip as he took a good look around, exposing a gleaming set of handcuffs. Lauren hoped he'd lose the coat altogether. Winter gear definitely impeded access to the tools you carried on your belt.

He began calling out orders, scattering his troopers around the building, having them sit on the various crime scenes. One he stationed outside Erica's room, one was sent to the third floor by the fireplace in the atrium, and the other took the small white cooler from Lauren after she'd made her sign and date the chain of custody sheet. The female trooper was given directions to the industrial freezer in the kitchen where she'd store the cooler, then keep guard over the evidence.

Once all his housekeeping was in order, Donovan swept his arm in front of him and Lauren in a flourish. 'Lead the way.'

Lauren needn't have worried about his coat because, as they crossed the lobby, he slipped off the dark navy-blue parka with the New York State Police patch sewn on the one shoulder and an American flag sewn on the other and tossed it over one of the chairs. He was wearing black nylon tactical pants with multiple pockets with a matching black shirt. At the collar she could see a thermal shirt peeking out. When he noticed her looking, he told her, 'My usual uniform is a suit and tie. The specialized unit that's attached to the ATVs brought me some gear to wear. The pants are a little too big, even over the thermal underwear, and the shirt's too tight, but beggars can't be choosers, right?'

'I'm walking next to you in my socks,' she reminded him as she led him to where their suspect was.

Passing under the big clock, she and Donovan walked into the lounge together. Reese was sitting at the bar, drinking a rocks glass full of whiskey with Owen, as Amanda sat next to her husband, black mascara smudged under her eyes. The separation of witnesses could be a problem for the prosecutors later, but it was out of Lauren's hands now.

Sitting calmly behind the long table in the corner where the group had had dinner the night before was Seth Creehan. Raphael Diaz sat directly across from him, eyes locked on his face, arms at his sides, hands clenched into fists, just daring Creehan to make one wrong move. Tyler sat next to him now, talking softly to him, keeping him from leaping across the table. Only hours ago, Raphael and Tyler had been trying to throttle each other. Now they were supporting each other against a common enemy. The black cloud of guilt they'd all been under had finally been lifted from them and had settled squarely over the right person and that changed everything.

Seth's hands were folded neatly in front of him, head down, his phone resting on the polished wood of the table. When Lauren and Donovan approached, he looked up at them with an expressionless face.

'Seth Creehan,' Donovan said, coming around the table and reaching for his cuffs, 'you're under arrest for the murder of Erica Diaz.'

'I want a lawyer,' he said simply, and hung his head again.

'You're gonna need one,' Reese called over, throwing back the last of the whiskey in his rocks glass. 'You son of a bitch.'

FORTY

Sitting across from each other at their kitchen table, Lauren looked over the top of her steaming cup of black coffee at Reese. He was propped up on his forearms, cradling his own stoneware mug in his hands, ignoring Watson at his feet begging for the last of his toast. Reese and Riley had both slept in until eight thirty, meeting like they usually did in the kitchen, with whoever got there first putting the coffee on. Today it had been Lauren.

They'd been back from the Sloane Spa and Retreat for two days now, not counting Saturday night they'd spent at the State Police barracks. Erie County District Attorney Carl Church had been briefed by Major Lyn Greenlee of the New York State Police and the Cattaraugus County District Attorney right after Seth's arrest. Church sounded pleased when Reese put him on speaker phone in the county snowplow as it sliced through the snowbound streets to take them to the trooper barracks.

Church had outlined everything he wanted done. Lauren could picture him ticking off the tasks on his fingers as he spoke. Lauren had to turn over her phone, with all its recordings, right away to the state police. Church would have another crew reinterview the witnesses, then when they got back to work, wanted them pulling all the evidence for retesting. That included having Jessica's secondhand computer brought out of secure storage and the State Police's computer expert examining it for the code to the original game and looking for Jessica's digital signature within it. When it was seized after her death the only thing the detectives had been interested in were her emails, which had turned up nothing. The key to the whole case had been sitting in a storage locker untouched for seventeen years. Somehow that fact made another little bloom of blackness open in Lauren's chest. The garden of dark flowers she was carrying was overgrown and starting to choke her.

Lauren had refused to go to the hospital that day, even

though she couldn't stop coughing. The last thing she needed was another doctor telling her what she already knew – her lungs were damaged. Probably permanently.

She and Reese had spent most of the rest of Saturday making statements and memorializing the events that had occurred during the previous twenty-four hours. The other members of their party were also taken to the barracks where, unlike Lauren, the troopers managed to successfully keep everyone apart. Lauren figured the next time the classmates would see each other again would be at Seth Creehan's trial.

Donovan had taken her aside to get all the gritty details as soon as they got to the barracks, while things were fresh in her mind. She watched another trooper take Reese in the opposite direction, hands stuffed down into his pockets, but head held high. For the first time in seventeen years there was no doubt as to what his involvement was in Jessica's death.

As she was writing down a timeline of events on a yellow legal pad in one of the interview rooms, she overheard a one-sided phone conversation between Donovan and the high-priced attorney Seth had immediately retained. Donovan had stepped out into the hallway, leaving the door open just a crack. From Donovan's responses, it sounded like a trial was an absolute certainty. *Good*, she thought. *Bring it on.* Then continued detailing her discovery of the burnt yearbook.

She and Reese had ended up sleeping on old, musty cots in the barracks' break room. She'd practically passed out from exhaustion, but not before catching the sound of Reese's familiar snore. Lauren's back was screaming when she got up the next morning to the steady drip, drip, dripping outside the window next to her.

The weather had broken. The temperature had risen and the snow, for the most part, was melting fast. There was some flooding in low-lying areas and a lot of damage to trees that hadn't lost all their leaves yet, the weight of the snow tearing branches down and cleaving others in two. Reese and Riley were driven back to their car on Sunday morning by a snow-plow, accompanied by an impossibly young-looking trooper who talked about his night of rescuing stranded motorists on the thruway the entire ride back to the hotel.

A tow truck driver was rigging Seth Creehan's snow-covered car on a flatbed when they pulled up. It was being impounded pending a search warrant for any evidence inside. Lauren watched a man with coveralls under his puffy black parka carefully handle the dark green Mercedes SUV, bitterly realizing that was what Seth had stolen Jessica's life for: luxury cars and multiple mansions. And he'd ended Erica's to hold onto them. She felt the bile rise in her throat as the tow truck driver took the vehicle away. It was such a horribly tragic waste, motivated by pure greed.

There hadn't been much conversation on the slippery ride home between Reese and Riley. They were both tired and drained. Lauren drove her SUV over the thin layer of ice and slush in her driveway. Her plow service had managed to get to her house once but not twice, and the accumulation that had built up was quickly melting. They both grabbed their bags and lugged them to the front door wordlessly. Retiring to their separate rooms, neither emerged until Charlotte had come to drop the baby off last night.

It was now Monday morning and the New York State Thruway was unclogged and mostly open again. Details from the murder were still only trickling out, the State Police doing a great job of releasing only what was necessary. Seth Creehan was the focus of the media attention: his millionaire playboy lifestyle, his past and present crimes, but not how he was caught. She had a few days before her involvement in his arrest came out. She'd spent part of the night before in her bed, flipping from one twenty-four-hour news station to the next, watching their coverage of the case until she decided it was unhealthy for her to obsess over it.

Seth's lawyers already had him out on bail. The county judge had taken his passport at arraignment Sunday morning after he pled not guilty to Erica's murder, frozen most of his assets and set a ridiculously high bail. Even that would do little to hinder a man of his means from fleeing the country if he set his mind to it. Lauren had to rely on the fact that Seth always thought he was the smartest person in the room. Watching him stand next to his lawyer with the smallest hint of a smirk on his face while he proclaimed his innocence in front of the Cattaraugus County Courthouse told Lauren he was looking forward to his trial, for another chance to pull one over on everybody.

The rest of Reese's classmates were evacuated from the trooper barracks the day before. Raphael intended to stay with relatives in the city until the trial. Owen and Amanda were holed up in a hotel by the airport, trying to catch a flight out of Buffalo, and Tyler was staying with his parents until the roads cleared up to drive back home. Chris had gone to a local hospital Saturday overnight for observation and was now back at his spa. Reese had been texting with him, and Chris had told him he was cooperating with the investigation and hoping to somehow salvage his dream. Without Seth's money, it was going to be hard to do. Lauren felt awful for Chris. He and his hotel were just more collateral damage to sociopath Seth Creehan.

Donovan had called her yesterday to tell her his Major wanted him and the State Police investigators working in tandem with the Buffalo Cold Case squad. She and Reese were off for one more day, then they planned to start putting together their own case against Seth for Jessica's murder. That would have to go in front of an Erie County grand jury because her murder had happened in Buffalo. Creehan's lawyers were already playing games, filing motions and demanding that their own experts examine the forensic evidence.

'Welcome to the shitshow,' Reese had joked after she hung up. 'It's a good thing we have alcohol.'

Yesterday, they'd just been glad to be back home. Today the mood was different. The morning sunlight streamed through the windows. Lauren could hear the steady dripping of snow melting along her gutter. It was almost fifty degrees out and the local news people were issuing flash flood warnings. Birds who hadn't yet flown south for the winter were chattering in the bushes on either side of her back door. Just another November morning in Buffalo. Except, somehow, it wasn't.

'I don't think I want to be a cop anymore,' Lauren said. Her voice was not emotional or full of angst. She was simply stating a conclusion she'd come to.

Reese nodded his head once and brought his mug to his lips to take a sip. 'I know the feeling.'

'Shirley Gizzo might have been onto something when she said sometimes it's better to cut your losses and walk away,' she said, biting back the bitterness in her voice.

'Do you think you can walk away?'

She studied his face for a moment. 'Could you?'

He didn't hesitate with his answer. 'After everything we've been through in the last few years, yes. Absolutely.'

'What would we do with ourselves?'

Now he sat back in his chair, letting his right arm dangle by his side. The sunshine splashed across his handsome face, lighting up his green eyes. 'I guess that begs the question I asked you back at Sloane's. What are *we* doing?'

She paused for a second, afraid her voice would crack. 'I look at myself in the mirror and I see a middle-aged woman, a physical wreck, who'll do nothing except hold you back,' she finally confessed.

'That's funny, because when I look at you, I still see the stunning, confident woman who greeted me at the Cold Case office door on my first day, coming at me with an attitude.' Her breath caught in her chest as he went on. 'Sometimes, when you get up before me and I walk in here, I see you with a cup of coffee in your hand, staring out the window, and I think you must be the most beautiful woman I have ever seen.'

Lauren's hand went to her short, choppy brown hair that had been long and sleek and California blond when they'd met. Her fingertips brushed the arm of the thick black glasses she now wore. Just as she once saw him as the handsome young ladies' man who was a rising star on the department, he remembered her as she was and accepted her now for who she'd become. They'd grown in different ways, but together.

'Both of us have aged over these last few years. I'm not a wide-eyed rookie detective anymore,' he said, echoing her thoughts. 'You'll never hold me back from going after what I want.'

Lauren knew it was now or never. In the comfort of the house that had somehow gone from hers to theirs, the nerve to say the words out loud finally came to her. 'If we left the department together, we could do whatever we wanted.'

They both let that sink in for a second, *whatever we wanted.*

'We can finish Jessica's case, finally give her justice, then both take a leave of absence.' Reese's voice caught a little on Jessica's name.

'You could work under my private investigator's license with me until something better comes our way.'

He reached across the table and took her pale hand in his warm brown one. It was strong and a little rough. A father's hand. A husband's hand. 'I could do private investigations. We could pick and choose our cases.'

'Only do cheating spouses and insurance fraud,' she agreed, squeezing his fingers. 'The more boring and mundane, the better.'

He propped his elbow on the table and cupped his chin with his free hand in mock seriousness. 'I could join an all-guys gentleman book club.'

That made Lauren laugh out loud. 'And I could take up yoga with Dayla.'

'Let's not get crazy,' he said.

There was a long moment of silence that stretched out before them. Possibilities and hopes and dreams they'd never dared believe could become reality suddenly seemed within their reach, if only they'd allow themselves to grasp them.

'Do you really think we can stay out of trouble?' he asked, cocking an eyebrow at her.

'Not really,' she admitted. 'But we can try to hide out from it as long as possible.'

His smile reached his eyes. 'That sounds like heaven.'

In the background, Gabe's cry punctuated the air. Charlotte had dropped him off the night before and Reese had just put him down for his mid-morning nap that he didn't seem to want but sorely needed.

'That sounds like heaven too.' Lauren smiled back.

'You want to come tame the little monster with me?'

He released her hand and they both stood up from the table.

Lauren's mind raced as she came around to his side. So many things could go disastrously wrong if they went down this road. They lived together but had never even been on a real date. He was the first person she saw every morning and the last person she saw every night. All of her life she'd made plans and not one of them had ever worked out the way she thought they would. Not one. She'd made bad decisions and more mistakes than she could count. But then she looked at the scars crisscrossing Reese's head and remembered the one in her side and across the palm of her hand, and the pain that came with just breathing sometimes, and she knew one thing was a fact: they'd earned an early retirement and had paid for it in blood. Their blood.

She slipped her hand back into his. 'Let's do this.'

AUTHOR'S NOTE

In this day and age, writing a contemporary mystery like this one can be quite a challenge for authors. Finding a believable way to strand a group of people together for a stretch of time with no outside help available to them is a tall order. I have always been a fan of locked-room mysteries, but I wanted the situation my characters found themselves in to be both believable and plausible.

It's a good thing I live in Buffalo, New York.

I referenced the infamous 2014 November storm numerous times in this book. Like Lauren Riley and Shane Reese, I found myself trapped in my home after a literal wall of snow dropped over five feet of accumulation overnight. I was stranded with my husband and two kids. Not for fifteen or twenty hours, but for four days! And just to be clear, I live in the city, not in a rural community or a suburb. While we could not physically open our doors, we never lost power, heat, or the internet.

Although the events in my book are fiction, the storm and its aftermath that inspired them were all too real. Hundreds of people were stuck on the New York State Thruway. Hundreds more were trapped at their jobs. A baby was born in the firehouse at the top of my street, where two maternity nurses happened to get stranded on their way to work at Mercy Hospital, just a few blocks away. The National Guard had to be called out. Tragically, at least thirteen people lost their lives.

I wanted to add this note because Buffalo and Western New York are known for copious amounts of snow and news-making blizzards. But it should also be known for the resilience of its residents to come together in such events, and help each other any way they can. People took strangers into their homes. Neighbors hand-shoveled for neighbors. New York State Troopers worked around the clock to rescue motorists. Local police, firefighters, nurses, doctors and other first responders stepped up, going above and beyond. Buffalo is called the 'City of Good Neighbors' and every few years Mother Nature likes to make us prove it. This book is dedicated to all the good neighbors of Western New York. I'm glad you've got my and my family's backs when needed.

ACKNOWLEDGMENTS

As always, I have to thank my children, Natalie and Mary, for being my inspiration every single day.

Much love to my husband, Dan, for supporting me throughout my book writing journey.

I must extend a huge thank you to the owners of the indie bookstores who have supported and promoted me over the years: Tom and Maureen from the Dog Ears Bookstore, Bob and Shannon Lingle from Good Neighbor Books, Sal and Penny Valvo from Turn the Page and everyone at The Bookworm in East Aurora and Talking Leaves in Buffalo. Thank you for keeping local authors on your shelves!

Thanks to Kevin Gallagher for answering all my questions, as well as his wife, Jill. Thank you to Eugene M. for the impromptu breakfast talks at The Poked Yolk. Special thanks to Mike Breen, for reading every word.

Thank you, John Schreier for continuing to keep our ragtag group of writers together on Thursday nights.

Thanks to Pat Carrington and Joyce Maguda, who weed out many bad commas!

Thank you to the team at Severn House: Carl Smith, Natasha Bell, and especially Piers Tilbury for the gorgeous artwork.

Thanks to my agent, Bob Mecoy, for keeping me on this rollercoaster.

And thank you to God, for blessing me everyday with the amazing people in my life.